M. C. Watson

Mates, They Say Things Come in Threes

Limited Special Edition. No. 23 of 25 Paperbacks

M. C. Watson grew up in Hartlepool, near the sea, with her family. There she went to Stranton Junior School and later to Brierton Comprehensive School. She moved to Durham in 1988 aged 16. She attended the Durham University Business College and Houghall College in Durham.

She married in 2005 and has three sons. After working for Durham University and the NHS, she is now a full-time author working from home.

This book is dedicated to my family and friends.

Family:
Sean, Damion, Michael and Naomi Brown; and Joanne Elborn, who I love dearly, you are my world, the light of my life.

Friends:
Alan Hardy, Richard Remalls, Byron Hardy, Luke Davison, Connor Flately, Jake Dowson, Joe Lund and Bethany Welsh.

M. C. Watson

Mates, They Say Things Come in Threes

Austin Macauley Publishers™
London • Cambridge • New York • Sharjah

A CIP catalogue record for this title is available from the British Library.

ISBN 9781788787321 (Paperback)
ISBN 9781528955973 (ePub e-book)

www.austinmacauley.com

First Published (2019)
Austin Macauley Publishers Ltd
25 Canada Square
Canary Wharf
London
E14 5LQ

I would like to acknowledge Joanne Elborn, who is not only my family, but also my best friend. She reads my books to me so that I am able to make amendments. Also, because she puts up with my crazy ideas and all the craziness in general.

I would also like to thank Austin Macauley for the publication of *Mates, They Say Things Come in Threes* and for also seeing the potential in my being an author.

To my children: Sean, Damion, Michael and Naomi, who inspired me to write about them; and their friends, Joe, Jake, Luke, Connor, Byron and Bethany.

And finally, my friend Ricky, who I have known for many years; and Alan, who I met as Byron's dad.

The Meet Up

HM Prison, Wormwood Scrubs, Du Cane Road, London

Gaz picked up his belongings from the tray on the desk in front of him and stood waiting for the doors to open for his release.

"I hope we don't see you back here again, Gaz, but don't worry, I will keep a seat for you at the table just in case you decide to come back. We will all be awaiting your return, especially me, so I can kick your arse at poker," said John, the head prison officer.

"Ha, ha, ha, ha, very funny, Shortie, you know I will always kick your arse at poker but don't bet on me coming back here, mate, because you won't win that bet in a million years. I have told you, I going straight, mate, from now on," said Gaz.

"Yes, well, we will see, Gaz, we will see. So, are you going back up the north or staying in London?" asked John. Gaz called John 'shortie' because he was really tall.

"To be honest, mate, I am not sure yet. I might fuck off abroad and get me some Mexican bird. We will see. But I do know one thing, I will never be coming back here, Shortie, so don't hold yer breath," said Gaz with a large smile on his face.

"Well, send us a postcard, Gaz, you know our address," said John, laughing.

"I will do so, mate. Right, I am off. I can't wait to see the back of this place." John walked over to Gaz and shook his hand.

Gaz nodded at John and John nodded back.

Gaz was finally free. He stood at the large wooden gates, looked up to the sky and took a deep breath in. Rick pulled up in front of him in a Mercedes Benz, all black with tinted windows. Gaz climbed in and shut the door.

"Is it all sorted?" asked Gaz.

Rick looked across at him.

"Yes, it's all sorted for tonight," said Rick.

"Good, take me for a cooked breakfast, I'm starving. I can't stand the porridge in that place." Gaz started to laugh and so did Rick.

Rick looked over at Gaz and nodded. Then they drove away into the distance.

Up the North of England Two Days Later

"This is the London news with David Dunn. The secret location where money is made for the Bank of England was robbed during the night in the early hours of this morning. Over four million pounds was stolen. The robbers were dressed in black with ski masks, as seen on the CCTV. The robbers were a professional gang and used a white transit van to make their getaway, with no number plates. Scotland Yard is leading the investigation and MI6. In other news today Theresa May is having a meeting with unions over pay rises and pensions…"

"Turn off that television, son, as we will have to leave now before the traffic gets bad. Are you ready, Michael?" asked Mum. Michael was being slow as usual.

"Come on, because I am supposed to be meeting Kim in the school yard," said Damion.

"There is your packed lunch," said Mum.

Damion went to the car and waited for his mum and brother.

"Hey, Damo, do yer fancy sleeping out tonight camping over the woods? There is going to be a few of us; it should be a laugh," said Conner, walking past to catch the school bus.

"Do you want a lift, Conner? I am sure my mum won't mind," Conner started to walk towards Damion.

"Well, if your ma's okay with it," Damion was getting impatient.

"Are yer coming or what?" shouted Damion up the garden path.

"Aye, man, hold yer horses," shouted Mum, waiting for Michael to walk out of the front door.

"God, you are so slow sometimes," said Damion to Michael.

"Shut up, it's just coz yer girlfriend is waiting for yer, creep," said Michael, brushing past Damion just to wind him up.

“Shut up, just coz yer jealous, coz you don’t have a girlfriend,” said Damion.

“Eh…who wants one? Yuck! Girls are stupid, shotgun!” Michael ran to get into the front of the car.

“He always gets in the front, Mum, it’s not fair,” said Damion.

“No he doesn’t, anyway, you can sit in the back and keep Conner company,” said Mum, climbing into the driver’s side once everyone was inside the car.

“Put your seat belts on,” everyone did.

Mum put the radio on and her favourite song was on.

“Because I’m happyeeeeee,” sang Mum.

“So will you be able to camp out tonight? Ask your mum now,” whispered Conner to Damion.

“Mum, can I camp out tonight? Coz everyone is.” Mum looked through the mirror.

“And who is everyone?” said Mum.

“I dunno, Conner! Can I use my tent?” said Damion, looking back at his mum through the car mirror.

“Yes, I suppose so.” Damion smiled at Conner and Conner gave Damion a cheesy smile back.

“Oh…this traffic is getting worse on a morning,” said Mum, as she did most mornings, as there was always queues on the way to school. Eventually, Mum pulled the car over.

“Have a good day, boys, and I will be in about six tonight, as I am working a bit late. I have left some money in the jar in the kitchen, so you two can get a kebab wrap or pizza,” the boys sat and listened.

“Okay, Mum, see you later, love yer,” Michael and Damion said together.

“Love you too, boys,” said Mum, as the boys where leaving the car.

“Oh, before you go, don’t forget to bring everything home out of your lockers, with it being your last day at school. Six weeks off school, boys, now. Okay, I will see you in the morning, if you two are sleeping out tonight, don’t be getting into any trouble,” said Mum, as the kids stood holding the car doors open.

“We won’t, I promise, Mum,” said Damion, shutting the car door.

Mum soon drove away into the traffic on her way to work.

“So who is camping out?” asked Damion, walking along the road with Conner.

Michael had run ahead as he had seen some of his mates in the schoolyard.

“Just me and you up to now. Why don’t we ask Joe, see if he wants to camp out?” said Conner.

Damion pulled out his mobile phone and rang Joe who goes to a different school.

“Hi, mate, fancy camping out tonight? If you’re staying at your dad’s,” said Damion.

“Yer, that sounds great. Where are we going to camp out at? Are any of the girls camping out?” asked Joe.

“I don’t know yet, I will have to ring you a bit later to let you know, as we have just thought about camping out. Even though, Conner reckoned everyone was camping out.” Damion gave Conner a look as if to say ‘you’re such a liar sometimes, Conner’. Conner just shrugged his shoulders.

“What time are yer coming over tonight?” said Damion.

“Straight after school,” said Joe.

“Right, we will all meet at mine then, coz me mum is out at work till late tonight,” Conner was trying to listen in on the conversation.

“Is your Michael camping out as well?” asked Joe.

“I don’t know, wait a second. MICHAEL, ARE YOU CAMPING OUT TONIGHT WITH US LOT?” shouted Damion across the courtyard of the school, as Michael was talking to a group of his mates.

“I DON’T KNOW YET, WILL LET YOU KNOW LATER, OLLI HAS JUST ASKED ME TO PLAY ON THE GAME WITH HIM TONIGHT, SO MAYBE AFTER THAT!” shouted Michael, back across the school yard to Damion.

“Right, Michael is going to be playing with Olli first, on the games and he will come down a bit later,” Damion was trying to move away from Conner.

“Okay, mate, will ring you a bit later, Damo,” said Joe.

“Okay, see you a bit later mate,” Damion put his phone back in his pocket.

“So is he camping out?” asked Conner.

“Yer, he’s coming over to mine straight after school,” said Damion.

“DAMO, DAMO!” shouted Jake, across the schoolyard and started to run towards Damion and Conner.

“Yer all right? Oh it’s great, last day at school, roll on one thirty, when we get finished. I can’t wait,” said Jake.

“Yer, me too, fancy camping out tonight?” asked Conner.

“Well, aye. Who else is camping out?” Damion was looking at Conner.

“Well, up to now, it’s me, Damo, Joe and Michael, but Michael is coming down a bit later coz he promised Olli he was going to play on the computer with him,” said Conner.

“We are all meeting at mine, after school,” said Damion.

“Great! I will bring my tent as well then,” said Jake.

“How many can sleep in your tent again?” asked Damion.

“Well, I can get four in mine.” They all started walking towards the entrance of the school.

“Are you bringing your tent like Conner?” asked Jake.

“Yer, but I can only get two or three in mine though,” Conner was going through his pockets.

“Well, that should be enough, unless all the girls are camping out as well,” said Damion, then he spotted Kim through the crowds.

“There’s Kim, come on,” Conner and Jake followed.

Kim was stood talking to her friends.

“Hey,” said Damion.

Kim’s face lit up, and she smiled.

“Fancy camping out tonight, Kim?” Kim looked at Damion.

“I wish, my dad probably won’t let me, but I will be able to come down for a bit. Fancy it, girls?” said Kim to her friends.

“Yes, sounds good,” said her friends.

“Where are we all going to meet up?” Kim raised her eyebrow and gave Damion one of her wicked smiles.

Damion’s smile grew bigger.

“We are all meeting at my place after school, so we will wait for you all there,” Kim winked at Damion.

“Okay, we will see you at yours then,” Kim and her friends slowly walked away towards the school entrance.

“That’s great, the girls are coming too. We should have a laugh. Come on, coz am going for a quick fag before we go in,” said Conner.

“You really need to pack them in, mate,” said Damion.

“Oh shut up, are you coming or what?” Conner started to make his way over to the smokers’ corner.

“Aye, but hurry up, will yer?”

The lads all walked over to the side of the school and Conner lit up his cigarette.

“Giza a couple of draws, Conner,” said Jake.

“Here,” said Conner, passing the cigarette over to Jake.

Damion stood and shook his head.

“Conner, Jake and Damion. I should have guessed you would be here,” said Mr Hunter.

Conner dropped the cigarette on the floor.

“I am going to let you off this time, as it is the last day of school, but if I catch you lot again after the holidays when we are back, you will have detention for a month. Do you hear me?”

The boys all put their heads down and looked at the floor.

“Yes, sir,” the boys all said together.

“Now go on, off to class,” the boys walked away.

Mr Hunter lit up his cigarette, started to smoke, shook his head and smiled.

“Conner, I knew we would get caught again and I don’t even smoke,” said Damion.

Conner looked at Damion.

“Sorry, mate,” Damion shook his head.

“I will let you off this time,” said Damion as they all started to laugh.

The day soon went by and the bell went for the end of school. All the kids where walking as fast as they could towards their lockers to get all their belongings, as school was now finished for the six weeks holidays.

The kids ran through the yard to catch up with their friends and to say goodbye to others, as they wouldn’t see them during the holidays. Damion and Conner where play fighting in the yard waiting for Jake as he had been in a different class.

“HURRY UP, MATE, WHEREHAVE YOU BEEN?” shouted Conner to Jake as he came out of the school doors.

“Don’t ask,” said Jake, walking towards them.

“Where is Michael?” said Jake.

“God knows, he wants to be at the bus stop when we get there,” said Damion.

The boys walked towards the bus stop and saw that Michael was there.

"Where have you been?" said Michael.

"We have been waiting for Jake."

"Is Luke camping out tonight?" asked Michael.

"I don't know, I haven't see him. We can give him a knock when we get back to the village," said Damion.

"Well, when we get home I want a shower first and to get changed out of these clothes. I will call for him then to see what he is doing," said Michael.

"Right, well, if you do that, I will get the tent out of the shed and find the sleeping bags and stuff. Then I can jump in the shower after you," Michael nodded.

"So what time are we meeting at your place?" asked Conner.

"I don't know, when you're ready," said Damion.

"Do you want me to order the pizzas and bring them down a bit later on?" asked Michael.

"Aye…I will grab a sandwich when I get in and we can have the pizza for later," said Damion.

The bus pulled up and the boys got on the bus and all sat up the back.

Damion jumped on Conner, play fighting, then Jake and Michael joined in. The bus was soon packed and overflowing with school kids. Everyone was shouting over the top of each other to be heard. Kim and her friends got on the bus and made their way up the back, squeezing past everyone to go and sit with Damion.

"Hello," said Kim.

Damion tried to sit up and pushed Jake and Michael off him. The boys all looked at Kim.

"Come on, lads, move along and let the ladies sit down," said Damion.

Kim and her two friends squeezed in on the seats.

One of her friends sat next to Conner and Conner started to blush.

"So, are you lot coming down tonight then?" asked Conner to the girl who sat next to him.

"I think so," said the girl.

"So what's your name again?"

The girl looked at Conner. "I am Beth."

Conner smiled.

"And what's her name again?" Conner moved his head towards the other girl.

"That's Kate," said Beth.

"Jake, ask Kate if she is coming tonight!" shouted Conner over the commotion on the bus.

"So are you coming tonight, Kate?" Kate looked at Jake.

"Yer, we will be going to Kim's first then we will come up to Damo's," Jake smiled.

"Great, the more the merrier," Kate smiled back at Jake and got up from her seat.

"Right, this is my stop. See you later, Jake. Kim, I will call for you about four o'clock," said Kate.

"Okay, Kate, see you then," Kim waved at her friend.

"Bye," said Jake.

"Bye, see you tonight," Conner bent over and winked at Jake.

"What?" Jake looked at Conner and Conner started to laugh.

Kate pushed her way to the front of the bus and everyone knelt on the back seat and waved at her, as the bus drove on. It was Beth's stop a bit further along the bus ride.

"See you all later. I will call for you at four with Kate as she is going to come for me first," Kim smiled and nodded then waved at Beth.

"Okay, see you later, Beth," Damion put his arm around Kim. Beth started to laugh.

"See you later, Beth," said Conner.

Beth squeezed through everyone and again everyone knelt on the back seat to wave at Beth as the bus drove off. Beth stood and waved back. Once Beth was out of sight, they all sat back down on the seat.

"So, Kim, is Beth seeing anyone?" asked Conner.

Kim started to laugh.

"No, Conner, why?"

Conner shrugged his shoulders.

"Oh, nothing, just asking," Conner smiled at Kim.

"You like Beth, don't you, Conner," said Damion, laughing.

"No," Conner started laughing and blushed again.

"You liar," said Damion and then jumped on Conner.

Michael and Jake joined in on the action.

"Will you lot stop it?" Kim kept trying to push the lads away from her.

"Come on, this is our stop," said Kim.

Jake and Michael got off Damion then Damion got off Conner.

"Ah, me ribs, I am going to get you back for that, Damo," Conner held his ribs.

"Ha, good luck," said Damion smiling at Conner.

The bus pulled up and they all squeezed their way through the kids and jumped off the bus. All their friends were waving and shouting out the windows.

"See you after the six weeks!" they shouted.

Damion, Conner, Michael, Jake and Kim all stood and waved till the bus was nearly out of sight.

"Do you want me to walk you home?" asked Damion to Kim.

"No, you go and get ready for tonight and I will see you later at yours," said Kim, kissing Damion on the cheek.

"OOOOW!" said Conner.

"Shut up, Conner, you're just jealous," Damion snarled.

Conner shrugged his shoulders.

"I'm not," said Conner.

"Bye," said Damion.

Kim walked away down the road.

"I'm going to just ring Luke when I get in the house to see if he is camping out," said Michael.

"Aye, all right, and, Conner, hurry up and get ready coz you take forever," said Damion.

"Aye, man, will see you round your place in a bit."

Damion and Michael walked on and Conner stuck his fingers up at Damion then walked into the house. Damion and Michael started to laugh.

"Have you got your key? I'm starving," said Michael.

"Me too, we can make some sandwiches when we get in and raid the biscuit tin."

Michael started to laugh. "Sounds like a plan to me."

They were soon at the front door. Damion unlocked the door and Michael barged passed him.

"Shot gun for the biscuits," Michael ran into the kitchen and grabbed the biscuit tin out of the cupboard.

“Oh, no, you don’t,” Damion ran through the house after him and snatched the biscuit tin out of Michael’s hands.

“I’m the oldest, so I go first,” he said, grabbing a load of biscuits out of the tin then passing it back to Michael. Michael shook his head.

Damion went and sat down in the sitting room and put the television on. Michael followed him carrying the biscuit tin.

“Oh, it’s so nice being off school, just think, we can lie in every morning if we want to,” said Michael, then stuffed a biscuit in his mouth.

“Right, I am going to get the tent out of the shed.” Damion got up from the couch, got the keys from the draw in the kitchen and went outside to the shed. He unlocked it and walked in. The tent was right at the back and he soon brought it out and put it in the kitchen on the floor.

“Are you going in the shower then or what?” Michael was sitting on the settee still.

“Aye, man, give me a chance.” Michael got up.

Damion walked upstairs, looked through the cupboards for the sleeping bags, soon he found them and chucked them down the stairs as Michael was walking up them.

Michael looked up at Damion. “You did that on purpose, didn’t you?”

Damion started to laugh.

“Shut up, and hurry up in the shower.”

Michael went into the bathroom and shut the door. The phone started to ring so Damion ran downstairs to answer it.

“Hello,” said Damion.

“It’s just me. Is me mum there?” asked Sean, Damion’s older brother on the other end of the phone.

“No, Na, she is at work, Sean.”

Sean sighed. “What time is she getting home?”

Damion thought. “Err…I am not sure, she said about six tonight.”

Sean looked at his watch.

“Where is our Michael at?” asked Sean.

“He’s is in the shower.”

“All right, well, when Mum gets in, tell her to give me a ring, just I can’t get her on her mobile.”

"I will have to leave her a note because we are camping out tonight and we won't see her."

"Oh…Okay, leave her a note, don't forget."

"Aye…no bother bro."

"Okay, speak to you later," said Sean.

"Aye, see yer later, Sean," Damion put the phone down.

Damion wrote a note, placed it in front of the kettle, then went back upstairs. Michael had just got out of the shower and went straight into his bedroom.

"Who was that on the phone?" Michael asked, trying to get dry.

"It was Sean, asking for Mum," Damion was looking for a towel to take with him camping.

"What for?" asked Michael.

"I don't know…none of your business."

Michael put on his high fi and cranked up the music. Damion barged into Michael's bedroom.

"Can you turn it down a bit, just the neighbours will start complaining and Mum won't be happy…if they tell her." Damion turned it down.

"Aye, man…yer frightened the shit out of me there." Michael looking at Damion.

"Well, if you want to get wrong then put it up, but I am not taking the wrap for you." Michael gave Damion one of his looks but thought about what he had said and decided to keep the volume low.

Damion jumped in the shower, got changed and spruced himself up for when he would see Kim.

"My god, how much sprays have you put on?" Michael was wafting his arms around in the air.

"Shut up!"

There was a knock on the door.

"Go and answer that for me, will yer? Please."

Michael obliged as he wanted to know who was at the door anyway. When he opened the door, it was Conner.

"Come in…"

Conner walked passed Michael.

"Where is he?"

Michael shut the door.

"Upstairs, in his room, smelling like a girl for Kim," Conner started to laugh.

"You don't smell much better, have you got a girlfriend as well?" Conner smiled.

"Ha ha ha," said Michael sarcastically.

"No…I haven't and I don't want one either," continued Michael.

"Can I go up?" asked Conner as he could hear Damion upstairs banging around.

"Please yourself."

Conner put down his bags and ran up the stairs.

Damion was just checking himself out in the bathroom mirror. Conner had walked straight past Damion and into the bedroom then came out again as Damion wasn't there.

"Oh…you're there, mate."

Damion looked at Conner walking towards him from his bedroom.

"Did you get some money off your mum for some pizza for later?"

Conner smiled.

"Aye, me mum gave me a tenna," said Conner.

Damion looked back in the mirror to start styling his hair again.

"Well, what we will do is that all of us go to the pizza shop a bit later and take it back to the camp to share," said Damion.

Conner checked his pockets, pulled out his tenna, flashed it to Damion, then kissed it and put it back in his pocket.

"Aye, yer…whatever," said Conner.

The doorbell started to ring.

"Go and see who that is, Conner, will yer?" Conner ran down the stairs and answered the door.

Jake was stood there.

"Come in, is that your tent?" Conner was looking at Jake's bags.

"Aye, and I've got some money off me dad so…I'm going to see if I can get some tabs at the shop," said Jake.

"How much have you got?" asked Conner.

"A tenna," said Jake.

"Well, me and you can go halves, if you like, on some tabs?" Conner flashed his tenna to Jake.

"Aye, all right then. Where's Damo at?" Jake looked up the stairs as he heard a noise.

"He is upstairs, getting ready," said Conner, putting his tenna back in his pocket.

Michael heard voices and came to see who it was at the door.

"I thought I heard your voice, he won't be long. Go and sit down."

Jake and Connor went and sat in the sitting room. Michael went and changed the channel on the television then Damion came downstairs.

"Do you want me to ring Luke?" asked Damion, looking at Michael.

"Aye, go on then," Damion picked up the house phone and rang Luke.

"Hi, mate, what are you doing tonight?" Damion looked at Michael.

"Knout, why? What yer up too?" asked Luke.

"We are all camping out, mate, fancy it?" asked Damion.

"Aye sounds good to me," Luke sounded quite excited.

"Well, get ready and come down here, coz we are just waiting for the others to come down."

"Who else is camping out?"

Damion started counting on his fingers. "Up till now there is me, our Michael, Conner, Jake, Joe, Kim, Beth and Kate."

"Sounds good," said Luke.

"We are just waiting for Joe getting over and the girls," said Damion.

"Okay, I won't be long, do I need my tent?"

Damion looked at Jake and then Conner.

"No, mate, we have three, just bring your sleeping bag," said Damion.

"Okay, be there in a bit," said Luke.

"See you in a sec," said Damion.

Damion put the phone down.

"Right, Luke is camping out too," Damion looked at Michael.

"Great, that's about nine of us then," said Conner.

The doorbell went again.

Everyone went to the door.

Joe was stood.

"All right, Joe?" said Damion.

"Aye, I am now that we are off school for six weeks."

Everyone started to laugh.

"Come on in, mate," said Damion.

Everyone went back into the sitting room and sat down on the settees.

"So who else is coming?" asked Joe.

"We are just waiting for the girls and Luke," said Damion.

"Which girls are coming?" said Joe.

"Kim, Beth and Kate," said Conner, all excited.

"Oh…okay, I know Kim, but I don't know Beth and Kate."

Damion nodded his head.

"Beth's lovely," said Conner.

Everyone started to laugh.

"You do like her, don't you, Conner?" asked Michael.

"She is all right," Conner started to blush.

"I knew it," said Damion, jumping on Conner to the point they both end up on the floor, rolling around.

There was another knock on the door.

"That will be Luke," said Jake.

They all went to the door.

When the door was open it was Kim and the girls. Everyone started to laugh.

"What are you lot laughing at?" said Kim.

"We all thought it was Luke, come in," said Damion.

"It's a good job we have plenty of seats in here," said Michael. They all went back into the sitting room and sat down.

"I have always wondered why you have three couches in your sitting room," said Jake.

"My mum says that it's because we all like to spread out, when we watch the telly, so we normally have a couch each," said Michael.

"Oh yer! Makes sense now," said Jake.

The doorbell went again.

"Right, come on that will be Luke, all get your stuff," said Damion.

Michael answered the door.

"You all right, mate?" said Michael.

"Aye, so are you going camping?" asked Luke.

"Yes, but I will be down a bit later, coz I promised Olli I would play on the computer for a couple of hours."

Luke looked disappointed.

"Right, well, do you want me to stay with you? I will have a couple of games with you and Olli if you like?" asked Luke.

Michael's eyebrows raised up and a smile came across his face.

"Yer, great, come on in then," said Michael.

"Damion, Luke is going to stay with me and come down later on," said Michael.

Damion walked up to Luke and they did their special handshake.

"Aye, all right, bro?" asked Damion.

"Well, I'm all right, I'm going to have a few games with Michael then we will come down. There is enough of you to put the tents up," said Luke.

"Aye, ne, bother," said Damion.

"Come on then, we will go and get the tents up and start a campfire."

Everyone got up, picked up their belongings and followed Damion out of the house.

"I am going to go to the toilet before we go," said Kim.

"Yer, just go there is a toilet upstairs or there is one just there near the front door," said Damion.

Everyone dropped their stuff and went to the toilets.

The girls all went to the toilet together upstairs. The boys just looked at each other and started to laugh.

"Why do girls always go to the toilets together?" asked Michael then looked at Conner.

"Don't ask me, mate, I haven't got a clue."

The girls were soon finished and came downstairs. All the lads started laughing.

"What yer laughing at?" asked Kate.

Which made the lads laugh even more.

"Nothing," said Conner and Damion together then burst out laughing again.

"Come on," said Jake.

Michael and Luke went into the kitchen to play on the computer.

“Okay, we will see you two soon. Don’t forget the money for the pizza, coz we are all going to go together. So just come straight down to the camp. We will be camping in the woods at the bottom of the bank!” shouted Damion.

The boys then picked up their tents and sleeping bags and left for the woods. On the way, they were all carrying on, laughing and pushing each other. They all decided to go to the shop first and hung around until they managed to get a man to go into the shop for some cigarettes for Conner and Jake. Eventually, they were off again on their journey and walked along the country roads till they reached the woods.

There was a small clearing in the woods where they could set up their tents. Everyone helped to get the tents up and they had lots of fun doing it. They decided to leave a large circle in the middle so they could build a campfire. Everyone placed their sleeping bags inside the tents.

“Right, we need some stones for around the fire, so it won’t spread,” said Damion.

“Yer, and we need to go and collect some sticks for the fire,” said Jake.

Everyone split up to find sticks and stones for the fire.

The girls decided to stick together and the boys went together.

They soon had loads of sticks and stones and brought them back to the camp.

“We should get some more sticks for later so we can keep the fire going,” said Damion.

“Well, we will stay here and help Jake and Joe, you and Conner go and get some more,” said Kim.

“Okay, Conner, you come with me,” said Damion.

Conner and Damion took two tent bags with them to collect and carry the sticks in. They walked quite deep into the woods and started to collect more sticks. Damion spotted a pile of sticks and leaves in a mound. He went over with his bag. He kicked at the leaves, picked up a load of sticks and placed them into his bag.

He then saw what looked like a black handle. Damion grabbed the handle and pulled it hard. It was really heavy. It was a black bag under the sticks and leaves. He moved some of the sticks off the bag and the bag was full of something. Damion opened the zip and he jumped back. He couldn't speak, he then knelt back up and looked in the bag again. Damion was shocked at what he had seen. He put his hand in the bag and pulled out a pile of money wrapped in a paper cover round the middle of it. It was a pile of twenty-pound notes. He flicked through the pile and found they were all twenty-pound notes.

"Conner, Conner, come here."

Conner was too busy picking up sticks and putting them into his bag.

"I have nearly done my bag, it's nearly full," said Conner, looking over at Damion.

"Conner, just come here," Damion was still on his knees looking at the bundle of money in his hands.

"What? I don't believe it, your bag's only half full," said Conner.

"Forget the sticks. Look!" said Damion.

"What?" Conner could then see Damion had something in his hand.

Conner walked over to Damion.

"Look in the large black bag," said Damion.

Conner came closer to have a look.

"What's in there?"

Damion chucked the bundle of money at Conner.

"What the FUCK!" Damion pulled out another bundle and it was fifty-pound notes. He flicked through the bundle to find it was all fifty-pound notes.

Conner dropped to his knees. Damion chucked the other bundle at Conner. Damion then dragged the bag fully out from the leaves and sticks and it was full to the brim with money. Conner was still in shock while looking at the money.

"What should we do?" asked Conner.

"Nothing, we do nothing yet. We need to leave it where it is for now. Say nothing to the others. Help me cover it back up." Damion snatched the money out of Conner's hands and placed it back in the bag.

"Can we not just take a little bit?" asked Conner.

"No, Conner, we can't just take a little bit, we need to leave it there for now and like I said, SAY NOTHING, RIGHT?" said Damion, starting to get annoyed.

Conner helped Damion cover the bag back up.

"Okay, Damo, no problem," Conner was still a little shocked.

"Look, if any of them find out about this they may tell their parents and then we will have to give it to the police," said Damion.

"Fuck that," said Connor.

"Right, help me cover it up then with sticks and leaves and we will get back to the camp. Remember: say nothing," Conner nodded.

"Yer, no problem, mate."

They made sure it was well covered up before they left.

"We will talk about it later when the girls have gone, okay?" Conner nodded again.

And they quickly got up and started to collect more sticks and went straight back to the camp.

Jake, Joe and the girls had the fire going and they were all sitting around it when Damion and Conner got back to the camp.

"Jake, Joe, will you stay here with the girls while me and Conner go and get Michael and Luke and we will bring back pizzas," said Damion.

"Yer, no, bother, will you bring me a pizza back? Here, take this money. There should be enough for a pizza," said Jake.

"Will you get me some chocolate, babe?" asked Kim.

"Yes, of course," said Damion, smiling at Kim.

"Right, come on, Conner," Conner looked at Damion.

Damion moved his head. Conner and Damion walked away from the camp heading back towards home.

Once they were well away from the camp and nobody could hear their conversation, Conner asked, "What are we going to do, Damo?"

"We are going to tell Michael and Luke and as soon as the girls have gone home. We will go and get it, all right? But we need to find somewhere else to hide it," said Damion.

Damion and Conner ran as fast as they could back to Damion's house.

They burst through the door and both of them were shouting of Michael.

"MICHAEL, MICHAEL!" shouted Damion and Conner together.

"What, man? We're in the kitchen!" shouted Michael from the distance.

"You are never going to believe what we have found," said Damion.

"What have you found?" asked Michael.

Luke was still playing on the computer.

"Turn that computer off and I will tell you," Luke looked up at Damion and then carried on playing with Olli.

"Turn it off," said Conner.

"Piss off, we are in a middle of a game," said Michael.

"Just turn it off NOW! Or I will turn it off," said Damion.

"Olli, mate, I am going to have to go, will catch up with you a bit later, mate," said Michael.

Luke looked up again at Damion and Conner.

"So what have you found?" asked Luke with a raised eyebrow.

"MONEY! LOADS OF IT!" shouted Damion and Conner together.

"Yer, right! Whatever," said Luke.

"Michael, I am telling you there are thousands of pounds in the woods," said Damion.

"Should we ring your brother Sean?" asked Conner.

"No! Not yet anyway," said Damion.

"Look, we haven't told the others, we are the only ones that know at the moment. I think we should wait till the girls go home then we will go and get it, right? And say nothing," said Damion.

"So Joe and Jake don't know?" asked Luke.

"No, not yet, they are at the camp with the girls waiting for us to come back with pizza and Kim wants some chocolate," said Conner.

"What should we do with it?" asked Damion.

"Well, if there is a load of money, we need to hide it somewhere else," said Luke.

"I wonder how it got there?" said Michael.

"Wasn't there something on the news this morning about a robbery in London or something like that? It could be from that," said Damion.

"Put the telly on and look at the teletext or the news, it should say something on there," said Luke.

Everyone rushed in the sitting room and Michael put the television on.

"Put the news on," said Damion to Michael.

Michael used the remote and he flicked through the channels until eventually he found the news on the screen. He turned the volume up so everyone could hear it clearly in the room.

"Other breaking news from London, a secret location where money is made for the Bank of England was robbed during the night in the early hours of this morning. The robbers were dressed in black and wore ski masks as seen on CCTV. Over four million pounds was stolen. The robbers were a professional gang and used a white transit van to make there get away, with no number plates. Scotland Yard and MI6 are leading the investigation. In other news today, Teresa May was meeting with unions over pay rises and pensions…"

"Turn it off," said Michael.

"So do you believe me now? That must be the money and there must be over four million pounds," said Damion.

"Right, we need a plan, are we going to tell Jake and Joe?" said Luke.

"Yer!" said Damion.

"Right, say nothing to them until the girls go home. We can let them know then," said Luke.

Damion, Conner and Michael all looked at Luke.

"Right, get the money out of the jar, Michael, and we will go to the shop for Kim's chocolate then go to the pizza shop. We need to get rid of the girls as soon as possible," said Damion.

Michael went to get the money and then they all set off to the shop.

"Hello again, Damion, did you forget something?" said the shopkeeper.

"No, Kim just wants some chocolate."

The shopkeeper then looked at Michael.

"Oh I see, and hello, Michael, how are you today? And how is your mum?"

Everyone looked at Michael.

"Aye, I am okay, thanks, and Mum, she is great, thanks for asking, she's at work at the moment," the shopkeeper took the chocolate from Damion.

“Aye, she’s a hard worker your mum, I hope you are all staying out of trouble,” said the shopkeeper, putting the chocolate on the counter after scanning it.

“Yer, of course we are,” said Luke.

Conner looked at Damion and Damion looked at Conner.

“That will be a pound,” said the shopkeeper.

Damion handed over a pound coin.

“See you boys later,” the shopkeeper said.

“Aye, see you later,” the boys all said together.

“Right what pizzas should we get?” asked Michael as they all walked out of the shop.

“Just get three sixteen inch with pepperoni on two of them and a margarita for the other. That should feed us all,” said Damion.

“Aye, that should do.”

They were soon at the pizza shop.

“Can we get two sixteen inch pepperoni and one sixteen inch margarita,” said Michael to the man behind the counter at the pizza shop.

“It will be about twenty minutes, is that all right?” asked the man.

“Aye, that will be fine, mate, how much will that be?” asked Michael.

“Right, I will just work it out. Mm, right, that’s twenty four pounds, son.”

Michael rummaged around in his pocket, pulled out a twenty-pound note and put it on the counter.

“Right, I’ve got twenty, Luke, have you got any money?” asked Michael.

“Here, I’ve got a fiver left,” said Conner.

“Great, mate, there you go, thanks,” Michael said to the pizza man.

“Come on, we will wait outside,” said Luke.

Everyone walked outside.

“Don’t talk about it out here right, coz it just takes one person to hear and we are all done for,” said Luke.

The boys looked at each other and all they could think about was the money. They were all very quiet just looking at each other.

“OH MY GOD, JUST THINK ABOUT WHAT WE CAN DO!” shouted Conner; he just couldn’t help himself.

Everyone started to laugh and started jumping on each other.

“Conner, man, yer just can’t help yourself, can yer?” said Damion, punching him in the arm.

“Aww, man, you just wait,” said Conner.

“What you going to do?” asked Damion.

They all started laughing.

“Pizza’s done!” shouted the man from behind the counter.

“Great! Should we get some bottles of pop as well?” asked Luke.

“Aye, you can buy them then,” said Michael.

“Here, squirt,” said Luke, passing a pizza box to Conner.

“Don’t drop it.”

Conner took the box off Luke. “I won’t.”

Michael then passed a box to Damion.

“Here, get this, Damo,” said Michael.

“Can I get three bottles of pop as well please?” asked Luke.

“Yep, that will be three pounds,” said the pizza man.

“See you later, mate,” said Luke.

They all started to walk towards the woods.

“So how can we get the girls to go home?” asked Michael.

“Well, Kim normally has to go in early anyway, so hopefully they will only be there a couple of hours then we can tell Joe and Jake and we can plan what we are going to do, and where to hide it,” said Damion.

“Right, that’s what we will do then, are we all agreed?” asked Luke.

“Yes,” said everyone.

They were soon at the woods and walked through the trees. Jake, Kim and Kate were sitting around the fire.

“Where’ve Joe and Beth gone?” said Damion.

Jake, Kim and Kate all pointed at one of the tents.

“What are they doing?” asked Michael.

Conner passed Jake his pizza box and walked over to the tent and pulled back the cover. Joe and Beth were kissing.

“Joe, man! I don’t believe you, get off her NOW!” said Conner.

Conner was upset and quite jealous as he liked Beth.

Everyone started laughing. Damion went to have a look.

"Come on, we have brought pizza and coke," Damion shook his head at Joe.

"What?" said Joe.

"Never mind," said Damion while Conner had walked away in a bit of a sulk.

"Conner, if Beth likes Joe leave it, mate, there is plenty more fish in the sea," said Damion.

Conner nodded.

"Aye you're right, mate."

Joe and Beth came out from the tent.

"Right, if we break the pizza boxes up we can use them like plates," said Michael.

"Did you get my chocolate babe?" asked Kim.

Damion took the chocolate out of his pocket and passed it to Kim.

"Thanks, babe." Damion and Kim sat on the grass together.

"Do you want some pizza, girls?," said Conner.

"Yes please," they all said together.

Conner dished out the pizza on to the boxes that Luke, Kate and Kim were ripping up. They all sat around the fire and ate their pizzas.

"So what time do you girls have to be in?" asked Luke.

"Why are you trying to get rid of us, Luke?" said Beth.

"No, No, I was just wondering, that's all," Luke looked over at Michael.

"I have to be in about six thirty, coz my mum and dad are going out and I have to babysit," Michael looked at Damion.

"Have you got the time on you, Damo?" said Michael.

Damion pulled out his mobile phone.

"It's now five thirty."

"So what do you girls fancy doing?" asked Conner.

"I don't know," said Kate.

"Well, why don't we have a look down to the river and have a laugh and skim some stones," said Conner.

"Aye sounds good to me," said Michael.

"I am up for that," said Luke.

Everyone agreed.

They placed the pizza boxes on the fire when they had finished and Joe and Beth decided to stay back until the fire was nearly out.

"Right as soon as the fire has died down, come down," said Luke.

"Aye ne, brother," said Joe, looking forward to spending more time with Beth kissing and cuddling. He was going to take full advantage of it while he could, he thought to himself.

Everyone else got up and they all walked between the trees towards the river. It was a warm day and as soon as the boys got there, they started to strip their t-shirts off. The girls took their shoes off and paddled in the water. The boys started a competition of who could do the most skims across the water with the stones and they were all really good.

"That was three that time," said Luke.

"That was four did you SEE IT!" shouted Michael.

Everyone was having a great time.

Back at the camp so were Joe and Beth.

Joe could see the fire was nearly out.

"Come on, Beth, we will go and see the others now."

Joe picked himself up off the floor and then helped Beth up like a true gentleman. Beth smiled and grabbed his hand and Joe pulled her up to him and kissed her on the forehead.

"Come on, we are going to miss all the fun with your friends." Joe smiled at Beth and Beth smiled back.

They ran off towards the river where their friends where.

"Here are the love birds," said Kate.

Beth started to smile and giggle and so did Joe. Joe took his t-shirt off, jumped in the water and splashed Damion.

"Right! That's it. You're in for it, Joe," said Damion.

Damion started to splash Joe and then everyone started splashing each other until everyone was soaking wet and having fun. The boys soon forgot about the money and were just enjoying themselves with their friends. It ended up girls against the boys and then the boys made it fairer and Damion and Joe helped the girls get Michael, Luke, Conner and Jake. They laughed and laughed until their bellies hurt. The time flew by and before they knew it, it was six thirty and the girls had to leave.

"Come on, we will all walk you back home and we should all go and get changed too back at the house," said Damion.

"Yer, good idea, mate, as it may get cold during the night," said Luke.

Everyone made their way back to the camp. The girls got their belongings, and Damion put his arm around Kim as they walked through the woods. Joe put his arm around Beth and Conner decided to chat up Kate.

"So, Kate, have you got a boyfriend?" asked Conner.

"No, why?" said Kate.

"Well, I was just asking, do you want one?" said Conner.

"Are you asking me out, Conner?"

He started to blush.

"Yes, why not?"

Kate started to smile.

"Okay, then, Conner," Kate took a hold of his hand and the others looked back at them.

Conner had the biggest smile on his face.

"Looks like Conner and Kate are now an item," said Luke, smiling.

Everyone turned around to have a look at Conner and Kate holding hands.

"I am sure I got a four with that last throw, you know," said Jake.

"No, it was defo a three," said Michael.

They were all happy and joking around.

"You better say goodbye here, Damo, you know what my dad's like," said Kim.

"Give me a kiss before you go," Kim slapped the lips on Damion.

Then Joe started kissing Beth. Conner decided to try and get in on the action too by going in to kiss Kate for the first time.

"Oh my lord, let's get up home and get changed while these lot are snogging on! I am starting to feel sick," said Michael.

Luke started to laugh and shook his head at them all.

"Damo, meet you at yours!" shouted Jake.

"Aye, I won't be too long."

The lads were already halfway up the street.

"So can I see you tomorrow then?" asked Damion.

"I am going to my nana's tomorrow, so I am not sure yet and what time yet either," Kim cuddled Damion tightly.

Camping out in the Woods

"So what time Sunday then?" Kim looked up at Damion.

"After dinner about two o'clock, is that all right?" Damion smiled.

"Yer, okay, babe, see you then," Damion let Kim go and watched her walk away.

"Come on, you two, are yer coming or what?" said Kim, walking backwards.

"Come on, lads, we will see the girls either tomorrow or Sunday, we are all meeting at mine for two o'clock Sunday," said Damion.

"See you later, Joe," Beth batted her eyelashes at Joe.

"Yer, see you, babe," Joe started to follow Damion up the street but he kept looking back to watch Beth.

"See you later, Conner," said Kate.

Conner just couldn't stop smiling.

"See you later, Kate," Conner bent Kate over, kissing her again then let her go. Kate nearly fell over.

"I'M IN LOVE!" shouted Conner, waving his arms in the air as he ran to catch up to his friends.

"I'M IN LOVE, I'M IN LOVE!" The boys looked back at Conner.

The girls all started to giggle. Conner had his arms in the air, jumping up and down in the middle of the road.

"Come on, dippy!" shouted Damion, shaking his head and laughing.

Joe couldn't hold his laughter either and they all started to laugh.

When they got back to Damion's house, Michael had jumped in the shower and Luke had popped up to his. Jake was borrowing clothes from Michael and was jumping in the shower after him.

The boys were still laughing when they got to the house.

"Right, mate, I'm off home for a shower, I think I need one now," said Conner.

The lads nearly fell over laughing at Conner's sexual innuendos.

"Conner, don't be long, coz we need to all talk remember," said Damion, who was trying to keep a straight face but couldn't.

"Aye, mate, I'll try not to be long," said Conner, still grinning for ear to ear. "Nor, mate, I am going to get a quick shower and change and I want my jumper in case it gets cold during the night," said Conner, still smiling like a Cheshire Cat.

"Good thinking, batman," Conner walked away up the street to his.

"Joe, do you want to have a shower at ours and borrow some of my clothes," asked Damion.

"Aye, cheers, mate, just I have only brought one set for tomorrow, that's all I have, they are at me dad's," Damion walked into the house and Joe followed him in and shut the door.

"Ne bother, mate. You can borrow some trackies, t-shirt and a jumper. My mum won't mind."

"Who's in the shower, Michael?" asked Damion, looking at his brother.

"Jake's in, he is borrowing some clothes till tomorrow. Mum said she will wash his," said Michael.

"Mum's back? Where is she?"

"She has just popped out over Sean's," Michael was putting clothes in the washing machine.

"What for?" asked Damion.

"I don't know, dippy, what you asking me for?" said Michael.

"All right, keep your hair on. Anyway, you want to start talking to me properly otherwise you get, knout, do yer hear me?" Michael looked at Damion.

Michael started laughing sarcastically.

"Ohhhhhh, is that right, is it? Keep going and I will tell Mum," Michael raised his eyebrows at Damion as if to say 'go on then push me and I WILL tell her'.

"You dare and I will smash your computer up, am telling yer," said Damion.

"Go on then but you will be buying me a new one, dipshit."

"What's up with you two? What yer on about? Telling yer Mum about what?" Damion and Michael looked at Joe.

"We will tell you when everyone gets back here," said Damion.

"Oh…Okay, sounds very secretive," Joe looked at Damion.

"That's because it is," Damion started to calm down.

Jake came down, rubbing his head with a towel.

“Right, Joe, you go in the shower next. There is more towels in the cupboard opposite my bedroom and I will sort yer some clothes out. I will put them on my bed for yer,” said Damion.

Joe went upstairs and jumped in the shower.

The doorbell rang.

“I will get it,” said Michael.

Damion went upstairs to get some clothes out for Joe and himself. It was Luke and Conner at the door.

“That was quick,” said Michael.

“Yer, I know,” said Conner.

“Have you got a hair dryer?” asked Jake.

“Aye, my mum has one upstairs in her bedroom on top of the dressing table, just use that and leave it in there,” Joe came out of the bathroom and went into Damion’s bedroom and closed the door.

“Are you going in the shower!” shouted Joe.

“Yer, the clothes are for you, take your wet ones downstairs and put them in the washing machine and we will wash them coz me mum said she is going to wash Jake’s clothes for him, so yours may as well go in. You can bring my clothes back tomorrow,” said Damion.

“Aye, okay, mate,” said Joe, stood with dripping wet hair and just a towel round his middle.

“I won’t be long, I am going in the shower,” Damion walked past his mum’s bedroom and saw that Jake was sitting on the stool in front of the mirror drying his hair. Damion quickly went in the shower and was soon out. Joe was ready and went in the bedroom where Jake was, to use the dryer after Jake.

“Hurry up, man, you’re worse than a girl doing her hair,” said Joe.

“Shut up,” said Jake, looking through the mirror at Joe.

Conner, Luke and Michael were downstairs.

“So is he lying, Conner?” asked Luke.

“No, Na, I have seen it with my own two eyes honestly, mate,” said Conner.

“I can’t wait to see this, just think of what we can spend it on, is there really that much, Conner?” said Michael.

“Aye there is loads of it, mate, bloody thousands,” Michael then walked to the bottom of the stairs and shouted. “Will you lot hurry up!”

Michael waited for a reply.

"Aye, we are nearly done, man!" shouted Damion.

Jake came downstairs.

"Put the telly on while we're waiting for him, will yer, Michael?" said Conner, getting up and passing Michael the remote off the arm of the chair. Michael put the telly on and Tom and Jerry was on. They all made themselves comfortable on the couches.

Damion quickly dried his hair, brought his wet clothes downstairs and walked through the sitting room to put them into the laundry basket which was in the kitchen. He came back into the sitting room.

"Right, are you lot ready then?" said Damion.

All the lads looked at him and Michael turned the telly off.

"Right, we have something to tell you, Jake and Joe," said Damion.

Joe looked at Jake and Jake looked at Joe.

"What?" said Joe.

Damion had a big smile on his face when they looked back at him.

"I have found something in the woods, but you are not to tell anyone and I mean anyone," Joe looked back at Jake and then back at Damion.

"I won't," said Joe.

"I won't either," said Jake.

"What is it?" Damion and Conner started to laugh.

"Money, loads of it," said Damion.

You could see the surprise come over both Joe's and Jake's faces as if they were in shock and they both just sat looking at Damion.

Damion started to grin from ear to ear. Joe knew that face well and he knew he wasn't lying about it.

"Well, how much money?" asked Joe, still shocked.

"Too much to count, we can't tell anyone, otherwise the police will just take it and we will get nothing," said Damion.

"And you can't tell your parents or anyone else, do you understand?" said Michael.

"When did you find that?" said Joe.

"Damo found it when we went looking for sticks for the fire, there is loads of it, Joe, honest, thousands," said Conner.

"We didn't want the girls to know in case they said anything to anyone. We are the only ones who know about it," Damion rubbed his hands together.

"We think it could be from the bank robbery the other night in London," said Luke.

"Bloody hell, what if the bank robbers come looking for it?" said Joe.

"Well, it won't be there, coz we are going to move it," said Damion.

"Right, I want everyone to get bags from around the house coz we are going to bring it back here and put it in the shed for now. Mum's at work in the morning coz I've just checked her rota in her bedroom, so we will bring it back then. She leaves at about five thirty in the morning coz she has to be at work for six. So we will get it tonight and start walking up here for about quarter to six in the morning so nobody sees us," said Damion.

Everyone got up. Michael went to the kitchen to the cupboard under the stairs and started chucking bags out of it. Everyone picked up the bags, most of which were school bags.

"Just empty everything out of them," said Damion, getting a large plastic bag from out of the cupboard under the sink.

"Just put everything in here."

All the lads emptied the bags and put the contents in the large plastic bag Damion was holding. Damion handed the plastic bag to Michael who put it in the cupboard under the stairs.

"Are you all ready? And don't talk about it in the street in case anyone overhears you, right?" said Damion.

All the lads made their way to the front door, all smiling at each other.

"Have you got your mobile, Damion?" asked Michael.

"Yer, it's in me pocket, come on then," Michael was the last one out and shut the door.

They all walked off down the street smiling and pushing each other and then they all started to run as none of them could wait to see the money. They got to the woods and Damion and Conner went in front to show them the way. The others all followed behind. Damion soon found the pile of sticks and leaves, knelt down on the floor and pushed the sticks and leaves away. The bag was still there.

He pulled at the handle and unzipped the bag and put his hand in it and pulled out a few piles of money.

"Bloody hell, Damo. Wow. You know, at first I thought you were just taking the Mick," Luke looked at Michael. "Sorry, mate, no offence," said Luke as 'takingthemic' is Michael's computer name.

Damion chucked the money at Luke and then some at Michael, Jake, Joe and Conner.

"I told you, didn't I? Right, I will share it out equally to carry it back to the camp ready for in the morning. Once we have emptied the bag we will fill it back up with leaves," Damion kept chucking money at everyone then filling his own bag. He pulled the large black bag out once it was empty and he saw another bag.

"There is another bag here," Damion pulled on it and dragged it out and unzipped it.

"This one is full of money too," said Damion.

"Damo, fuckin' hell, it must be the money from the bank robbery, it has to be," said Michael.

"Right, quick, put this lot in your bags as well," said Damion.

Everyone's bags were full to the brim with money. Everyone helped put leaves and twigs in the black bags. Damion started to move the leaves and sticks again and there was another black bag. Damion put his hand to his mouth in disbelief and started to shake his head.

"I don't believe it. There is another bag here, who has room in their bags?" said Damion.

"I can get a few more in," said Michael.

"So can I," said Jake.

"Right, everyone fill your bags to the brim then what's left we will take out. Fill the three bags with leaves and sticks and stuff then cover the top with the money, right? So if the robbers do come back they think all the money is still in all the bags," said Damion.

"Sounds like a plan to me," said Joe.

All of them helped fill the bags with stones, leaves, sticks, and anything they could pack them with. Then they covered the bags back up as if they had never been touched. Everyone picked up their bags and carried them back to the camp.

"Put the bags in your tents and zip them up," said Damion. Everyone did, and then came and sat round the fire.

"Conner, get your sticks and we will put the fire on," said Damion.

"Do you think the robbers will come back tonight?" asked Conner.

"I don't think so, maybe in a couple of days or so when the news settles down on the telly, that's what I would do anyway," said Damion.

Everyone helped and picked up sticks and chucked them in the middle of the fire.

"Get that pizza box that someone has left and light that," said Luke.

Conner got his lighter out of his pocket and lit the box. It soon started to smoulder and set alight. Everyone sat and watched the fire and was quiet for a little while. Jake and Conner lit a tab up each and they all sat staring into the fire as if they were in a trance by its beauty. It was nice and warm against their skin and the smoke bellowed up into the air with little sparks coming off the fire which seem to dance against the now darker night sky. They all sat and contemplated for a little while about the money.

"So what are we going to do with it, Damion?" asked Conner.

"Spend it, of course, but remember we are going to have to be careful what we spend it on," said Luke.

"We can all decide together," said Damion.

"Can I get some new games?" asked Michael.

"No, because Mum will wonder where you got the money for the games," said Damion.

"Oh, well what else can we spend it on then?" said Michael, quite disappointed with his brother's response.

Damion started to smile.

"The shows are coming on Monday, we can all go to the shows and take the girls and we can go on every ride if we want," Michael started to cheer up a bit and then he started to smile.

"Yer, that sounds great." Michael's thoughts then turned to the shows.

"First ride I am going on is the Waltzer's. Mum took me last year and it was great." Michael reminisced.

"Well, if Mum's off work we will have to make an excuse and tell her we are all going together this year, all agreed?" said Damion.

"Yer, we will have to ask Mum for money though," said Michael.

"Well, you can tell her you have been saving your pocket money up, right? That goes for us all, we can't tell our parents every time we are going somewhere, otherwise they might wonder where we are getting the money from," said Luke.

"This is going to be the best six weeks ever; we can have so much fun. Fancy going to the shop for some sweets and pop?" said Conner.

Everyone started to laugh.

"Yer, grab a twenty pound note out of one of the bags. You and Michael and Luke go to the shop get everyone a large chocolate bar, oh and get one of them twelve packs of pop," said Damion.

Conner jumped up and so did Michael and Luke.

Conner went inside the tent and flashed the twenty-pound note with a big smile on his face. Luke and Michael smiled then looked at each other.

"This is great; we can get anything we want," said Luke.

Everyone started to laugh.

"Won't be long," said Michael.

They all walked off into the woods together. Damion, Joe and Jake started laughing.

"Damo, god, I just can't believe it," said Joe.

"I know, the girls are going to love us when we take them out to the shows and pay for everything," said Damion.

"It's going to be wicked, man. We will be able to go and see the new film *Atargatis* and go to get burgers after, we can all go swimming," said Jake.

"Yer and we have the trips coming up with the youthie too. We can take twenty quid each on the trips and we can take more when we all go to Alton towers. I may even buy a new top to go in and just tell Mum I have been saving my pocket money for a few weeks," said Damion.

"We must be the luckiest kids in the world at the moment," said Jake.

"I think we are, Jake," said Joe.

Damion laid back on the grass and put his hands behind his head.

"I think you're right, Jake," Damion closed his eyes.

"Do you think your mum will look in the shed?" asked Joe.

"No, Na. She always sends Michael or me in the shed coz she frightened of the spiders. We have a massive wood box at the back of the shed; we can just put all the money in there. Michael is always in and out of the shed to get his bike out or scooter, so we are in and out of there all the time. Mum likes it locked every time we have been in so nothing gets stolen. Mum won't know a thing," said Damion.

They were all quiet again. Damion just lay there, thinking about all the fun that they were going to have. Jake laid back too and Conner sat watching into the fire. They all had big smiles on their faces and started daydreaming of what they would like to do with the money until they heard someone talking and the noise of leaves and sticks being broken under someone's feet.

"It will be Michael, Conner and Luke back, man," said Damion as Joe's face was a picture as he sat up quickly.

Damion sat up and watched as Conner, Michael and Luke came through the trees.

"See, stop panicking, I am telling you them robbers won't be back for a few days or weeks," said Damion.

"How do you know?" said Joe.

"It's always in the books me and my mum read, they lay low for days or weeks at a time then come back once things die down a bit. So stop worrying, anyway, from now on we will just camp up in the park instead of down here," said Damion.

Michael, Luke and Conner were stood listening to Damion.

"Damo's right, man, stop worrying," said Michael.

"Did you get the chocolate?" asked Jake.

"Yer, no problem," Conner looked in the plastic bag he was carrying.

"Here," said Conner and chucked everyone a chocolate bar and then took out the cans, broke into the box and passed everyone a can of pop. Everyone opened their can of pop. Luke raised his can in the air.

"To best mates and spending money."

Everyone raised their cans in the air.

"To best mates and money," said everyone, then took a drink of their pop and started laughing.

"We have just been talking about what we can spend the money on and we have decided to take the girls to the shows on Monday. Tuesday we are going to the pictures to see that new film *Atargatis* then go to get burgers and milkshakes after. What do you think?" said Damion.

"Yer, definitely," said everyone.

"So that's all agreed then?"

Damion lay back down on the grass.

"What are we going to say to our mums?" said Conner.

"Just say we are all going down the town together and just ask for some money. Keep all the money in a jar under your bed that you get off your mum and save it up," said Damion.

"Yer, okay, Damo, good one," said Conner.

"We were also on about going to the swimming baths, we could all go to the metro centre at Newcastle to do a little shopping, we also have the trips with the youth club. We can all take a bit extra money and have a whale of a time," said Damion who had now sat up so he could see everyone.

"Oh yer, I forgot about that, we are going camping, go karting, Altin Park and we are going to South Shields too," said Michael.

"You forgot paint balling as well," said Jake.

"Oh yer, paint balling, get on, I can't wait," said Joe.

"Do you think we should tell Sean?" said Michael, looking at Damion.

"I don't know yet, let's just keep it between us for now, yer. We can all top our mobiles up, but we should never talk about the money on any phone, just in case, and don't tell the girls anything, if they ask where we are getting the money, it is pocket money," said Damion.

Everyone agreed.

"Can we count one of the bundles, Damo?" said Luke.

"Yes, come on then."

Everyone got up and into Damion's tent.

"Zip the tent up, Conner, behind yer and be quiet coz you never know who's in the woods," said Jake.

Damion zipped open his bag, passed everyone a bundle and zipped the bag back up.

“Twenty, forty, sixty, eighty one hundred, this is going to take forever,” said Conner.

“I wouldn’t like to count it all,” said Joe.

“Yer, me neither,” said Michael.

“I have an idea,” said Damion.

“Right just count how many is in your bundle and then we can work it out on the calculator on my mobile,” Damion got his mobile out of his pocket.

“Yer, that sounds better to me, one, two, three, four,” said Joe still counting.

“Joe count quietly coz you’re putting me off,” said Michael.

Everyone started to count their bundle in their heads.

“Right, how many have you got in your bundle? I have a hundred,” Damion looked at Michael.

“Yer, I have the same,” Damion looked at Joe.

“Me too.”

“Yep, I have the same,” said Luke.

“Me too,” Damion then looked at Conner.

“I have a hundred too.”

Damion picked up his mobile phone again and put it on to calculator.

“Right, I have fifty pound notes,” said Damion.

“100 x 50 = £5,000.00, look, that’s just in my bundle,” Damion looked at Conner.

“I have twenties in my bundle,” Damion worked it out on the calculator. “Right, 100 x 20 = £2,000.00 so that’s £7,000.00 with just mine and Conner’s bundle. Wow, we have over twelve bags full to the brim with money. We have thousands of pounds,” said Damion.

“Bloody hell, Damo, we will never spend all this,” said Luke.

“So what if we don’t, who cares, we are rich. Do you all want to hand it in to the police?” asked Damion.

“What? Are you MAD, no way,” said Joe.

“Right, we will have a vote on it, hands up who wants to hand it in to the police?”

No one put their hands up.

“Let the good times roll,” said Damion.

Conner jumped on top of Damion then everyone jumped on each other and started laughing.

"Let's have some fun," said Joe.

The boys talked all night and they just couldn't sleep; they were all too excited about spending the money, they all brought their sleeping bags into the one tent and sat and talked all night long. Damion's alarm went off. It was 5:30 am.

"Come on, lads, it's five thirty in the morning, we need to move the money now. We will keep a bundle of the twenty's out and split it between us and just lock the rest in the shed, all agreed?" said Damion.

"Yes, well, it is your money, Damo, you found it," said Conner.

Everyone agreed.

"Come on then. Mum should be leaving for work now," said Michael.

One by one, they came out of the tent with the bags of money and all walked towards the woods. Conner was talking to Luke and started laughing.

"Keep it down! We don't need anyone seeing us or hearing us," Conner soon shut up and started to whisper to Luke instead.

They walked along the road and they were all quiet like ninjas. The boys soon got to the house. They all walked round the back to check the drive to make sure the car had gone and their mum had gone to work.

"She's gone, we can go in," said Michael.

The boys all walked around to the front door as the back door was still locked. They all went inside Damion and Michael's house.

"Well, I don't think anyone's seen us," said Conner.

"Put the kettle on, Luke," said Joe.

"You put the kettle on, I need the toilet," said Luke.

"Just go," said Damion.

"Yer, I need to go too," said Jake.

"Are you making everyone a cup of coffee, Joe?" asked Damion as he was parched.

"Yer, I suppose I'll have to," Joe said sarcastically to Damion.

Damion got the keys for the shed out of the draw. "I will start putting the bags in the shed, give me a hand, Conner."

Luke came back from the toilet.

"Give me a hand, mate, will yer?"

They picked up three of the bags and took them to the shed. Damion unlocked it and it was quite light outside so they could see without any problem. Damion opened up the box—it was empty—and placed his bag in. Conner then passed his bag to Damion then took Luke's bag off him and passed it to Damion.

"Go bring the other bags, Luke, Conner give him a hand, will yer?" said Damion.

Luke went back in the house and picked up one of the other bags and passed it to Conner the bags were quite heavy and they could only carry one at a time.

Sean had been sleeping over with his girlfriend and the boys didn't know. Michael was on the toilet upstairs and Sean came walking in on him.

"Sorry, son," said Sean and shut the door.

Sean walked downstairs. Jake was on the other toilet and Sean walked in on Jake.

"Oh, sorry," said Sean and shut the door quickly.

Sean walked in the kitchen and saw Luke passing a bag to Conner then saw Joe making cups of coffee for everyone.

"Make me a cup, son," Joe turned round.

"Yer, no problem, Sean," Joe turned back around and got another cup out of the cupboard and started to make another cup of coffee.

Joe then stopped and turned around quick and looked at Sean. Sean had walked outside as Luke turned to come back for another bag.

"What are you doing?" said Sean.

Luke just looked at Sean with a surprised look on his face.

"Are you all right, son? It looks like you have just seen a ghost."

Luke nodded then Conner came out of the shed and saw Sean.

"Damo, Damo," said Conner.

Damion had just placed the bag in the box and was making room for the next bags to come.

"What?" said Damion.

Damion turned around and Sean was stood behind him.

"What are you doing?" said Sean.

"Knout," said Damion.

"What's in the bags?" said Sean.

"Knout," said Damion.

His heart started beating faster.

"Right, so there is nothing in the bags?" Sean looked at Damion, smiled and then started to laugh.

"Well, they look full of something to me," Damion looked at Conner and Conner shrugged his shoulders.

"Damion, what's in the bags?" Damion tried to think but couldn't think of what to say, except the truth.

"Come in the house and I will show you," Sean turned around and walked back in the house. Luke walked into the kitchen and there were still quite a few bags on the floor. Conner followed Luke in the kitchen then Damion came in and shut the door.

"Sean, don't tell anyone, will you promise me?" Michael and Jake came into the kitchen too. Everyone was looking at Damion.

"Right so what's in the bags?" Sean was still smiling and looking at Damion.

Damion's heart flipped as he walked over to the bags and got on his knees and unzipped a bag. He pulled out some of the bundles and showed Sean. Sean looked at the money and then picked up a bundle.

"Where the FUCK have you got this FROM?"

Everyone started to talk at once. Sean put his hands in the air and everyone shut up.

"Damion, where has all this came from?" Sean didn't know what to think.

"I found it in the woods," said Damion.

Sean looked at Damion and then flicked through the bundle of money in his hand.

"Are all of them bags full of money?"

Damion put his head down. "Yes."

Sean was shocked

"And you found it in the woods?" Sean looked back at Damion.

"Yes," Sean flicked through the money again, his brain ticking over at a million miles per second and he took a very big breath and let it out.

"Michael, go and lock the doors now and shut the sitting room door on the way back in. We need to talk, put the rest of the bags in the shed and lock it now, Damion. You lot, go in the sitting room." Sean couldn't believe it.

"Joe hurry up with the coffee, will yer?" said Sean.

"They are all ready," said Joe.

"Give everyone their cups then go and sit down with the rest of them," Michael soon came back and Joe passed Sean a cup of coffee, trying not to spill it.

"Chill out, Joe, and go and sit down," Luke came back in and Sean handed Luke a cup.

"Go and sit down, son," Damion came back in after locking the shed.

Sean handed Damion his cup of coffee.

"Go and sit down and give me the keys," Damion handed over the keys and walked into the sitting room. Sean followed behind him and sat on the floor so he could see all of the boys.

"Right, tell me from the beginning. Damion, where has the money come from?" said Sean, then took a sip of his coffee.

"Nice cup of coffee, Joe, right, Damion, fire away," Sean sat and listened carefully to every word.

"We were down the woods looking for sticks for the fire and there was a pile of sticks and leaves. Conner was with me and the others were back at the camp, starting the fire but we thought we would get loads of sticks to keep the fire going all night. Anyway, I saw a pile of sticks and leaves and went over to collect the sticks that's when I saw a black handle. It was a bag full of money. I showed Conner and we left it there till later, until the girls went home. We all went to get it, we took it to the tents until Mum went to work and then we brought it up here and now you know about it too. Are you going to tell the police, Sean? Just we have spent twenty pounds on sweets and coke," said Damion.

"So there was just one big bag?" said Sean.

"No, I found another two when we went back, there were three big bags. We emptied two and a bit and left the rest. We filled the bags with stones, sticks and leaves then placed the money over the top of the sticks so it looked as if the three bags where still full," Sean started to smile.

"Damion, you're not daft, are yer, lad?" said Sean.

"Where do you think the money has come from?" Sean looked around the room at the others.

“We think it’s from that bank robbery that was on the telly yesterday morning,” said Damion.

Sean raised his eyebrows.

“So what did it say on the news about the robbery?” Sean looked at Michael.

“It was a secret location,” said Michael.

Sean shook his head then took another drink of his coffee.

“Right, I need a tab, stay where you are and don’t move.” Everyone was quiet.

Sean got up, went into the kitchen and shut the door. He picked up his cigarettes off the windowsill. He lit up his tab, opened the back door and tried to think. He paced up and down, thinking of what they needed to do. Sean could hear the boys trying to whisper to each other.

“Do you think he will phone the police?” said Conner.

“No! I don’t think he will,” said Michael.

“I don’t know. What if he tells your mum?” said another voice.

“He won’t, man, shut up,” said Damion.

Sean shook his head, picked up the bundle of money, flicked through it, shook his head then rubbed his chin.

The front door bell rang and everyone went silent.

“Go and get Sean to answer it,” said Luke.

Michael got up off the couch and went into the back garden. Sean was just finishing his cigarette.

“Someone is at the door, Sean,” said Michael.

Sean looked up at Michael, nodded and walked into the house through the sitting room where everyone was still sitting quiet. Sean shut the sitting room door and opened the front door.

“Is Damo there?” said a strawberry-blond kid, stood with his scooter.

“You’re up early, what’s your name, kid?” said Sean.

“I am Byron, don’t you recognise me? I was here once a few weeks ago when you were here,” said Byron.

“Oh yer, two minutes, Byron,” Sean shut the door in Byron’s face, walked back into the sitting room and shut the sitting room door.

“It’s a kid at the door called Byron,” said Sean.

“Can he come in, he normally knocks about with us?” said Damion.

"Well, I am not sure if that is a good idea at the moment, do you, with what's going on, Damion?" Sean looked flustered and annoyed.

"Byron won't say anything, Sean, we will give him twenty quid to keep his mouth shut," said Damion.

Sean shook his head.

"He better not, otherwise I will give you a good scudding, I am telling yer," Sean went back to the door and opened it again.

"Come in, Byron," Sean said nicely.

Byron walked past Sean and stood in the passage as Sean shut the door.

"Right, Byron. We are having a meeting in the sitting room at the moment and what is said in this house is never repeated outside this house, do you understand?" said Sean.

"Eh, eh, yes, Sean, no problem, mate! Is there something wrong?" said Byron.

Sean rolled his eyes at Byron as if to say 'you have no idea, son'.

Byron opened the door and everyone shouted. "BYRON!" Byron started smiling from ear to ear.

"Wow, man, you frightened me there."

Everyone started to laugh. Sean walked in behind Byron.

"Go and find a seat, son, as this is serious in here at the moment," Bryon looked at Sean and raised his eyebrows, still smiling and wondering what was going on. He sat in between Damion and Luke.

"What's going on? What have you been doing?" said Byron to Damion.

Damion just looked at Byron and shook his head.

"Listen up. This is how it is going to go. You are all going to get twenty pounds each on your mobile phones. If you see anything suspicious going on when you are in the woods, you ring me. You all need to go to different shops for your top up otherwise the shopkeeper will think something is up. Nobody touches the money without my say so, right?" Everyone nodded.

Byron looked around at everyone.

"What's going on?" said Byron.

"Damion will fill you in on the situation as soon as we are finished. Nobody says anything to anybody about this, if you need to discuss anything you only talk face to face, not on your mobiles and only when you know there is definitely nobody listening in on your conversation. Never, EVER, discuss it outside. Always whisper and shut windows and doors when talking about it. You say nothing to your families or other friends. Only talk amongst the people in this room, any other mates call they are told nothing about it, right. Byron, welcome to the gang. Joe, go and put the kettle on, will yer?" said Sean.

"Sean, we planned to go out to the shows with our girlfriends and we were all going to take some money with us to go on the shows and go and get something to eat. We were also on about going to the cinema to see *Atargatis* with the girls and then maybe go for burgers and milkshakes after," said Damion.

Sean shook his head then pulled out a bundle of the money which Damion had handed him earlier. He stood up and shut the sitting room curtains then opened the packaging off the money. Byron's eyes nearly popped out of his head.

"Have you won the lottery, Sean?" said Byron.

"No, not exactly," Sean passed everyone twenty pounds.

"That is for your mobile phones for when you all go to the town on Monday. All go to different shops to get your top ups, do you hear me? None of you go to the same shop. Nobody go to the village shop, right?"

Everyone started to nod their heads in agreement.

Sean then handed everyone another forty pounds.

"This forty pounds is to go to the shows. You can all walk into town and spend the full forty on the rides and get your dinners out of it too."

Everyone was smiling and happy and looking at each other. Sean then handed everyone another forty pounds each.

"This forty pounds is to go to the cinemas on Tuesday and you are getting forty pounds to pay for your girlfriends and to be able to get them something to eat. If anyone needs anything, ask Damion face to face, not over the mobile phone. Damion will come to my home and ask me then he will let you know face to face. Do you all understand?" said Sean.

Joe came in carrying two cups in his hands and passed Sean a cup of coffee. "Thanks, son. Joe, this is your money, did you hear what I told the others?"

Joe nodded.

Sean gave a hundred pounds to Joe from the bundle.

"There you go, son, right you know the plan, stick to it and everything will be fine, okay?"

Everyone was smiling and looking at their money.

"Wow, it's like it's my birthday," said Byron.

Everyone started to laugh.

"Put it in your pockets now and, Jake, get up, so I can sit down," Sean shoved the rest of the bundle in his pocket.

The door of the sitting room opened and Sean's girlfriend walked in.

Everyone went quiet and looked at Naomi.

"What's going on, babe?" she said, yawning and rubbing her head.

"Nothing, the lads have been out camping, princess, and just come back. They were all cold and wanted a cup of coffee, Joe's making cuppas if you want one, babe," Sean looked at Joe.

"Aye, go on then," said Naomi.

Sean and Joe got up off the couch and went into the kitchen and Naomi followed them. Everyone started smiling at each other.

"Joe, mate, can you make Naomi a cuppa?"

Joe smiled.

"Yes, you all right, Naomi?" asked Joe.

"Yes, I just wasn't expecting everyone in the sitting room when I came through, that's all," said Naomi.

"How do you like your coffee?" Naomi looked at Joe.

"Two sugars and milk, thanks, Joe."

Joe got a cup and put the coffee and sugar in then went to the fridge and got the milk out.

"Whose are all these cuppas on here?" said Naomi.

"They are for them lot in there," said Joe.

Sean walked back into the sitting room and put the telly on.

"Lads, go get your cuppas from the kitchen," said Sean.

The news was on the television. All the lads got up and went and got their cuppas.

"Whose is whose, Joe?" said Conner.

"They are all the same, just get one Conner," said Joe.

"Do they all have two sugars in?" asked Michael.

"Aye, mate."

Everyone picked a cup up and went and sat back down in the sitting room again except Joe and Naomi. Naomi walked back into the sitting room.

"Where's the fags, Sean?"

Sean got up.

"On the windowsill, babe." He picked his cup off the floor.

"Get me one out, I will have one with yer," Conner looked at Jake.

"Fancy a fag, Jake?" said Conner.

"Aye, how many have we got left?" Conner took the box out of his pocket.

"We have six left, so three each," said Conner.

"Aye, go on then," Conner and Jake got up and went in the back garden with Sean and Naomi.

"So what's the crack then, Damo?" said Byron.

"Look, we will tell you later coz we don't want Naomi knowing anything about it," said Damion.

"Oh right," said Byron.

"Michael, turn the television over, mate, will yer?" said Luke.

"Why, like what do you want to watch?" said Michael, picking up the remote control.

"Anything but the news," said Luke.

Michael gave Luke a cheesy smile and switched the television over to the cartoons.

"This better for yer?" asked Michael, smiling.

"Well, aye man, the Shan, I like the Shan, yer can't beat him." Everyone started to laugh. It went quiet while everyone watched the super hero the Shan, being drunken and getting himself into trouble as usual.

"Babe, the shows are on Monday, fancy going?" said Sean.

"Yer, sounds good. It's been years since I've been to the shows. Oh I'm all excited now, we have never been to the shows together before," said Naomi.

Sean smiled and then looked at the lads.

"Are you lot going to the shows, Conner?" Sean gave him a look as if to say 'just play along'.

"Aye, we are all going to the shows, we are walking in to the town," said Conner.

"Oh well, we will probably see you lot there then. Are you lot sleeping out again tonight?" Sean was looking at Conner.

"No, I don't think so," said Conner.

"Are you going, Jake?" Sean looked at Jake.

"Aye, mate, I'm going."

Naomi started to get excited.

"It will be good. We can have some candy floss," said Naomi.

"You can have anything you want, princess."

The lads had big smiles on their faces while looking at Sean.

"My lord, it is a bit nippy this morning, no wonder you are all up so early," Naomi rubbed her arms.

"Come on, we will go back in."

Everyone followed Naomi back into the house from the garden.

"What time is it?" said Naomi.

Jake looked at his mobile phone.

"It's seven thirty," Naomi looked at Sean.

"I am going back to bed, are you coming?" Sean smiled.

"No, babe, I am going to have a look round the shop for a newspaper. Do you want anything while I am there?"

Naomi tried to think. "Mm…no."

Sean walked back into the sitting room.

"Okay, go on, get yourself back to bed," Naomi walked through the sitting room and everyone was still watching the Shan on the telly. Naomi shut the sitting room door and went back to bed. Sean stood in the doorway. Conner and Jake sat back down on the couches.

"Right, what are you lot doing today?" said Sean.

"We have to go back down the woods to get the tents," said Damion. "Right, come on then, I will come down with you. The more of us the quicker we get the tents down and get you lot back up here. I want all of you to keep out of the woods for a few months, right?"

Everyone nodded.

"Come on then the quicker we get there the quicker we all get back."

All the lads stood up and Michael knocked the telly off.

They all left the house and walked towards the woods. They soon got to the camp.

"Damion, you come with me, everyone else take the tents down and get everything packed up. Also get rid of them stones and cover up where you have had a fire. Make sure you don't leave anything, pick up all the cans. There is a plastic bag near the tent, there, look."

Sean pointed at the bag. "Put all the cans and chocolate wrappers in that, we won't be long," said Sean, starting to walk away and followed Damion.

The lads soon got to work. Michael picked up the rubbish while the others got on dismantling the tents.

"Show me where the bags are, Damion."

Damion showed Sean the way through the woods and they were soon back where the bags were. Damion started to move the sticks until one of the bags was in clear view. Sean bent over and unzipped the bag, which looked as if it was full to the brim with money. Sean nodded at Damion.

"Right, good job, bro, just cover it back over," Sean zipped the bag back up and they both started to cover the bag with sticks and leaves.

They got up off their knees and started to walk away back through the trees back to the camp. The lads had done a good job and everything was nearly packed up. Sean and Damion helped to finish off packing up the tents and they were soon off walking back up through the wood and headed to the shop to get a newspaper. Sean looked around just to make sure nobody else was around and took the bundle of money out of his pocket. He took a twenty from the roll of money in his hand.

"You lot stay here and I won't be long and be quiet," Sean went into the shop and bought three packets of bacon, two loaves of bread, some cigarettes and a newspaper.

"Hello, Sean, are you over watching the boys for your mum?" said the woman behind the counter.

"Yes."

The shopkeeper looked at Sean.

"Are you hungry, son?" Sean looked at the shopkeeper funny.

"Oh, the bacon? I just fancied a bacon sandwich and I thought I would make Naomi breakfast in bed," Sean smiled at the woman.

"Oh that's lovely, Sean, well, that will be twelve pound thirty," Sean handed over the money.

"Enjoy your breakfast, son," said the shopkeeper.

Sean smiled again.

"I will, see you later," Sean said, leaving the shop.

Sean looked at the lads who were being really quiet. He moved his head in the direction of home and they all walked along together.

When they got a bit further along the road, Sean said, "Have you told Byron yet what is going on, Damion?"

Damion looked at Sean.

"No, not yet."

Sean nodded.

"When we get back to the house, I want you all to be quiet, just sit and watch the telly. I will make you all a bacon sandwich."

Everyone started smiling at each other, but kept quiet so as not to upset Sean.

They all walked in the house one after the other and piled up the tents and bags in the hallway. They all sat down and made themselves comfortable on the couch again.

"Damion, tell Byron what is going on before you put the telly on and remember to be quiet!" said Sean.

Damion nodded at Sean who went into the kitchen and started making the bacon sandwiches while Damion explained to Byron what was going on. Byron was shocked. Damion and Byron came into the kitchen.

"Sean, can I go and show Byron the shed?"

Sean looked at Damion and shook his head.

"Aye, man, hurry up and don't forget to lock it back up. We are going to have to move it out of the shed as soon as we can to a better hiding place."

Sean chucked the keys at Damion.

Damion went outside and Byron followed him. They both went into the shed. Sean watched them coming out of the shed and Byron's face was a picture. Sean shook his head and then walked back over to the cooker with a smile on his face, still in disbelief that his younger brother had found all this money. He then continued making breakfast for the boys.

After breakfast, Sean told everyone to leave and go play out over the park. The lads all went out and Sean went back to bed and took Naomi up some breakfast. Sean needed to think about where they could put the money and it needed to be in a safe place where nobody knew it was except Damion, Michael and himself. As the lads walked towards the park, Michael spotted a football near the fence and there was nobody else in the park but them.

"FOOTBALL!" shouted Michael.

Everyone ran towards the football and Michael managed to kick it first. He kicked it over in the direction of the football field. Everyone ran after the ball and soon the game was on.

Byron ran for the ball and then passed it to Conner. Conner then kicked it to Damion and Jake ran to get in the goal. Luke decided to go in the other goal. Damion quickly passed it over to Michael and Michael scored. Everyone jumped in the air and shouted "GOAL!" They soon decided to pick teams and the match was on.

The boys played for a couple of hours and they were all tired after the match and thirsty.

"Who fancies going to the shop and I will buy a couple of bottles of pop," said Luke.

Everyone was red faced and hot.

"Oh yes," said Jake, trying to catch his breath.

"Last one there is a rotten egg," said Luke.

No one was moving and then all of a sudden Joe set off as fast as he could across the field towards the shop. Everyone started laughing and all started running after him. Joe got to the shop first and everyone came running towards Joe. Joe was bent over and all puffed out with his hands on his knees and started laughing as they all ran towards him.

Joe stood up and put his hands out in front of him to protect himself, as he thought everyone was going to dive on top of him, but they stopped as they got closer. Joe started to laugh and so did the others. Three of them came in last so they decided to argue about who was last outside the shop. Luke went into the shop and picked up two large bottles of pop. The woman put them through the till and gave Luke his change and he walked outside and passed a bottle to Michael. They soon passed the two bottles around as everyone was really thirsty.

"Are we going back to the park?" said Jake.

Everyone was so tired after camping out and the game of football.

"What time is it?" asked Michael.

"It's about twelve o'clock, why? What are you doing, Michael?" said Luke, putting his phone in his pocket.

"I was thinking of going to get some sleep for a couple of hours, because I am so tired now," Michael was looking quite shattered.

"I thought you may have wanted to go on the computer or something," Luke started to laugh.

"You're joking, aren't you? I don't think I could. I could sleep on me mum's washing line, I am that tired," said Michael.

"I could do with some sleep as well. Maybe we should all go home for a couple of hours and meet up later at the park," said Joe.

Everyone agreed and they all walked together.

"So what time are we all meeting up?" asked Jake.

"How about five o'clock?" said Damion.

"If we all set our mobile phones now then we won't forget when we get in," said Luke.

Everyone took out their mobile phones and set their alarms.

"Right, five at the park, so what do you fancy doing later?" said Conner.

"I don't know, I can't think straight now, I am that tired. Look, we can all decide when we meet up," grumbled Damion as he could hardly keep his eyes open.

"Come on then, I am walking home now."

Everyone followed and then they all said their goodbyes as they went off in different directions to their homes.

Michael and Damion walked through the door of their home, nearly tripping over everyone's tents and belongings. The boys went straight to their rooms and as soon as their heads were on their pillows they went straight to sleep. Sean and Naomi were cuddled on the couch and heard the boys come in and go straight upstairs to their rooms. Sean knew it was the boys and he was too busy watching a movie with Naomi.

"Do you think they will be hungry, Sean?" said Naomi.

“No, Na, they are tired. If they were hungry they would be in here tormenting the life out of me for something to eat,” Sean smiled.

Naomi shook her head and they cuddled in again to watch the film.

Damion and Michael slept until their alarms went off on their mobile phones. Kim had been texting Damion but he didn’t hear the texts coming through since two o’clock. It was now five o’clock. Damion got up, rubbed his head and walked towards the bathroom. He could hear footsteps along the passage and it was Michael getting up too and also heading towards the bathroom. Damion moved faster in case it was someone else going to the toilet. He opened the door and Michael was walking out of his room to at the same time.

Damion gave Michael a slight smile then they both tried to get into the bathroom at the same time, pushing and shoving each other and eventually Michael won and Damion backed down. Damion went to the toilet downstairs instead and washed his hands. He took a look in the mirror and he still looked tired. He wanted to go back to bed but knew he had arranged to meet up with his friends at the park. He walked into the sitting room and Sean looked up at him. Sean and Naomi where still on the couch watching movies.

“You all right, son?” asked Sean.

Damion smiled.

“Yes, but I am still tired, I promised the others I would meet them at the park for five o’clock but I didn’t realise how tired I would be.”

Naomi paused the film.

“Do you want something to eat, son?”

Damion looked at Naomi and shook his head to say ‘no’.

“No thanks, I am not hungry just yet.”

There were footsteps coming down the stairs.

“Michael might though,” said Damion.

Michael walked in the sitting room and walked passed everyone and straight into the kitchen.

“Michael, do you want something to eat?” asked Sean.

“No, I am just going to have some biscuits. I will get something a bit later on,” said Michael.

"Are you coming down the park?" Damion walked into the kitchen.

"Yes, are you going down now?" Michael grabbed a few biscuits and put them in his pockets.

"Do you want some?" Michael offered the biscuit tin to Damion.

"Aye, go on then," Damion grabbed a load of biscuits and put them in his pockets too. Michael walked passed him.

"Come on then," Damion followed him out of the back door.

They walked down to the park Kim, Beth, Kate, Joe and Conner were there. They started to all wave as they noticed Damion and Michael walking towards them.

"What happened at two o'clock?" said Kim.

"I was shattered, man, we didn't get any sleep last night as we were up all night talking. Anyway, I thought we were meeting up on Sunday not today?" said Damion, starting to yawn as he was still tired.

Kim smiled at him.

"I was just telling the girls I forgot and thought it was Sunday today for some reason, how silly am I?"

Damion started to laugh. "We all know that, man," said Damion.

Kim gave a wrinkled nose smile as if to say 'I know how dumb I can be, there is no need to remind me'.

"We were thinking about going to the shows tomorrow," said Conner.

"Yer, that's right, would you like to come?" said Damion to Kim.

"Yes, I would love to go." Kim smiled at Damion.

"That's great! Have you asked your girlfriends too?" Damion looked at Joe and Conner.

"Well, aye man, of course, I've asked our lass," said Conner.

Everyone started to laugh.

"Are you bringing a girl, Michael?" Conner looked at Michael, who shook his head.

"Well, what do you think, Conner?" Michael gave a funny smile.

"Why on earth would I want to spend my money on a girl?"

Conner's eyebrows went up and he looked at Kate.

"Why not?" said Conner.

"Coz I don't want to! That's why not," said Michael.

Luke came walking over the field towards them.

"Yer all right, mate? Tell this lot, will yer, I don't need a girlfriend just coz they have them. I would rather spend my money on myself. What do you think, Luke?" said Michael.

Luke started to laugh.

"Michael, mate, you don't need a girlfriend yet, man, just get one when you're ready. That's my advice anyway," Michael had a smug grin on his face.

"Are you taking anyone to the shows, Luke?"

Everyone looked at Luke.

"Am I, hell… I want to have a laugh, man, not get all soppy like you lot."

Michael started to laugh.

"We can stick together, mate. Let all the lovebirds do their thing and we will do ours yer?" Michael nodded.

"Sounds good to me," Luke smiled at Michael.

"Anyway, we might meet someone at the shows that we like," said Luke.

Michael shrugged his shoulders.

"What time are we all meeting up tomorrow? If we sort it out now then we all know," said Joe.

"Well the shows start at ten in the morning, so it's up to the girls coz they take longer to get ready than we do," said Damion.

Kim nudged Damion.

"What?" Kim and Damion started laughing and pushing each other.

"Well, we should meet up at nine thirty then. What do you think, Beth?" said Kate.

"Yer… I am good with that time. So is that agreed?" Everyone agreed.

"So where at?" asked Kim.

"We should all meet at Damion and Michael's," said Conner.

"I wonder where Jake and Byron are?" Michael looked at Luke.

"Should I give them a ring and see if they are coming down?" Luke said to Michael.

"Why don't we all have a walk up to theirs? Are you lot coming for Jake and Byron?" asked Luke.

“Aye, come on then and we can all go down the youth club and have a couple of games of pool if you like. Byron will be there now, helping his dad open up,” said Damion.

Everyone got off the swings and apparatus and they all walked up to get Jake from his grandma’s house. Damion put his arm around Kim and Conner put his arm around Kate. Joe held Beth’s hand and Michael and Luke talked about the trailers for the new films coming out soon.

Conner went and knocked for Jake.

Jake answered the door.

“Are you coming down the youth club mate?” asked Conner. Jake looked a bit fed up.

“Aye, two minutes while I get some money off me Gran,” said Jake who then turned and went back inside shouting Gran.

“He doesn’t look too happy. Conner, ask him what’s wrong,” said Damion.

Jake was back quite quickly.

“Yer ready?” asked Conner.

The Youth Club

“Aye, come on then,” said Jake, closing the front door.

“What’s up, Jake? You don’t look too happy, mate,” Conner looked at Damion.

“Me mum has just been on the phone and we are moving,” Jake looked sad.

“Where are you moving to?” asked Conner.

“Apparently we are moving to Scotland,” Jake looked at the floor.

“SCOTLAND, OH MY!” said Conner.

Damion walked over to Jake and put his arm around his shoulders.

“Well, don’t worry, mate, you can always come home to see us at any time coz my mum will let you stay at ours, you know that. So don’t worry, mate, and we will be able to keep in touch over the X box man. Come on, we will have a good time before you have to leave.”

Damion smiled at Jake.

“We can come to see you as well. We can come up to Scotland on the train.”

Jake started to cry and everyone crowded around him and cuddled Jake.

"We are going to miss you, mate," said Michael.

Luke also had tears in his eyes.

"So when will you be going?"

Everyone started to back off a little.

"At the end of the six weeks," said Jake, wiping the tears off his cheeks with the cuffs of his hoody.

"So we have six weeks to enjoy ourselves then. Come on, mate, forget about it for now and just enjoy yourself with your mates. Fancy a couple of games of pool?" said Damion, placing his arm back around Jake's shoulders.

Jake nodded and they all walked off down to the youth club, which was at the bottom of the road. They walked through the door and Byron and his little brother was there playing on the game console on a racing game.

"BYRON!" shouted Conner and Luke together.

"You all right? Give me a sec while I just beat him on this race and I will be with you," said Byron, smiling and happy to see his friends.

They all walked over to the pool table and Kim sorted the balls out in the triangle.

"See if you can find the white ball, will yer? Just it's not here," said Kim, looking in the holder where all the balls drop into.

"Jake, you can play first, mate," said Michael.

Jake smiled and nodded and tears came to his eyes again.

"Do you want a can of pop, mate?" Damion asked Jake.

"Yer…go on then thanks, Damo."

Damion smiled, and went and got everyone a can of pop from the machine in the corner.

"Hello, lads and girls, sorry… nice to see you all. So our Byron said you are all going to the shows tomorrow eh?" asked Alan, Byron's dad.

"Yer, yer…we were all thinking about going together, we are all going to walk into the town to the shows," said Damion.

"So who is going?" asked Alan.

"Just us lot," said Damion.

"Okay, son, as long as you are all sensible that is fine." Byron had come over and was now stood next to his dad.

"Great so can I have some money tomorrow Dad to go on the shows?" asked Byron.

"Yes, son, you can have twenty quid. Will that be enough?" Alan looked at Byron.

"Yer…great, Dad, thanks." Byron had the biggest smile on his face.

Damion started to laugh. He just couldn't hold it any longer as they both knew Byron already had forty pounds to go with.

Alan walked away as more kids were entering through the doors of the youth club. Byron watched his dad walk away then looked back at Damion. Damion shook his head still smiling.

"This is great, I am loaded," said Byron.

Damion started laughing. Kim came over.

"It's your turn on the pool table, Jake won against Conner," Damion turned and walked towards the pool table and Byron followed him.

"Me dad has organised a disco and a barbeque for next Friday night in here. Are you lot coming or what?" asked Byron.

Kate and Beth looked at each other and smiled.

"We are coming. Conner, are you coming to the disco?" said Kate.

"Well, aye man, of course I'm coming. You don't think I would miss out on seeing you in all your good clobber, do yer," Kate started to blush and Beth giggled at her.

Jake was racking up the pool balls on the pool table while Damion picked a cue to play with. The girls got their cans of pop that Damion had brought over and were talking amongst themselves about the disco and what they were thinking about wearing. Conner and Byron went outside because Conner wanted a cigarette. Luke sat with Michael and Joe talking about what shows they were going to go on, the next day at the shows in the city.

The night flew by and Alan decided to change the disco to a fancy dress disco to make it more fun. All the lads were excited about this and were talking about what they might go as, but none of them were quite sure just yet and said they would all talk about it later.

Everyone had agreed the time was still going to be nine thirty in the morning as it would take a good half an hour to walk into the city and they wanted to be there early to get on all the good rides with not so many ques.

At the end of the night, Damion said goodnight to Kim. Joe said goodnight to Beth and Conner, of course, said goodnight to Kate. They were all tired and looking forward to getting in their own beds. The lads said their goodbyes and Damion and Michael went in their home as Jake, Conner, Joe, Byron and Luke all took their own direction's home.

The boys went into the sitting room and Mum was back from work.

"Hi, Mum," said the boys together.

"Have you been good, boys?" asked Mum.

"Yes, we had a good time camping out. Mum, we are all going to the shows tomorrow, are we okay to go with the lads, Mum? As Conner, Jake, Joe, Byron and Luke are going, also some of the girls are going too. It's just Kim, Beth and Kate," said Michael.

"I don't see why not, that will give me time to go out shopping and get a bit of housework done, as I am off work tomorrow," said Mum.

"What time will you have to be up tomorrow then? And I will set the alarms for you," said Mum.

"We can do that, Mum, we can put our alarms on our mobile phones," said Damion.

"Oh okay, you two are growing up too fast, come here and give me a hug. I've missed you both," said Mum.

Damion and Michael hugged their mum tightly and they both towered above her.

"Mum, are you getting smaller?" asked Michael.

"HU, yer cheeky bugger," laughed Mum.

"Are you hungry, boys?" Mum was smiling and happy after getting a hug.

"I'm starving, we have only had some biscuits," said Damion.

"Did Sean not make you anything?" Mum looked disappointed with Sean.

"We didn't want anything, Mum, but I am hungry now," said Damion.

"Me too," said Michael.

“Okay, what do yer want to eat?” Mum started looking through the cupboards to see what food was in. She then looked in the fridge.

“How about bacon and egg sandwiches?” Mum looked at the boys still holding the fridge door open.

“Yer,” said the boys together.

“You two go and get a shower and I will do the sandwiches, go on now then we can watch a film before bed.”

“Okay, Mum,” said the boys.

“Michael, you can go in first if you like?” said Damion, putting the kettle on.

“Okay, make me a cup of tea, please, Damion, will yer?” said Michael.

“Go on then, hurry up in the shower,” Damion got three cups off the cup holder.

Michael went upstairs and Damion could hear the shower go on.

Mum was placing the bacon under the grill.

“Mum could we have some money tomorrow for the shows?” Damion looked at his mum with his big brown eyes.

“Of course you can. How much do you think you will need?” Mum started buttering the bread.

“Do you want two sandwiches?” Mum got the frying pan out of the cupboard and placed it on the cooker.

“Yes, Mum, I think Michael will want two as well.” Mum went to the fridge and got the eggs out.

“How much do you think, Mum?” Mum looked at Damion.

“Will twenty pounds each do?” Mum smiled.

“Yer that will be great, are you sure, Mum?”

Mum smiled.

“Yes, I am sure; I want you two to have a good time. We can’t afford a holiday so why not and I will have to see Alan tomorrow to pay the money for your trips away with the youth club. When is your first trip away?” asked Mum while cooking the eggs.

“It’s next week. We are going to the lake district to camp in Giza Forest and watch *The Hunger Games*.”

“Oh yer, I will have to get you new sleeping bags, you will have to put the tents back in the shed as well. I nearly tripped over them all in the passage at the front door, okay?” said Mum, then carried on cooking and Damion was wondering where the keys were for the shed, as Sean had them earlier.

"So did you take Sean and Naomi home?" asked Damion.

"Yes…I just got back not long ago, our Sean is on about decorating again but he is on about plastering the walls first as he said he is not happy with the walls as they are. I told him not to bother with it being a council house but he is having none of it." Damion wondered what Sean was thinking; he had just decorated his bedroom last month.

"Mum, can I use the house phone please? Just to see if Sean is going to the shows tomorrow." Mum looked up at Damion.

"Yes, of course you can, tell Michael to hurry up in the shower, will yer, when you go through," Mum was just finishing the sandwiches.

"Okay Mum," Damion went upstairs and knocked on the bathroom door.

"Mum says hurry up coz the sandwiches are done, Michael,"

"Okay, I am nearly finished!" Michael shouted back through the door.

Damion went into the bedroom and rang Sean.

"Hello," said Naomi.

"Is Sean there Naomi?"

"Yer, two minutes, SEAN, DAMION IS ON THE PHONE FOR YER!" Naomi shouted and Damion had to take the phone away from his ear as it was quite loud.

Damion shook his head.

"Yer all right bro, what's up?" said Sean.

"So are you going to the shows tomorrow?" Sean looked at Naomi.

"Yer, we are going."

"What time will you be there? Just we need to talk."

"We should be there about eleven o'clock."

"Okay, where do you want to meet up?"

"Meet you near the band stand and then we can talk, is Kim going? Just to keep Naomi company while we talk," said Sean.

"Yer, Kim's going, we are getting some money off Mum so we are going to put that other money away and save it." Damion felt horrible taking money from his mum knowing she works really hard and all the money was in the shed. But what could he do?

"I feel horrible, Sean," said Damion.

"Don't be silly, you wouldn't be feeling like that, if this didn't happen. Look don't worry about it and we can talk tomorrow okay? Go and get a good night's sleep and we can get things moving tomorrow, I promise," Sean tried to reassure Damion.

"Okay, bro…no problem. See you at the bandstand at eleven o'clock okay?"

"Okay, bro, see you then," Damion felt a little better and put the phone down.

Michael was just coming out of the bathroom covered in towels.

"Who are you phoning?" asked Michael, towel drying his hair.

"Sean. We are going to meet up to talk tomorrow at the bandstand for eleven o'clock, to talk about what we are going to do. Sean is going to get Naomi and Kim to go off and do what they want to for a while together while we talk," Michael listened carefully.

"Yer…I think we need to get things sorted," Damion nodded.

"Right, I am going in the shower, I won't be long. You and Mum can pick the film if you like," Michael smiled.

"I was going to anyway," said Michael, giving Damion a cheeky grin.

Damion started laughing.

"Oh were you now?" said Damion.

Michael went off into his bedroom laughing.

The boys spent the rest of the night watching a movie with their mum and they all went to bed straight after. It took Damion and Michael a while to get to sleep as all they could think about was what would happen if the money was from the robbery and would these robbers find out that they had took the money and what would they do to them if they did find out it was them. The boys imaginations went wild each going through different sonorous but eventually they did manage to fall asleep.

Before they knew it, the alarms were going off on their mobile phones. Damion reached out to his bedside cabinet, stopped the alarm, made a big sigh and stretched out his legs on his bed.

A wave of excitement soon came over him. He jumped out of bed, went to the bathroom and looked in the mirror. He could hear Michael's alarm going off and Michael moving around in his room. Michael wasn't so excited about the prospects of getting out of bed and buried his head under his pillows. Damion decided to get a quick shower and brush his teeth while he had the bathroom, because if he came out now Michael would take it over then he would have to wait. He locked the door and switched the shower on.

Michael jumped out of bed quickly after remembering they were going to the shows.

He knocked on the bathroom door.

"How long are you going to be?" he asked.

"Just getting out now, put the kettle on, I won't be long!" shouted Damion through the door.

"Aye okay…hurry up then," said Michael, making his way downstairs.

Damion was soon finished. He got dry and gelled his hair while it was still wet as it stayed in place better. Michael had put the kettle on and went back upstairs to sort out what he was going to wear as he wanted to look good, as he may meet a girl at the shows, even though he wasn't really interested at the moment. He thought he would be prepared just in case. Damion was soon ready and made Michael a cup of tea.

Michael was ready too. It was now nine thirty and there was a knock at the door. Everyone was there outside.

"Yer both ready?" asked Conner.

"Well, aye man, we are, we can't wait, man," said Michael.

Damion started to laugh.

"I am just shocked the girls are here and ready, to be honest."

Kim looked at Damion.

Show Time

"Cheeky," said Kim, smiling at Damion.

"Come on then, have you got your money, Michael? And did you get the money off the kitchen table Mum left for yer?" asked Damion.

"Yer, I can't wait to just get to the shows now. Oh that reminds me, Byron text me this morning. He is going to meet us there, he going in with his dad. He said he couldn't be bothered to walk in," said Michael.

"Oh okay never mind, I am going to get some breakfast when I get there. You didn't have anything either, did you?" asked Damion to Michael.

"No Na, I forgot, to be honest, I was too busy thinking about the shows," said Michael.

"Well, I am just going to eat sweets all day long," said Conner to Kate, walking along the road holding her hand.

"Well, I don't think that's a good idea, do you, Conner? You may end up feeling sick off the shows if you eat too many sweets and I don't want you being sick on me, mind," said Kate.

"Oh yer, I never thought of that, oh well. I will just wait until we have finished going on the shows then eat a load of sweets. Does that sound better?" Conner raised his eyebrow at Kate.

Kate shook her head and started to laugh.

"Conner, you crack me up," said Kate, bumping Conner with her hip.

They all walked along the country road and they had to walk in single file in case of traffic coming, as there was no path anymore. Luke was the last one and if any traffic was to come, he would warn the others. They soon came to the end and were back on the path. They walked past the old dairy and up the steep bank then down the other side and were soon in the city.

There was police patrols out in the city as the traffic was starting to get quite busy and there was traffic police parked up, and down some of the streets.

"They must be expecting it to be really busy today just with all the police out," said Luke to Michael and Jake.

"Yer…well, as long as we keep out of trouble we will be okay," said Jake.

"I am pleased we walked, can you imagine what the bus station is going to be like today? And we would never be able to get a taxi," said Luke to Jake and Michael who both nodded.

They could soon see crowds of people as they walked over the bridge and up the street towards the field were the shows were taking place. There was stalls with people selling balloons and different flashing gadgets and small windmills for children.

There was stalls with sweets and candy floss, toys, hotdogs and burger stands and vans the smells drifted towards them and it made Damion hungry.

"That's it…I need a burger. I am starving. Would you like something, babe?" Kim looked at Damion.

"No, not yet, maybe later on thanks, Damo."

Damion bent over, kissed Kim—just a peck on the lips— and walked over to a burger van. Michael and Joe and Jake followed him, they all got burgers with onions and cheese with plenty of tomato sauce on them. They bit into them and they tasted so… good!

"Mm, these are lovely, aren't they?" said Jake as he watched Damion take another bite of his burger. Damion nodded and so did Joe. Joe ended up with tomato sauce down his chin and it had dripped onto his t-shirt. Conner started to laugh at him and pointed to Joe's t-shirt. Kate started to laugh and so did Beth.

"We can't take you anywhere, can we?" said Beth as she tried to wipe it off with a scrunchie she had just took out of her pocket.

As they walked further along, they could hear the music playing loudly and they all followed the crowd's on to the field. They could see all the shows. There was the Waltzer and the Dodgems, the Big Wheel, a large Merry-go-round with all the horses and loads of more stalls of food and goodies. Everyone was excited and headed towards the shows there was the Ali Baba ride which looked wicked and they could see the Evolution in the distance.

"Oh my look, it's the FRISBEE!" shouted Conner in Kate's ear and nearly made her deaf.

"Look, isn't that the…oh I have forgotten the name of it, what's that one called over there, near the Ghost train?" Everyone started pointing at it.

"That's the Round Up," said Joe, looking as if to say 'don't ask me to go on there with you'.

The rides all looked great and dangerous, so the friends were in their element. They stayed close to each other, as not to end up splitting up and they all decided to go on the Big Wheel first. They waited in line. It was two people per seat and they soon were in pairs. Damion and Kim, Joe and Beth, Conner and Kate, Michael and Luke, and Jake.

"Who is going to go on with Jake? It's a pity Byron isn't here yet," said Damion, then a voice came from behind him.

"I will go on with Jake," Damion turned around.

It was Naomi and Sean.

"Yer, all right, bro," said Damion to Sean.

Sean smiled a big cheesy grin smile.

Naomi had the biggest bag of candyfloss Damion had ever seen.

"That bag is nearly as big as you, Naomi," said Damion, laughing at her shoving more candy in her mouth.

Naomi slapped him on the arm.

"What are you trying to say?" said Naomi.

Damion started to laugh harder.

"Well, you are only four foot, knout."

Naomi giggled and looked at Sean who was laughing.

"What are you laughing at?" said Naomi with her hands on her hips and a quirky smile on her face.

"Nothing, princess," said Sean quickly.

"So are you going on with Jake then?" said Sean, looking down at her, as she really was only four foot nothing and very slim with it.

"Yes, coz you won't come on, chicken," Sean shook his head and smiled.

"Take care of her mind, Jake, don't let her fall out, will yer?" Jake started laughing.

They all started to climb into the seating and as the two were seated and strapped in, the next carriage came down and the next two climbed into the next carriage available.

Sean stood and watched them all as they moved up the wheel. Naomi and Jake were the last to get in the carriages once the man was happy that everyone was in safe, he went to the controls to operate the Big Wheel.

Naomi was waving frantically at Sean and Sean waved back holding her candyfloss for her and smiling. Naomi was like a child loving every minute of it. Jake laughed at her waving over to Sean. The wheel started to move and they went backwards so Naomi and Jake would go round the wheel first. Naomi screamed as the wheel jerked and the carriage started to rock backwards and forwards. Jake wasn't sure what to do his face was a picture and Sean started laughing at them.

"Are you okay, Naomi?" asked Jake, a little worried after the scream.

"Yes, I just got a shock when it jerked, that's all. I will be fine."

The wheel started to move around and it got quite fast. Sean waved and laughed at Naomi's face as she was trying to be brave but her face was white as a sheet. She held on as tight as she could. The ride was soon over and they all started to get off the ride two by two.

"Babe, your face was a picture on that ride. I thought you were going to be sick at one point your face was that white," said Sean, trying not to laugh too much.

"No, I wasn't, anyway it has been a long time since I have been on a Big Wheel. I must have been about thirteen years old," said Naomi as she started to feel a little better and the colour came back to her cheeks again.

"Fancy going on the Dodgems, you lot," asked Sean.

"YER, YER!" shouted everyone, they all made their way over to the Dodgems.

"What do you reckon boys against girls, lads," said Damion.

Kim looked at Damion and she didn't look too happy.

"What?" said Damion, laughing.

"Come on, girls!" shouted Kim.

All the girls started running towards the Dodgems, even Naomi ran to get a car.

The lads all started laughing at them and they soon all ran to get in a car themselves. The man came and collected their money and the game was on.

Damion bumped into Joe. Sean rammed into Jake and Luke rammed into Conner. Then the girls started to ram into the lads before they knew it they were all chasing each other around the Dodgem circuit. The music was loud and everyone was really enjoying the fun of it all. The ride soon came to a halt.

"Oh, is it finished already?" shouted Kate to Conner.

Everyone could have played on them all day but there was other people now queuing up to go on them. The shows were starting to get more and more people coming and it was really busy. The music was blearing out different songs from different rides then Joe spotted Byron and his dad and brother near the Ghost Train.

"Come on, are we going on here? There is Byron," said Joe, pointing towards the Ghost Train and Byron.

The girls were all talking at once as they headed over towards the Ghost Train. They all had to wait their turn to get on and it was two to each carriage.

The girls all got on with their partners. Jake and Michael got on together and Luke was on his own as Byron didn't want to go on as he was going to get some pop at the stall next door. Luke soon had a partner to go on with a girl about his age sat down next to him. Luke smiled at her and she started to blush but smiled back.

"Are you easily frightened?" said Luke to the girl.

"No, not really," she replied, giving him a sideways glance.

"Well, if you need a cuddle, I am here, I don't mind," said Luke, trying to look into her eyes.

The girl started to giggle and then the train started to move. Sean looked behind as he overheard the conversation with Luke and the girl and he smiled a toothy grin. Luke then saw Sean smiling at him and Luke started to laugh as he knew what Sean was thinking by his facial expression.

"Hold on tight!" shouted Sean.

The carriages were now starting to pick up a bit of speed they couldn't see anything entering the tunnel except black strips that hug down from the roof of the entrance which went in their faces as they entered the ghost ride. They heard growls but they couldn't see anything as it was pitch black then all of a sudden there was a large scream and skulls and spiders jumped out in front of their faces. The girls all screamed then it went black again. The carriages moved along fast. There were witches that floated from the walls towards them and skulls that popped out when they approached. There were high-pitched sirens and creepy faces with axes covered in blood. The girls screamed most of the ride and the boys laughed at them for screaming. The ride didn't last long and they were soon off. Byron was stood waiting for them, he smiled as he saw them coming out of the ghost train.

"Was it any good?" shouted Byron as they pulled up in their seats.

They all looked at Byron. The girls were saying it was good but the boys thought it was crap.

"I am pleased I didn't waste my money on it now," said Byron then took a drink of his can of pop.

"So where do you girls want to go now?" asked Sean, looking at Naomi.

Naomi wanted to go and see if she could win on the catch a duck game as she had spotted a large teddy she wanted.

"Okay, girls, why don't you all go with Naomi and then we will meet up with you in about half an hour. I just want to talk to the lads," said Sean.

Naomi looked puzzled, looked at the girls and shrugged her shoulders.

"Come on then, let's see if we can win a teddy," said Naomi.

Sean pulled out forty pound and handed it to Naomi.

"Thanks, babe," Naomi kissed Sean on the cheek.

"That's ten pounds each," said Sean.

The girls looked surprised and they all thanked Sean then wandered off though the crowds towards the catch a duck.

Sean and the lads wandered off in the other direction to find a bit of a quiet spot to talk about what was going to happen about the money.

They soon found a place and all sat on the grass where nobody could listen in on their conversation.

"Right, I have decided that I am taking the money out of the shed as soon as I can and I am taking it and putting it back. I will leave some bundles out for everyone to share, are we all agreed?" said Sean, looking around at everyone's face.

"I just think these robbers could be dangerous men and I don't want anyone here to get hurt," said Sean.

"Put your hands up if you don't agree," said Sean, looking at everyone.

No one put their hand up.

"Right so we all agree that the money Damion found needs to go back and he has been very generous giving you all money, so you can enjoy yourselves and you all will, over these six weeks, I promise you that."

Everyone nodded in agreement and smiled at each other. Sean was right the money needed to go back as it was putting everyone in danger.

"So as from today, it is up to Damion what money is left out and what it is spent on." Everyone was quiet and just nodding.

“Right, now that this is sorted, we can go and enjoy ourselves,” Sean got up from the grass and looked down at the others.

“Are you lot coming then or what?”

The boys all got up and followed Sean over to the ride called The Bullet.

“Who wants to come on with me?” Sean looked up at it, spinning around as high as a four-storeyed building.

“You can count me out,” said Conner.

Sean looked around at Conner smiling and then he looked at the others looking back at him.

“Well, anyone?” Damion nodded and Michael shook his head with one eyebrow raised, as if to say ‘I can’t wait to see this’ meaning Damion’s and Sean’s face.

Jake and Joe decided to give it a go too but they were not looking forward to this ride as it looked quite frightening. It had two carriages shaped like bullets with a very long arm in-between them, which then spun, once you were in the air. Some lads were just coming off and were white as sheets and one even ran over to a bin and was being sick in it. All the lads cringed at the sight of him being sick.

Damion, Joe and Jake were just a little worried now and they weren’t even on the ride yet. It was soon their turn and Sean and Damion got on first and sat down on the seats.

“Here goes,” said Joe, looking at Jake.

“You’re not going to puke, are you, Jake?” said Joe, looking at bit worried.

“No, are you?” said Jake, watching Sean and Damion being lifted into the air four stories high.

Damion already looked terrified.

“I bloody hope not,” said Joe, climbing into the carriage and then sitting down. Jake followed him in and the man locked the door.

“My stomach is flipping already,” said Damion to Sean.

“Just hold on tight, bro, you will be fine, I promise you,” said Sean reassuringly.

The bullet started to move down slowly until the lads could see each other in their carriages and then all of a sudden Damion’s carriage dropped and Joe’s and Jake’s carriage went up. Damion’s stomach flipped. The bullets started to rock from side to side and the long arm between them spun and spun and spun. One minute they could see nothing but sky, the next they were heading at high speed towards the ground. Damion started to feel sick and wished he had had nothing to eat at all now. Sean laughed and laughed and Damion screamed out.

"Are you okay, Damo? You have gone white. Don't worry, you are with me you will be fine," said Sean, laughing at Damion's colour changing from white to green.

The colour did eventually come back to his face as he listened to Sean's voice and just held on tight and closed his eyes as tight as he could.

Joe and Jake were terrified and were both screaming at the top of their lungs. Sean caught a glimpse every turn of them holding on for dear life which made him laugh even harder. Damion, Joe and Jake felt as if the ride was never going to stop but thankfully it eventually did and Sean and Damion were the first to get off while Joe and Jake were still in the air rocking clinging on to the sides of the cage. Damion legs were weak when he got off and he bent over and held his knees.

"I am never going on that ride again."

Sean patted him on the back.

"You all right, bro?"

Damion stood up, smiled and shook his head at Sean. Sean was grinning like a Cheshire cat.

"I am now that we are off that ride."

They both turned and watched as the other bullet came down from the sky rocking Joe and Jake were white as sheets and Joe came out and was sick. Everyone cringed and looked away.

The man off the ride came over, gave Joe a tissue to wipe his mouth with and showed him where the bin was to place it. Sean shouted over at him.

"Are you okay, Joe?" Joe still looked white but felt better now he had been sick.

Jake was also feeling better now that he was off the ride.

"I am never going on there again," said Joe once he had cleaned himself up.

"Me nether, my stomach is still flipping round," said Jake, still looking a little pale.

"I am just pleased the girls are not here, I would have been so embarrassed me puking up, getting off the ride," said Joe.

“Well, not to worry, I won’t tell her,” said Sean, starting to laugh again.

Then they all started laughing. Michael, Luke, Conner and Byron were so pleased they didn’t go on after seeing their friend’s faces as they went around the ride screaming but they did have a laugh at them.

Michael had filmed the whole thing on his phone and was thinking of putting it on his YouTube channel for the world to see. They decided to wander around to see if they could find the girls.

They soon found the girls who had all been enjoying themselves and had all won something. Naomi won a teddy and Kim, Kate and Beth had won a gold fish each.

“Have you been having a good time, princess?” said Sean.

Naomi made Sean cuddle the teddy.

“He is lovely, isn’t he, he is so cuddly, these lot won fish they will have to find goldfish bowls for them now, but I told them they can put them in our fish tank if they like, until they get theirs.”

Sean placed his arm around Naomi, looked down at her, smiled and said, “That’s fine, anything you want,” then kissed her on the forehead.

Damion was telling Kim about the ride they had just been on and how frightened he was. All the lads started talking at once and were trying to explain to the girls about the ride. Sean said he would take the girls if they wanted to go on but they all declined his offer, after hearing the stories off the boys. Sean started laughing at them all again and everyone had a great day together walking round the rest of the shows they stayed till late and then decided to order a mini bus back home to the village.

The mini bus dropped them off at their front doors and they had arranged to meet again at Damion and Michael’s house as they were all going to the pictures the next day to see the new film *Atargatis*. The boys and girls all jumped out of the mini bus. Sean and Naomi were the only ones left in.

“Are you two going to come tomorrow with us?” Sean looked at Naomi.

“Do you want to go tomorrow?” Naomi looked at Sean and smiled.

"Are you sure, babe? Just we spent a fortune today," Sean smiled.

"Yes, I am sure, why not, I haven't got a lot to do tomorrow and I can catch up with work," Sean looked at Naomi smiling.

"Yes, yes, we will come too, see you tomorrow about three o'clock then?" said Naomi.

Sean nodded, smiled, then shut the door of the mini bus and the boys watched and waved till it was out of sight. Damion and Michael walked into the house and shouted at their mum who was in the kitchen with Conner's mum, having a bottle of wine and she was a little tipsy.

"Here they are, my boys," Mum got up from the kitchen table and cuddled the boys.

"I have missed you two, have you had a good time?" The boys told the story of the bullet and how Joe had been sick.

"Did Conner not go on?" said Conner's mum.

"No Na, he stayed off with Michael, Luke, and Byron. Mum you should have seen our Damion's face, it was as white as a sheet when he got off."

Mum started to laugh and so did Conner's mum.

"Well, honey, I better make my way over to see Conner now he is home," said Connor's mum.

"Okay, I will give you a text tomorrow," said Mum then took another sip of her wine and got up and walked Connor's mum to the front door.

"Bye, hun, watch how you go!" Mum shouted at her as she walked over the road.

"See you later!" Conner's mum shouted back.

Mum came back in, shut the door and came back into the kitchen.

"I am pleased you saw Sean and Naomi there, I am sure Naomi will ring me tomorrow telling me all about it too," Mum smiled.

"Are you two hungry?" Mum looked at the boys.

Damion was getting a drink at the sink.

"No, Mum, we got something while we were there."

Mum smiled.

"Okay then boys, I am going to bed to read my book, don't make it too late coming to bed, will yer?" Mum was swaying a little. She poured the rest of the wine into her glass and went upstairs to bed.

Michael and Damion decided to watch a horror film before going to bed.

They made themselves some hot chocolate then sat and watched the film together. When the film was over, they turned everything off downstairs and locked all the doors then went upstairs. Mum had fell asleep reading and Michael went into her room to take her glasses off. Damion stood in the doorway to watch Michael to see if he managed not to wake her up. Michael was very gentle as he slipped Mum's glasses from around her ears. Damion was trying hard not to giggle out loud and wake her. Michael looked back at Damion in the doorway, shook his head and smiled as he managed to get them off without disturbing her at all. He then turned the light out and tiptoed out of the bedroom and closed the door.

"I can't believe she didn't wake up. Mum is out like a light tonight. It must be the wine," Michael smiled and nodded.

Getting Rid of the Money

"Right, goodnight, Michael, I'm off to bed," said Damion, yawning.

"Yer me too, night, bro, get me up when you get up, will yer?" Michael also started to yawn and stretched his arms into the air then flopped his arms back down to his sides and slouched over a little.

"Yer, okay, bro, night," Damion turned to walk into his room.

"Night," said Michael, following suit.

The boys slept really well and soon Damion's alarm went off

"It can't be morning already," said Damion to himself.

He looked at the alarm clock then flopped back into his pillow. He grunted and decided he needed to get up and go and wake Michael up too. Damion knocked on Michael's door and he didn't get an answer. He opened the door and Michael was flat out snoring. Damion decided to leave him there until after he had his shower otherwise they may end up arguing over who was going in first. Damion enjoyed his shower and when he came out he knocked on Michael's door again and went in with just a towel round him.

"Are you getting up, bro, the bathroom is free at the moment. Mum is still asleep. You want to get in there now coz you know how long Mum takes when she is off work," Michael opened his eyes and looked at Damion.

"Aye, what time is it?" Michael started to get up.

"It's about half past eight. I am going to ring our Sean to see if he has gone to work or not, as I wanted to know when we are going to put the money back down the woods," Michael yawned and stood up.

"Oh okay," Michael looked shattered and was still half asleep.

Damion went to get ready and Michael went into the shower. Damion was soon ready and went downstairs to phone Sean.

"It's just me, are you going to work today or what?" said Damion to Sean.

"No, Na. I am coming over in a sec to pick up the stuff," Damion was surprised.

"Oh, okay, see you soon," Damion could hear Sean moving around then he heard what sounded like keys.

"Right, see you in a sec, make a coffee, will yer?" said Sean, still walking around and making noises.

"Okay, see you in a bit," Sean put the phone down, left the house and jumped in his work van.

Damion put the kettle on. He got three cups out and made coffee. He could hear Michael had got out of the shower and was walking around upstairs.

It didn't take long and Sean came through the door.

"Thanks, Damion, I need this coffee to wake me up a bit, my head feels like cotton wool this morning," Sean picked his cup up.

Michael came into the kitchen and saw the coffee on the bench.

"Is one of them mine?" He walked over to the cups.

"Yer, so what's the plan, Sean," Damion looked a little worried.

"Right, we are going to move the money this morning over to mine. I have been up early this morning and made a start in the bedroom and I am going to put it behind a false wall until the time is right."

Damion looked at Michael and Michael looked at Damion.

"Sean, I thought we were going to take it back to the woods?" said Damion, a little confused now.

"No, we are keeping it, I told everyone that to stop them from having to worry about it anymore," said Sean.

"Do you think the police will know it is up here?" Sean shrugged his shoulders and took another drink.

"We need to get it out of the way from here, because if the police do get wind that it is up here, they may come around asking questions and looking around. If we get it out of the way now and behind the wall, it is gone and we don't have to worry about it," Sean looked out of the window at the shed.

"Go and get some old clothes on then you can help me get it sorted," Sean looked back at the boys.

"What about Naomi?" Damion went and picked his coffee up off the bench and took a drink.

"She is taken care of, I gave her some money to go down into the city, and get her mum's birthday present and some new boots she's been going on about for a few weeks now. I told her not to rush and enjoy her morning shopping. That gives us chance to get back, finish the wall and get it plastered before she gets back. Oh, and she is shopping for paint as well. That should keep her busy for a couple of hours," Damion was impressed by Sean's organisation of managing to get rid of Naomi.

He thought that he would have had to tell her everything by now.

"Right, go on get sorted and I will start moving the bags into the van. Michael, you can keep an eye out at the van while Damion gets sorted then swap over while you get sorted. Make sure they are old clothes, mind, coz they will get covered in dust and plaster and it doesn't come out easy."

"Okay, bro," said Damion.

"Oh and be quiet don't wake up Mum, will yer?" Damion shook his head then he headed upstairs to get some old clothes on.

Sean and Michael headed outside and opened the shed door. Sean chucked the keys for the van at Michael.

"Go and open up the back door of the van, will yer?" Michael made his way down the path and opened up the back doors of the van wide then went back to the shed. Sean handed him a bag and Michael carried it into the van. Then Sean came and handed him another bag and he looked around it was all quiet; no one was in sight.

"Stay here and I will carry the bags to you, okay?"

Michael nodded then Sean went back to get some more bags. It wasn't long and Damion was back and Sean passed him a bag to carry to the van.

"Right, you help me get these in the van then Michael can go and get changed. It will take less time with two of us carrying."

Damion nodded while Sean passed Damion another bag to carry. It didn't take too long and all the bags were in the van. Sean locked the door and Michael went to get changed. Mum had woke up and was on her way down stairs in her dressing gown, her hair all over as if she had been rolling around on the bed all night long. She walked into the kitchen.

"Good morning, what are you doing here?" She wasn't expecting Sean to be there.

"Morning, Mum, the boys are going to help me today, we are going to sort that wall out in the bedroom by re-plastering it," Mum looked surprised.

"It can be a bit of work experience for them, it is something to write about when they get back to school that they helped their brothers at work plastering." Mum smiled at Sean and gave him a cuddle.

"You're a good lad, son, thinking of your brothers like that. It will do them good a bit day's graft. Are you going to give them a little money for helping?" Mum looked at Sean holding his arms.

"Of course, Mum, they can have twenty pounds each."

Mum smiled then went and put the kettle on.

"Good lads, aren't you," Mum looked at Michael and then at Damion.

"My head's not my own this morning, no more wine for me, I think, for a while."

Sean started to laugh.

"Conner's mum came over last night, we got on talking and we drank quite a bit two bottles of wine, yer know," Sean smiled and so did Damion and Michael.

"Great, yer right, come on then, you two, the quicker we get over, the quicker we get it done and you get paid."

Michael started to giggle and so did Damion. Sean kissed Mum on the cheek and then so did the boys.

"See you later, Mum," they all said together. They were soon in the van. Michael had to sit in the back on the made seating Sean had put in place.

"Hold on tight," said Sean as they started to move out and then drove off away from the house.

The roads are all country roads and winded this way and that. Michael was finding it hard to sit on his seat, in the back of the van. He started to laugh as it was like being on one of the shows rides.

"You all right, Michael, in the back?" said Sean, looking thought his mirror.

"Yer, yer, fine just a little bumpy, that's all," said Michael, clinging on for dear life.

They were soon at Sean's house and Sean went to check to make sure Naomi had left to go shopping. He soon came back to the van.

"Right she has gone, come on," said Sean.

The boys jumped out of the van. Sean opened the back door so Michael could get out. Michael grabbed one of the bags and passed it to Sean then passed another to Damion. Michael stayed with the van to keep passing them the bags until they were all gone. Sean locked the van up and went back into the house. They had put all the bags into a cupboard in case anyone came in. Sean took the boys into the bedroom and it had been emptied out of everything and there was wood and plasterboards in there and some wall lights as that was Sean's excuse as well to Naomi to redecorate the bedroom, as he wanted wall light in there, plus he wanted the wall smoother. Sean had been busy.

"Wow, I was expecting to have to move everything out of the room," said Michael, looking around the room with a wall light in his hand.

"Right, open up the work bench and let's get started. The quicker we get this done the better," said Sean.

The lads soon got to work measuring the wood to build a frame to be placed around the back wall. Sean drilled through the wood once cut to size with a special drill bit and through the wall to keep the wood in place, he then placed wall plugs into the wall and screwed through the wood and through into the wall plugs to keep the wood in place. They worked non-stop and before they knew it the wooden frame was in place and ready to be boarded up.

"Right, we will have a quick coffee then board it up. We will have to take the money out of the bags and stack it in the gaps between the wall and the boards and put the wires in for the lights then it's gone and hidden. We just need to plaster it after that and get the skirting boards back on. Go and put the kettle on Michael and make a coffee while Damion and I get the bags and start filling the inside with the money and make sure the door is locked downstairs. We don't want anyone just walking in," said Sean.

Michael went to put the kettle on and Sean and Damion got to work packing the false wall with the money. Sean got the bags and Damion emptied them and stacked up the cash.

"This is a great idea, Sean, you are clever."

Sean smiled at Damion. "Aye, not just a pretty face, after all eh!"

Damion started to laugh. Michael was soon back with the coffee.

"Give Damion a hand to pile up the money, will yer, I will go and get another couple of bags," said Sean, walking off.

Michael and Damion carried on getting the money out and stacking it up.

"It fits in well and once it gets plaster boarded you would never know it was there at all," said Michael.

Sean was soon back with two bags and while they were placing the money in the wall Sean started to cut the plaster boards to size so then they could be soon nailed on. The boys watched Sean as he cut the boards. He made it look really easy to do. It took a little while but the money was soon piled up and a quarter of the wall from the floor to the ceiling was soon full of money. Sean had put the wires in for the wall lights. Michael and Damion went to get more bags from the cupboard. They could hear Sean hammering and when they got back the money was all hidden by the plasterboards.

Damion and Michael smiled at Sean.

"Looking good?"

The boys both nodded. Sean got on and moved out of the way so the boys could carry on piling the money up as he placed the wires ready for the other side for the other wall light. They all worked hard and before they knew it the money was all covered up with boards except five bundles of fifty and twenty pound notes.

"Right, now to get it plastered, come on, we need to mix this outside and then we can carry the buckets in."

Sean unlocked the door and showed the boys how to mix the plaster. Once it was ready, it needed to go straight on to the wall quickly before it went off. The boys all worked really hard and never stopped until it was totally plastered and nice and smooth. Just the skirting boards back on, they dabbed all along the wood with blobs of plaster and they all held the wood to the wall until it had stuck into place. Sean, Damion and Michael all stood back and looked at the wall: it looked great.

"Well done, lads, nobody will ever know now, will they?" said Sean, taking a drink of his coffee.

"There we go, all done. It just needs painting now and the light's wired in place and screwed on then we are done. Go and put them bags in the back of the van. We can take them all back over Mum's. Don't forget to put the stuff that was in them back in and put them back where they were so Mum thinks nothing is out of the ordinary."

The boys collected up all the school bags and chucked them into the back of the van and locked the doors.

"Fancy making a coffee, Damion? I am parched," said Michael.

Damion looked at Michael.

"Yer me too, I could do with something to eat as well, are you hungry?" said Damion, rubbing his stomach.

"Yer starving now," Sean came to the door.

"Fancy an egg sandwich or what, you two?"

The boys helped and they all went and sat and looked at the wall while they ate their sandwiches.

"What do you think will happen now, Sean?" said Damion, a little worried.

"Nothing will happen, we just need to keep your mates happy then and maybe pay them all off at some point to keep their mouths shut." Damion looked at Sean and so did Michael.

"What do you mean, Sean, do you think they might say something?" Sean looked at Damion.

“We just have to hope they don’t, kid, or we could be done for.” Sean looked doubtful.

“They won’t say anything, I know they won’t. They are our mates, man,” Sean nodded but he knew the best way to keep them quiet was to maybe pay them off.

If they all got a few thousand pounds each they would be done for too for accepting and taking the money as they would become accomplices to a crime. Sean needed to be sure that they would not talk. Even though the boys trusted their friends, Sean was not a hundred percent convinced.

“Okay, bro, you know them better than me, what can I say. I am just trying to protect you two, that’s all.”

Michael and Damion smiled at each other.

“We know you have our best interests at heart, bro, but we know our friends and they are good friends. I just know that they wouldn’t do anything like that,” said Michael.

Sean smiled at Michael and then got up off the floor.

“Don’t tell your friends what we have done, this is between us three, as we ARE the three super warriors, ALL FOR ONE AND ONE FOR ALL.”

The boys all laughed and laughed.

Sean picked up a piece of wood.

“On guard,” he started waving the wood around like a sword, Damion and Michael joined in on the action.

“On guard, on guard,” said Michael, bashing his piece of wood against Sean’s stick then Damion hit Michael’s stick.

“Come on then,” said Michael, getting all excited.

They all bashed their sticks against each other’s and were play fighting. Then all of a sudden Sean stopped and looked at the door.

“What’s going on in here?” It was Naomi back from shopping.

“Did you get anything nice, babe?” asked Sean.

Michael and Damion had turned to look at Naomi too.

“Is the wall finished already?” said Naomi, walking towards it to take a better luck at the work they had done.

“Well, you should take these two to work with you, Sean, you could do with a little help now and again.”

Sean smiled at the lads.

"I know; they have done a great job, haven't they? It just needs to dry out now and then we can paint it and get the new lights up. It will look really romantic, babe."

Michael and Damion started to giggle at Sean with him saying 'romantic'. They never thought of their brother being romantic before.

"You two just wait till you're older, you will want to be romantic with the girls too. Won't they, babe?" Naomi smiled at Sean.

"Aye, he is right, lads, you will. I got a nice pink for the back wall, babe?"

Sean stood with his mouth open.

"PINK, did you say PINK?"

The boys started to laugh again.

"Yes pink, why, what is wrong with pink?"

Sean shook his head.

"Look what I have to put up with, lads, a pink bedroom my, WHAT EVER NEXT. Pink!" Sean shook his head.

"Well, I think it will look lovely, anyway, pink is supposed to be a relaxing colour." Naomi was not going to budge away from pink.

Sean was beat.

"What time is it now, babe? As we will need to start getting ready for the cinemas."

Naomi looked at her mobile phone.

"It's now half past one," Naomi walked out of the room and went to the kitchen.

"Right, come on, you two, we will get you back home so you can get ready. We will be over about three o'clock, okay?" Damion and Michael nodded.

"Babe, I am just taking these two home. I won't be long," Naomi came and gave Sean a kiss on the cheek.

"See you in a bit." Sean and the boys left and Sean was carrying the money he left out in a bag over his shoulder.

Michael jumped in the front of the van this time and Damion went in the back no arguments.

"Good job, lads, I am quite proud of you two today, I tell yer. You make good little grafters," Michael looked at Sean.

"What do you mean 'little'? I am as tall as you."

Sean started to laugh. "Well, you know what I mean."

Damion started to giggle in the back of the van.

It didn't take long and they were all giggling and laughing as Sean was actually the smallest one out of the three of them even though he was the oldest.

"You must have got Mum's genes, Sean," said Damion.

Sean gave Damion a look through the mirror. Then they all burst out laughing. They were soon home. Sean took a bundle of money out of the bag and told Damion to put the rest in the box in the shed and he gave him the key back.

"Lock it up and ring me if you need any of it, okay?" Damion nodded and went straight to the shed and hid the bag in the box and locked the shed back up. Mum had made a dinner and was just dishing it out onto plates.

"Do you want some dinner, Sean? There is plenty, you can take a plate for Naomi as well," Mum turned round, away from the cooker, to look at Sean.

"Aye, okay, Mum, plate Naomi some as well, it will save us making something later. Thanks, Mum." Mum smiled and got to work dishing out everyone a plate of dinner.

"So how did it go did you manage to get the wall lights in?" Sean looked at the boys and smiled.

The boys gave him cheesy smiles back.

"We got the wires in and it is now all plastered the lads did a good days graft today, Mum. I am proud of what they have done. We got it done in half the time. We make a good team. That reminds me…" Sean went in his pocket and pulled out a bundle of money. He took forty pounds each out for the boys and gave them the money.

"There you go, thanks, you two. You have been a big help." Michael and Damion smiled and took the money from Sean.

"Thanks, Sean," said Michael, looking at Sean and then at Damion.

"Thanks, Sean," said Damion looking at Sean and then at Michael.

They all sat at the table then Damion got up and made a coffee.

"Mum, you know we are all going to the pictures this afternoon, don't yer?"

Mum looked at Damion.

"I am sure you did mention something to me about it. What are you all going to see again?" Mum started to wrap the plates with Clingfilm to cover them for Sean to put into the van.

"*Atargatis,* Mum, would you like to come?"

Mum smiled at Damion, walked over and gave him a hug.

"Oh, aren't you sweet? Bless yer. No, son, you lot go and enjoy yourselves. I have some things I need to do myself. Maybe next time you are all going, I will come then."

Mum smiled and went back to sorting out the dinner onto the plates.

The Cinema, Meal out and the Bet

"Right, Mum, I am going to go and we will be back over in a bit."

Sean left with the dinners for Naomi and himself and drove back home. Michael and Damion ate their dinner with Mum then got showered and ready for everyone coming. They were soon nice, tidy and clean again. They sat and waited for the knock at the door. Conner came early, sat and waited for the others with the boys. All of them were excited to be going to the pictures. Sean and Naomi pulled up outside and parked up.

"Once everyone is there, I will phone us a mini bus to get us to the pictures and we can order a one later to come home. Are we going to go and get something to eat after?" said Sean to the boys.

"Yes, that was the plan," said Damion.

"Conner, have you got enough money? If you need any just let me know?" said Sean, looking at Conner.

"Yes, I should be fine, Sean, thanks. If not I will let you know," Sean winked at Conner and nodded.

"Do you lot fancy going to the all you can eat restaurant after, or is it a burger house?" Sean looked at Damion.

"Well, we can all decide after the pictures, Sean, that might be better," said Naomi, picking some fluff off her dress.

The others were soon at the door.

Naomi then ordered a mini bus. The mini bus pulled up outside.

The boys were quite impressed as the girls had come dressed up and looked really nice. They got out of the mini bus and queued to get their tickets for the box office.

"Do you want some popcorn, you lot?"

Everyone wanted popcorn and drink to take in with them. Damion, Conner and Joe made sure that they got the seats next to their girlfriends. The room went black. There were a few adverts on the screen at first and then the film started. Damion put his arm around Kim's shoulder and cuddled her in to him. Joe did the same with Beth and Conner watched Damion and Joe making their moves on the girls. So he decided to put his arm around Kate. Sean was also watching them. He giggled to himself and whispered to Naomi about the lads. Naomi looked along the line and could see them with their arms around the girls and smiled back at Sean.

"No kissing, you lot," whispered Sean up the line to them all.

Damion stuck his fingers up at Sean and Sean raised his eyebrows at Damion then smiled.

Michael, Luke, Byron and Jake giggled on quietly between themselves until a man behind shushed at them and Sean gave the man a funny look. As if to say, 'they are just being teenagers for goodness sake, leave them alone'.

Everyone got into the film and they all really enjoyed it. At the end, the lights came on and everyone had a great time and were telling each other their favourite bits in the film. They were soon back outside. It was still early and everyone was looking forward to something to eat.

"So where are we going to then? Have you lot decided yet?" Sean asked the others.

Everyone started to talk about where they should go to eat. They all had different ideas about what they wanted to do.

"Right, we will vote on it then, who wants to go to the burger house?" Damion, Michael, Conner, and Luke put their hands up Damion was trying to rise Kim's hand too into the air.

"That's cheating, Damion, I want to go to All You Can Eat," said Kim.

Everyone stood and looked at Kim.

"Right that's four for the burger house. Well, lads it's going to be All You Can Eat, you know you will be allowed a glass of wine with your meal there, don't you," said Sean.

The lads were soon happy again at the prospect of getting a glass of wine with their meal.

"Just the one, Sean?" asked Conner.

Sean shook his head.

"Yes, Conner, just the one."

Conner looked a little disappointed but soon got over it.

They all walked along together and Naomi and Sean lit up a cigarette each. Conner looked at Jake.

"Have you got any tabs, Jake?" Jake looked at Conner.

"Well, aye man, do you want one?" Conner smiled.

"Aye, if yer don't mind, that is," Jake chucked Conner a cigarette and Conner caught it.

"Have yer got a light as well, mate?"

Kate didn't look too impressed with Conner.

"Aye, do yer want me to smoke it for yer as well?" asked Jake, smiling.

"No Na, yer all right, I can do that myself."

Kate watched Conner light up the cigarette.

"Conner, you need to stop smoking, I am going to take you to the doctors to get some of them patches so you can quit."

Sean started to laugh as he knew what it was like to have a girl tell him, what you can and can't do.

"Just agree, son, as you are better off, but I do agree you shouldn't be smoking at your age. Kate has a point." They walked a bit further to some shops and Conner peered through the window.

"Sean, would you go in the shop for me and get some cigarettes?" Sean looked at Conner and laughed out loud then his face changed.

"No, Conner, I won't, sorry, mate. You're too young to be smoking so don't ever ask me again."

Conner started to blush and Kate smiled at Sean.

"If you were Damion or Michael you would be getting your arse kicked right about now."

Damion and Michael started laughing at Sean's comment. They were both pleased they didn't smoke.

They were outside the All You Can Eat restaurant and Conner disposed of his cigarette into a nearby bin with the others who had been smoking.

"Right, I will try and get us a table where we can all be together," said Sean, going in first.

There was a woman at a bar counter when you first walked in. None of them had been before and were looking forward to eating as much as they could. Michael, Luke, Byron and Jake were starting bets at who would eat the most out of all of them.

"Well, Naomi is out of the running she is tiny she would never eat anything like us, I think it will be our Sean," said Michael, looking at the others

"Well, how much are we betting?" said Byron, getting some money out of his pocket.

"Put your money away for now. How about five pounds each that means between the four of us, one of us should come out with twenty quid," said Luke.

"Well, who do you think then, Luke? You can't have the same person as Michael, mind, coz that isn't going to be fair."

They all started to move as the woman showed them all to a large table at the back of the room. The couples sat next to their partners and the lads sat together placing their bets.

"I am going to pick Damo," said Luke, looking at Damion.

Damion looked over at the lads all whispering on.

"What are you lot on about?" asked Damion.

The four of them looked back at Damion and laughed.

"We have got bets on who is going to eat the most out of you lot."

Damion started to laugh.

"How much are yer betting?"

The lads looked at each other.

"Five pounds each," said Luke.

Sean also wanted in on the action.

"Okay, I will have a bet on that," Sean chucked a five pound note in the middle of where everyone was sitting.

"So who are you going to pick, Sean?" Sean looked at Naomi and started laughing. Naomi nudged him in the ribs.

"What? I pick Naomi," said Sean, starting to laugh.

"Cheeky," Naomi gave him another dig to the ribs. Sean tried to move away but she caught him just right.

"OW!" Sean was only joking and rubbed his ribs as if they hurt him.

All the girls started to laugh at Sean rubbing his ribs.

"I have picked Sean," said Michael.

Naomi started to laugh.

"Yer, you may be right there, son." Naomi said to Michael.

"I am going to pick Conner," said Byron.

Conner pointed to his chest with a shocked look on his face.

“Don’t act all innocent in front of Kate, Conner, you know you can eat loads. We have all see you,” said Byron, smiling at Conner.

Conner started to laugh.

“Damion, who are you going to pick?” Damion looked around at everyone then stopped at Joe.

“I am going to pick Joe, I think he is a secret eater,” Joe looked at Damion and started to blush in front of Beth.

“What do you mean?” Joe blushed more and his face was bright red.

“Ha, I am going to win, Joe’s blush say’s everything, he is a secret eater,” laughed Damion.

Beth started to laugh at Joe being so red.

“You just wait, Damo, I pick Damion,” said Joe still red and pouting his lips.

“You can’t pick, Damo. Luke picked Damo, man,” said Jake, laughing.

“Okay then I will pick you then, Jake.”

Jake’s eyebrows went up and then he smiled.

“I am going to pick Kate,” said Jake.

Kate smiled at Jake.

“You know you are going to lose, don’t you, Jake?” Jake shrugged his shoulders.

“Okay, well, I am going to pick Beth coz I know Beth likes to munch, no holding back, mind, Beth, we could split the winnings,” Beth started to laugh and her laugh was infectious and everyone started to laugh with her.

“Oh I haven’t laughed as much for ages, my cheeks are killing, man,” said Kim.

“Beth, who are you picking?” Sean piped up. “Well, who is left? I think it is just Kim, isn’t it? Conner, have you picked anyone?” asked Sean, looking across the table at him.

“No Na, not yet I wasn’t sure who to pick,” Conner looked around.

“It will have to be Kim then, OH NO I PICK BYRON!” shouted Conner.

People from another table looked around at Conner as if to say ‘really!’ Conner stooped down a bit in his chair trying to hide behind Sean so they couldn’t make evil eyes at him.

"Right, Beth, who are you going to pick?"

Everyone looked at Beth as there was only one person left to pick.

"It will have to be Kim then, you better eat, mind, girl," said Beth.

Kim started to laugh.

"Well, who am I supposed to choose?" Sean tried to think. He rubbed his forehead.

"You will have to pick Michael, Kim or Luke," said Sean.

"Okay, I will pick Michael," said Kim, looking up the table at Michael.

"Babe, you will have to pick Luke. He is the last one left to pick."

Naomi looked at Luke and stuck her thumb up at him and he stuck his thumb back up at her and smiled.

"Get your money in the middle of the table, you lot," said Sean.

Everyone placed the money in the centre of the table.

"How much is there?" Jake picked up the money to count it.

"There is sixty five pounds," said Jake.

"That's not bad, I will be stuffing my face," said Joe.

"Right are we going for the first round then?"

The cooks were filling up the bay marries with more hot food everyone got up and walked to get a plate of food and then made their way back to the table. Once they were all back, the waiter came around asking what drinks they would like.

Sean took over.

"We would all like a nice cold glass of white wine, thank you," Sean looked at the waiter.

"Yes, sir," the waiter walked away to get the wine and came back with four bottles and placed them on the table. Sean nodded and the waiter smiled.

"Right, dig in, everyone," said Sean.

The lads soon had the wine and passed it around and everyone soon had their glass full.

"Ha this is great, a night out and drinking wine," said Conner, tucking into the wine.

"Make it last, son, because you're only allowed one, mind, that's the law," Conner looked disappointed.

"Never mind be thankful you have that."

Everyone started to tuck into their meal and it was nice. They were all back for second's to try another dish.

Damion picked the curry the next time and it was really hot, he quickly took a drink of his wine.

"Did anyone else get the curry?" Naomi waved her hand as the other hand was wafting over her mouth.

"It's hot, isn't it?" said Damion.

Sean started to laugh.

"Well, it looks like Damion and Naomi are out all ready."

Damion tried again but he couldn't eat it. Naomi wasn't keen too.

"Never mind," said Naomi, getting up.

"Where are you going?" said Sean, looking up at her.

"To get a sweet, I fancy the chocolate cake, it looks lush." Beth and Kate got up and followed her over to the sweet counter.

Michael was holding his stomach, and he couldn't eat another thing.

"That's it for me, I am stuffed," Kim looked at Michael.

"Don't give up now, man, otherwise I am out," Michael shrugged his shoulders.

"Sorry, I couldn't eat another thing," he took a drink of his wine.

"It's okay," said Kim.

Everyone else went back again for thirds and they were soon back at the table but the pace was slowing now.

Beth, Kim, Kate and Naomi where all out now, which just left. Sean, Luke, Byron, Jake, Joe and Conner. They tucked into the meal and Joe managed to get half eaten then stopped.

"Joe, man, what are you doing?" Joe held his belly and shook his head.

Sean was also full and couldn't eat another thing.

"Oh, man, I am disappointed in myself, but I am stuffed you lot must have hollow legs or something."

There was only Byron, Luke, Jake and Conner left.

Everyone watched them getting slower and slower. Byron and Luke were the next to go.

"Come on, Jake, my son, you can do it!" shouted Joe.

Jake jumped up and ran towards the toilets.

"NO, NO," Joe followed him to make sure he was okay.

"Conner, mate, you are the winner, son."

Conner's mouth was full of food and he spat it onto his plate and stood up and yelled out.

"YES! YES! I AM THE WINNER!" Then sat back down in his chair everyone started laughing at him. Other people in the restaurant however were not amused at his outburst.

"So who picked Conner then?" Byron stood up and grabbed the money out of the centre of the table.

"It was ME, I AM THE REAL WINNER," said Byron, stuffing the money into his pocket.

"You Jammy sod," said Conner, moving his plate away from him.

"Aye, tell you what, Conner, because you won for me, we will go halves."

Conner's face lit up as he looked at Byron.

"Really, Byron?"

Byron chucked half the money over to Conner.

"Thanks, mate," Byron sat back down on his chair.

"Oh, Byron, that was a really nice thing to do," said Beth, Jake and Joe came back from the toilet and sat down.

"Yer, all right, mate?" asked Sean.

Jake looked over at him.

"I am now, I feel as if all my food has just been wasted, I feel hungry again now."

Everyone laughed as he got up to get a sweet from the counter.

"Right we will wait for Jake then we will make tracks, okay?"

"What do you all fancy doing when we get back?" asked Michael.

"I don't know, why have you got something in mind?" Michael started to smile.

Luke knew he had something up his sleeve but he didn't dare ask again.

"Fancy camping out?" Michael whispered to Luke.

"I heard that, Michael. Remember that if you are going to camp out camp over the field," Sean gave Michael the look as if to say you know what I mean.

Sean started listening in on the conversation going on, on the next table as they were talking about the robbery.

"Well, on the news they say that they have some leads to where the money might be," said the man at the next table.

Sean listened closely to what was being said.

"They said they think the van headed up to the north east of England as they have it on CCTV on the motorway apparently. They think it is near here somewhere. Lucky sods, I hope they do get away with it. They show you the van but the number plate is missing. Then on the next CCTV the number plate is there on the van but they think it is a false number plate." The woman then started to talk.

"Babe, have you got a pen in your bag?"

Naomi looked in her bag, found a pen and passed it to Sean.

Sean quickly got a napkin and waited in case they knew the number plate.

"Can you remember the number plate?" asked the woman.

"Yer it was ROB 8RY can you believe it. It is like they were taking the mick out of the police, apparently they are searching the registration companies to see where the number plate came from. The couple started to laugh. ROB 8RY, it is like they want the police to find them," said the woman.

Sean started to laugh.

"What are you laughing at, babe?" asked Naomi, looking at Sean and wondering what he was thinking about.

"I was just thinking about me and you camping out tonight under the bed covers."

Naomi shook her head.

"I know what you are thinking about," she whispered back.

Sean drew a bed with a cover over it like a tent and put the number plate on the other side. He showed Naomi the picture. Naomi started to laugh and he then stuffed it in his pocket out of the way. Jake was back and soon munched up his sweet.

"Come on then, you lot," Sean looked at his mobile phone to see what time it was. It was now eight o'clock.

"So are we going to order a taxi back or what?"

Nobody was sure. The waiter came over with the bill and gave it to Sean. Sean took a look.

It said one hundred and five pounds which worked out five pounds each and ten pounds each for the bottles of wine which wasn't bad really as there was thirteen of them.

"Right, lads, get your money out, what's one hundred and five divided by thirteen anyone?"

Everyone got out their mobile phones to work it out.

"Damion, what do you get?" said Sean.

Damion looked at his phone.

"I get eight pounds and seven pence each, well, technically, eight pounds and eight pence each. So Joe and Conner and me and you need to pay sixteen pounds and fifteen pence each."

Everyone started to get their money out.

"Just round it up to a ten pounds and a twenty to give the waiter a tip, lads."

Everyone was happy with that as they all ate quite a bit. They left the waiter a twenty-five pound tip. The waiter came over and Sean gave him the money and told him to keep the change.

"Sir, are you sure? That is a twenty-five pounds tip, you know?" said the waiter.

"That's fine, we have had a great time and the food was lovely, thank you."

The waiter had the biggest smile on his face.

"Please come again soon and tell all your friends to come too," he said.

Sean smiled and then stood up.

"Come on then, you lot."

Everyone left the restaurant and Jake spotted the bus to the village coming into the bus station.

"Look, the bus going home, come on, you lot," said Jake.

Everyone hurried to catch the bus and they caught it just in time.

They all got on the bus and the lads paid for the girls. It only cost a couple of pounds each and they all went up to the back of the bus.

The bus moved away and they were soon on their way home.

"Who is camping out tonight?" asked Michael.

"I will have to ring my mum to see if it is okay to stay over again tonight," said Joe.

Everyone started getting their phones out of their pockets to ring their mums.

"Do yer fancy staying at my mum's tonight, babe? We could get a couple of bottles and watch a few movies with Mum. We can always get up early and go over home just with the bedroom still being upside down that's all."

Naomi agreed. The bus drove past the woods and Sean spotted a white transit van parked up near to the woods. He watched to see what the number plate was and he read it out in his head.

Oh my god, that's the van! It has the same number plate on it as the man said, Sean's face went white.

"Babe, are you okay? You look a little pale," said Naomi.

Sean cuddled Naomi.

"Yes, babe, I am fine, I think I just had a little too much to eat that's all. We can get off at the shop, go and get some wine and walk back. WE ARE GETTING OFF AT THE SHOP. ARE YOU LOT COMING OR WHAT?"

Everyone was chatting and the bus was quite noisy.

"So that's us lot camping out over the park, yer?" said Michael. All the lads replied yes.

"Well, I want to get changed first like coz these are my good clothes and we need to get the tents," said Luke.

Everyone agreed.

"Babe, I will be going out a bit later coz I am going to frighten the shit out of this lot," said Sean.

That was his excuse to get away and see what was happening with the white van. Sean wanted to see if he could find out who it was who robbed the bank and this would be his only chance.

"You are cruel, Sean, frightening your brothers."

Sean smiled a wicked smile.

They soon got the wine from the shop and Jake got a guy to get some cigarettes for him and Conner.

"Sean, we are going to walk the girls to Kim's as they are sleeping at hers tonight, so we will see you in a bit," said Damion, walking off with Kim, Joe, Beth, Conner and Kate.

"GET EVERYTHING READY FOR WHEN WE GET BACK, WILL YER, MICHAEL!" shouted Damion.

"AYE, MAN!" shouted Michael back at Damion.

They all walked off in different directions. Michael, Sean, Luke, Jake, Byron and Naomi all walked together.

"Right, this is me," said Jake.

"Meet you at yours in a bit with the tent," Jake walked off up the path to his Gran's house.

"Right, see you in a bit," said Luke. "Won't be long."

Luke ran up the pathway and went inside his house.

"Right, Byron, see you in a bit, mate," said Michael as he walked off to the house.

"Mum will be pleased you two are staying over tonight. Mum is always on about getting a big house where we can all live together and have our own rooms and stuff she keeps saying when she wins the lottery."

Sean laughed and cuddled Naomi.

"How would you feel about living with my mum, babe? If she won the lottery?"

Naomi shrugged her shoulders.

"Well, it would be all right as long as everyone helped with the house work and stuff."

Sean smiled and so did Michael.

They soon reached their door and they went inside. Mum was sitting watching the soaps on catch up telly.

"Oh here you are, have you all had a nice time?" said Mum, smiling.

"Mum, can we stay here tonight? Just I can't drive. I have been drinking."

Mum looked at the bottles of wine in Sean's hands.

The Robbers Are Back

"Yes, son, it looks like you are intending to do some more of that as well, have you not got any work on tomorrow?"

Michael turned and went upstairs to get changed into some old clothes.

"Yer, we thought we would have a drink with you because you are back at work soon, as well," said Sean.

Mum got up and went into the kitchen to go and get some glasses for the three of them. Sean and Naomi followed Mum through into the kitchen.

"Mum, the lads are all camping out again tonight," Mum passed a glass to Naomi.

"Where is Damion?" Mum took a bottle off Sean and passed it to Naomi and Naomi opened up the bottle on the bench.

"He has gone to walk Kim home with Conner and Joe and their girlfriends."

Mum nodded and poured out some wine into her glass.

"So what was the film like then, Naomi? Was it good?"

Naomi smiled and reflected upon the film and told Mum all about it. Sean went upstairs to talk to Michael he was just getting the sleeping bags out of the cupboard.

"I have seen the van the robbers used to do the robbery," said Sean.

Michael looked at him; his face went white.

"How do you know it is the van?" Sean pointed for Michael to go into his room and Sean followed him in and shut the door.

"I overheard a conversation when we were in the restaurant about the robbery and they were talking about the registration number on the van. I wrote it down and there was a van parked outside near the wood. I am going to go down in a bit to have a look. It was definitely the same registration number that they said. You will never guess what it is!" said Sean.

"What?" said Michael in anticipation.

"It is ROB 8RY, it is nearly robbery funny fuckers or what? They are going to get a shock when they open them bags up. I just hope they don't come from around here, that's all. One of them must know this place, but god knows who that is like. I just can't think of anyone that has lived here that would do that sort of thing. Can you?" Michael tried to think and he couldn't think of anyone either.

"So what are we going to do?" said Michael, sitting on his bed.

"Well, I am going to tell Mum and Naomi that I am going to give you a hand with the tents. Instead, I will go and have a look. It is a pity we didn't have a dog so I could walk it through the woods but there again I don't really want them to see me. I will just watch and see if I can get any photos of them on my mobile phone then at least we know what they look like and then you all will know to keep away from anyone that looks like them. Anyway, hurry up so I can get down there before they go, bro," Michael nodded and took a deep breath as he was a little worried about Sean going on his own.

"Do you want me to come with you, Sean?"

Sean chewed his lip while he thought.

"No…you stay at the park. I can be more stealthy on my own," Michael smiled at him.

"Stealthy you mean like playing a stealth game?" said Michael, smiling.

"Yer, stealthy like that," smiled Sean.

Michael was worried for Sean and didn't want him to go on his own or go at all.

"Come on then, as we need to move now."

Michael picked up the sleeping bags and followed Sean down the stairs. Mum and Naomi where sitting at the kitchen table.

"Babe, I am going to give Michael a hand to put the tents up and I forgot we could do with some more cigarettes at the shop babe," Naomi nodded.

"Okay, babe, love yer," said Naomi.

Mum thought they really did make a good couple. Michael went into the shed, to get the tent out.

"Come on then," said Sean.

"Mum, when Damion gets back will you tell him to hurry up and come down the park, please?" Mum stood up and grabbed Michael's cheeks.

"Love yer, son, be good and I will see you in the morning. I will leave the door open in case you want to come home, as it may get too cold out there."

Michael kissed his mum on the cheek.

"Okay, Mum, love yer."

Mum smiled.

"Love yer too, son. Sean, could you pick up some bacon and eggs for in the morning and I will make us all a cooked breakfast?" Sean nodded.

"Okay, Mum, won't be long." The boys soon left and Mum turned her attentions to Naomi again.

"So when are you and Sean going to get married then?" Naomi started to giggle.

"Did you hear me mum then? She has just asked your lass when you two are going to get married," Sean smiled and looked at Michael and shook his head.

"Oh take no notice. Mum is always going on about us getting married."

Michael started to laugh.

"So can I be your best man then?"

Sean looked surprised at Michael.

"You can be an usher," Michael looked puzzled.

"What does an usher do?" Sean shook his head.

"They are the ones who make sure everyone gets to their seats in the church and stuff."

Michael raised his head as if to say 'oh I see'.

They were soon at the park.

"Right, Michael, I need to go now otherwise they may be gone."

Michael nodded and dropped the stuff on the floor and cuddled Sean. Sean knew Michael was worried about him and made light of it.

"Don't worry, bro, I will be fine." Michael started to get upset and breathed deeply. Sean took a hold of his arms.

"Don't worry, I can look after myself, right, you know this," Michael nodded.

Both of them knew that the robbers may have guns and Sean could be shot if they notice him there checking them out.

"Come straight back here if you are gone over half an hour, mind. I am coming in case there is something wrong, okay?"

Sean nodded and he soon left. He looked back at Michael.

Sean ran as fast as he could back to the woods. There was nobody about but the van was still there. He decided to hide in the woods and lay and wait then catch them on his mobile phone. He made sure the volume and the vibration was off in case anyone rang him. He turned the light down then he ran across the road further up from the van he walked through the woods and tried to be quiet and not to break any twigs as they may hear him.

He moved slowly and got as close as he could he sat on the floor with his mobile phone and took a photograph of the van. He didn't have to wait long and he could hear men talking and the breaking of twigs. Sean knew the countryside these people didn't obviously otherwise they would have been a lot quieter than what they were. He listened closely as they came closer. He sat as still as he could. He could make out one of the voices was a southern accent then other voices were foreign and they were very close now. Sean focused his mobile on the van. He then saw them in the mobile. Sean tried to slow his breathing down. He had a good view of the men on the video he pressed the button and it started to record the men. They were all dressed in black and one of them was a black man the other three were white or lighter skin colouring. They were all carrying the black bags from the woods.

"Gaz, have you got the keys or what?" the black man said to the white man.

"Yes," said the white man.

He fumbled around in his jacket, pulled out the keys and gave them to the black man. He put a large black bag on the floor and then unlocked the back of the van. They all put the black bags in the back and two of them jumped in.

"Rick, you will have to change the plates now just in case," said one of the white men to the black man.

"Are we going straight back to London now then or what?" said the black man called Rick.

"Yer…I think we need to go straight back to Peckham and lay low for a while," said Rick then changed the van's registration plates, which now were saying G002 YER. Sean knew that one of them was a joker. That was for sure with these number plates they had.

Sean focused hard but he didn't recognise any of them. The men were soon in the van and Sean laid there as quiet as a mouse. The van turned around and then he got a better picture of the man driving which was the other one of the white men. They were soon out of sight and Sean listened carefully before he moved and got up from the wet ground. He felt as if he had been there for a long time. He checked the time on his phone. It was now nearly nine o'clock and the shop was closing soon. He checked to make sure no one was around before coming out of the woods; he couldn't see anyone.

He then walked off up the road. He walked over the grass and saw a couple of women talking outside the shop. He decided to fall over as his clothes were a little dirty from sitting on the ground. He did a dive on the grass as if he tripped and the two women came running over to him to help him up.

"Are you all right, son?" said one of the women concerned.

"Yer, I just tripped look at the state of my clothes, I don't know," The women helped him to his feet and dusted him off.

"Are you sure you are okay, son? Aren't you Sean?" said the woman.

"By, you have the look of your mum, you do, lad," said the other women.

“Yes, I am Sean, I am just on my way to the shop for my mum,” said Sean.

“Okay, son, we will let yer go because the shop shuts soon, mind, lad,” Sean thanked the women and went into the shop.

He looked around and picked up three packets of bacon for his mum then went to the counter to buy some cigarettes.

“Twenty of them cigarettes as well please,” Sean pointed to the ones he wanted and soon left the shop and went back to where Michael had put up the tents.

There was now three tents up and the lads where all huddled up in one.

Sean unzipped the tent. Everyone went quiet and he climbed in.

“Thank god for that, the lads know where you have been. We have all been worried,” said Michael.

Sean took out his mobile phone, put on the video and passed it around.

“Take a good look. Do any of you know the white guy driving? He comes from here, as he has our accent.”

All the lads took turns in looking at the video, but none of them knew the man. Sean rubbed his head someone must know him he thought.

“What are you lot doing tomorrow?” asked Sean.

“We have been on about going on the internet to look at some fancy dress outfits because there is a fancy dress disco on Friday at the youth club,” Sean nodded.

Sean pulled out some money and gave them all twenty pounds to go to the youth club.

“Oh and we are going go karting on Thursday as well,” said Michael. Sean shook his head and gave the lads another ten pounds each.

“Right that should be enough money for you lot for now. I am going to have to go as Mum and Naomi will be wondering where I am.”

All the lads said their goodbyes.

“Yer, see you all later,” said Sean.

All the lads were happy and they now just had to get an outfit to wear.

They all talked about what they might go as and were looking forward to looking at the outfits the next day on Damo’s laptop and in the catalogue. Sean was soon back at his mum's and Naomi and Mum had polished off a bottle of wine already. They both smiled as he came in.

"Do yer fancy watching a film son before bed?" asked Mum, getting up and poring Sean a glass of wine.

Sean put the bacon in the fridge then took the wine glass off his mum.

"Aye, what do yer fancy watching, Mum?" asked Sean.

Mum picked up her glass and the wine and went into the sitting room and sat in her favourite spot to watch the television.

"Could we watch the news first, son? Because I haven't managed to watch it for a few days now and everyone is on about the robbery at the moment," said Mum.

Sean wanted to know about what was happening himself. Mum put the television on and then put on the news. The newsman was on about something about the prime minister and the government as usual but Sean wanted to see what information they had managed to find out about the robbery.

"Oh here it is coming on now," said Mum.

The three of them sat quiet and listened to the report. It showed the van on the motorway at Scotch Corner heading north. The news showed the number plates and the police were saying they had a lead.

The Police and the Robbers

Mum turned the news off after that. The police knew it was four men but Sean knew they were pulling at straws at the moment and the least Mum and Naomi knew the better.

"Lucky sods, I hope they get away with it, come on, everyone is struggling no wonder that people are turning to crimes like that. Look at me working two jobs and for what? I can't even afford to take my family on a nice holiday, everything is that expensive."

Naomi agreed and they soon got on about winning the Lottery.

"That's what we need to do, son, win the lottery then we can all live together somewhere nice and hot with a nice pool outside. I would love to open up a nice little cafe and work for myself or a florist," Mum sighed as she came back down to reality.

"Well, Mum, you never know, you have to be in it to win it, Mum," Mum nodded.

She thought of how lovely it would be to be able to be debt free and no worries ever again. Sean could see his mum thinking about things and so wanted to tell her and Naomi but it was just not the right time just yet.

"What would you want to do, Naomi, if we won the Lottery?" Naomi thought about it for a little while then looked at Mum.

"I would love to do what your mum wants to do. We could all work together in the cafe and have a nice villa with BBQs and parties and swimming pool or a nice florist shop. You could teach me the ropes. Who wouldn't want that?" Naomi's mind was now working overtime as well and Sean sighed a loud sigh as he also would love for that to happen.

"Well, we can all put the lottery on, on Friday, Mum, the euro the three of us, the more lines we have the better chance we have," Mum smiled and took a sip of her wine.

"Well, come on then we should watch a film, what do yer fancy watching, son?" Sean looked at Naomi and shrugged his shoulders.

"Let's look through the on demand films. We should watch a comedy. I could do with a good old laugh," said Mum, looking through the comedy section.

"You pick, son, will yer? I can't decide or give it to Naomi to decide."

Sean passed the remote to Naomi and Naomi looked through the films.

"Oh this one looks good," Sean nodded and so did Mum.

"This should be really funny," said Sean.

The three of them all settled down and started to watch the film.

****

Back at the camp, the lads all had their torches on and were telling each other ghost stories.

"Shhh, can you hear that?"

Everyone went quiet and listened in the distance. They could here police sirens and it sounded like they were heading towards the village. It sounded like there was quite a few of them the lads sat quiet and just listened as the sirens went past the bottom of the football field.

"Come on, let's go and see what is happening," said Damion.

They all scrambled out of the tent and headed towards the sirens. They started to run along the street and in the distance, they could see police vans and cars near the wood where Sean said he had seen the van earlier.

"Shit, what should we do?"

All the lads looked at each other. "We should go back to the tent and say nothing to no one or we are all done for," said Damion.

Everyone agreed that was the best thing that they could do.

"You don't think they will find us, do you?" Conner was worried.

"Conner, everything will be fine, they are not looking for us, they will be looking for the van and the robbers. Remember the money is all gone now. Sean said we have nothing to worry about." Conner still looked worried.

"Come on, we need to go back to the tent and go to sleep. Hopefully we will have better news in the morning," said Damion.

All the lads followed Damion and kept looking back at the police vans and cars. They were soon back at the tent and they all climbed into the same tent.

"I don't think it is a good idea to discuss anything now as we don't know who could be listening," said Michael.

Everyone agreed, so they talked about what they all wanted to wear for the youth club again.

"So what do you want to go as, Conner?" asked Damion.

Conner looked up and his mind was soon off the police and he was back to his normal self.

"I want to go as a, you know, YER BABY."

Everyone started laughing again and they soon forgot about their worries.

"Michael, what about you?" asked Damion.

Michael was into computers and Damion knew it would have something to do with a game.

"I have decided that I want to make my own costume and go as a creeper."

Everyone liked that idea and was now thinking of what they would like to be.

"How about you, Damion?" Damion thought for a little while,

"I think I will go as the new superhero Jack Union."

Everyone liked that too.

"Well, I want to go as him out of the pirate film," said Joe.

"I think I will go as the Beatle," said Jake.

Everyone laughed.

"I have seen the costume in the catalogue. It looks great, we can have a look at it tomorrow, I will show you it," said Jake.

"Well, I think I want to go as a robber," said Luke.

"It is a good idea but I bet there is half a dozen or so robbers there with what is going on, man," Luke looked disappointed.

Damion felt horrible.

"Okay, I suppose it will do no harm at the end of the day," Luke felt a bit better.

"Right what do you want to be, Byron?" asked Damion.

Byron looked around the lads.

"I might go as a policeman then," Damion laughed and then everyone laughed.

"Well, I think we are going to look great and the girls will love us," said Damion, smiling.

Damion then yawned and it soon set everyone off yawning.

"I am shattered, are you lot?" said Byron, starting to feel cold as well.

"I am going to go to sleep, who is coming in the tent with me?" Jake and Luke got up, went over to the other tent and snuggled in for the night.

"Well, we better go and get some sleep too," said Joe to Conner.

"Aye, come on then."

The boys left and went to their tents Michael and Damion made themselves comfortable and climbed into their sleeping bags. Michael looked at Damion and gave a slight smile.

"Everything will be okay, won't it, bro?" Damion smiled a slight smile back.

"Yes, I promise it will be fine. Don't worry, remember they are not after us they are after the robbers," Michael nodded and settled down for the night.

It took a long time for the boys to get to sleep again, as their minds were on the police and what would happen next. Damion would talk to Sean in the morning about it.

****

The robbers were well on their way back towards London and to their secret hideout they had rented between them. It was an old shop with a flat above it in Peckham London. It took them six hours to get back and they made sure no one was around before taking the large heavy bags out of the back of the van and up into the flat. They had bought some beers earlier to celebrate their victory. They put the massive bags into the middle of the floor and each of them stood around the bags with a bottle of beer in their hands.

"Well, we have pulled it off," said one of the robbers.

"Here is to us," said another.

They clinked together their bottles over the bags and each of them took a drink.

"Let's get the money out and have a look at it," said another robber.

They all dropped to their knees, unzipped the bags on the floor in front of them and pulled out some bundles of the money.

"How come there is leaves and mud in the bags?" said the other robber.

They all looked at each other and then started to quickly empty the bags out onto the floor and to their horror they found that the bags were mainly full of mud leaves and sticks.

"Where the FUCK is the rest of the money?" said Gaz, the main robber who had organised the whole robbery.

Each of them looked at each other and shook their heads in disbelief that they had actually been done over. Gaz pulled out his gun and pointed it at the others each in turn. The other robbers started to panic as they knew Gaz wasn't messing about. Gaz stood up.

"Where the FUCK IS THE MONEY?"

They all looked at each other and none of them dare speak. They shrugged their shoulders and just looked horrified.

"Someone has had us over," one of the men piped up eventually.

"Yes, I fucking know that, but by who? We were the only people in the world that knew where it was. Have any of you told anyone else about this?" said Gaz, pointing the gun at the robber that had just spoke who was still on his knees.

"NO, GAZZ, I HAVN'T TOLD ANYONE," said the robber who had just spoke and was as shocked as everyone else.

"What are we going to do, Rick?" Rick shook his head and tried to think.

"If none of you took it, then someone has found the money in the wood and took the fucker. We have lost it now. I just can't believe it! It is no good going back to find it. What could we say? Oh mate, have you found a load of money in the woods in three very large black bags and then filled the bags with fucking mud and leaves? We have lost the fucker, that's it. We are going to have to go back and do it over again. This time we can just bring the money here instead, now we have this place. Let's just count up what we have and we can then discus our next bank robbery."

The robbers were all fed up and were trying to think of what they could do. They all sat and looked at each other, disappointed and upset that they had been well and truly done over and would never be able to find out who had took the money. None of them wanted to go back and do another robbery but what choice did they have as Gaz would kill them all if they didn't do as he said.

Gaz put the gun away back in his jacket then went and picked up four bottles off the floor of the empty flat and handed the other robbers a bottle each and opened his. He drank it straight down. He shook his head and looked at the money and mud all over the middle of the floor.

"Right, pile up the twenties in a pile and count the bundles and do the same with the fifties."

Gaz sat back down on the floor and started to help the others count the money. When they had finished he totalled up the money on his calculator on his mobile phone.

"Right, we have about two hundred and fifty thousand so quarter of a million. So the ones who have the money have at least a few million," said Rick, shaking his head and looking at the others.

"So what are we going to do over now?" said one of the others.

“I am thinking about going back to where we did this robbery and doing it over again,” said Gaz.

“When Gaz?” said Rick.

“Sunday night as we now know they have limited staff on a Sunday night,” Rick sighed deeply and started to place the money into one bag.

“Come on, we should get home now and we will meet up on Saturday night to discuss the plan again.” Gaz picked up the bag of money and placed it into a cupboard in the kitchen of the flat.

“Right, come on, I will drop you all off home to get some sleep.”

The robbers left the flat and all went home to bed after their disappointing night.

****

Morning soon came around. Back up north at the field, the lads had packed up their tents and belongings. They all walked up the road together and decided to meet up after one o’clock that day to go on the laptop to look for costumes. Everyone said their goodbyes and Michael and Damion went into their home and put the tent away in the shed. Michael and Damion checked on the money which Sean had put in a bag in the shed and it was still there.

Sean came downstairs as soon as he heard the lads come in and left Naomi in bed still asleep as it was quite early in the morning.

“You all right, you two?” said Sean, following the lads into the kitchen and lighting up a cigarette. Sean opened the back door and stood there smoking.

“Yer, we have just been on about what we are going to go to the disco as,” said Michael.

“Sean we need to talk like as the lads are worrying all the time about the money and getting caught,” said Damion.

“I have already told them I have put the money back in the bags in the woods and just kept the money that’s left in the shed,” said Sean.

Sean looked at Damion seriously and paused for a little while. He thought about what he had just said.

"Right, when you see them later on today just explain to them again that we put the money back in the bags in the woods and we only kept a small amount that's in the shed. The robbers wouldn't even notice that a little bit's gone. I have been thinking as well, Damion, I think we should phone the police and show them the video that I have of the robbers then they will look for them and hopefully they will get caught and then everything is off us," Damion looked at Michael.

"What do you think, Michael?" said Damion.

"What are you going to say though about why you were in the woods, Sean," Sean looked at Michael then flung his cigarette butt outside on the grass.

"I can just say that I was looking for you lot to check up on you all as I thought you were camping down the woods but when I got there you weren't there and I spotted the van on the edge of the woods with the number plates the police had described on the news. Then I heard some people talking and I lay down in the woods near the van and took the video of the robbers." Michael and Damion nodded at Sean.

"Sounds good to me," said Damion.

"What if they ask us any questions?" said Michael, looking at Damion.

"Look just tell them the truth but nothing about the money. We camp down the woods all the time or on the field and if they ask about the last time we camped in the woods just tell them about Friday night except without the money. We were up most of the night telling each other ghost stories as we usually do and about playing down the river and that," said Damion.

"Right so is that the plan then?" said Sean.

All of them agreed that's what they should do.

"What about Naomi and Mum?" said Damion.

Sean pointed to the kettle for Michael to put it on. Michael started to make the three of them a cup of coffee.

"Right, I will give Naomi some money to go and get some shopping and Mum can take her. I will say I have promised you two I would play on the computer with you, that should give us time to phone the police and they should be out straight away as soon as I ring them."

Michael's heart went in his mouth.

"Oh god," said Michael.

"Don't worry, you know the plan, just stick to it and nothing will go wrong. Look, you two go and get showered and changed and I will butter up Mum and Naomi by making them breakfast."

The boys nodded and went upstairs to get showered and changed while Sean started cooking breakfast. The smell of cooking soon drifted through the house and it smelt good. Naomi came downstairs first and she wrapped her arms around Sean's waist.

"Morning, babe, that smells good."

Sean turned around and gave Naomi a peck on the lips.

"Morning, I was going to bring you and Mum breakfast in bed," said Sean with a wicked smile.

"What are you after?" said Naomi, looking at him with one eyebrow up.

"Well, the boys have asked me if I can play on the games with them for a few hours today, so I thought you and Mum could go shopping for some food, as we could do with some at home. I thought you could get a chicken for Sunday and we could ask Mum and the boys to come for dinner over ours this week for a change. What do you think, babe?" said Sean, looking down at Naomi still hanging on his waist.

"Aye, okay then, I don't know boys and their toys," said Naomi, walking away, picking up the cigarette box then lighting up a cigarette and walking into the garden.

Mum had also smelt the bacon and managed to drag herself out of bed and walking into the kitchen with her hair all over and her dressing gown on.

"Morning, you two. That smells lovely, son," said Mum, sitting down at the kitchen table.

"I am making us all breakfast, Mum," said Sean, smiling at her.

"Yer, he wants you to take me shopping, Mum," said Naomi.

"That's all right, I fancy a look out. It will be nice going shopping together, we haven't done that for a while," said Mum, getting up and putting the kettle on to make everyone a cup of coffee.

"I see the boys are back and getting ready," said Mum.

"Yer, I told them to hurry before you two got up to use the bathroom," said Sean.

Mum smiled and stood and made everyone coffee and brought them over to the table. The boys were soon ready and back downstairs and sat at the table with their mum.

"Morning, Mum, did you have a good night last night?" said Michael, picking up his cup.

"Yes, it was lovely watching films, son. Did you two have a good night camping out?" asked Mum, looking at Michael and then at Damion.

"Yes, it was good, we just told each other ghost stories most of the night as usual. Conner makes me laugh. He is always the one who get scared first," said Michael, starting to laugh.

Damion soon followed, laughing at the thought of Conner getting frightened at some of the stories and he was also frightened of the dark. Mum had a big smile on her face.

"Yes, I can just imagine. I know what Conner is like he makes me laugh too," said Mum, starting to cough as some coffee went down the wrong way.

"Are you okay, Mum?" said Damion, leaning over and patting Mum on the back.

"Yes, son, I am fine, it just went down the wrong way, that's all."

Sean was soon finished cooking and brought over the bacon sandwiches to the table for everyone. Naomi was now sitting down too and they all tucked into their breakfast.

"I am going to pick us up some lottery tickets for Friday night, son, do you want one?" Mum stuffed some bacon into her mouth.

"Yes, Mum, you have to be in it to win it, I guess."

Mum smiled at Sean.

"Right, I am going to go and jump in the shower first," said Naomi getting up of her seat.

"Okay, just give me a shout when you're finished," said Mum.

Naomi nodded, smiled and went upstairs to get ready.

"It's nice that you three are going to spend some time together," said Mum.

"Right, you two, get up and do the washing up for Mum so she can go and get ready. One wash the dishes and the other one dry and put away," said Sean.

The boys looked at each other, got up, cleared away the dishes and Damion started the washing up.

"Thanks, son," said Mum, smiling at Sean and getting up from the table.

"Right, I am going to go and get sorted."

Sean smiled at Mum and Mum left the kitchen to go and get ready. Sean went and got the computer console and put it onto the big television in the sitting room and pulled up the three seated couch as close to the television as possible. He looked through the games in the kitchen then brought all the three player games to play on with the boys. The boys were soon finished the dishes and came into the sitting room. They took a seat on the couch and picked up their controllers, ready to play.

"So what do you two fancy playing?" The boys both looked at the games.

"How about fight and flight? It's been ages since we have played that," said Michael.

"Aye okay, sounds good," said Damion.

Sean picked up the game and took it out of its box and placed it into the computer console then started the game.

The boys were soon into the fight and flight game and forgot about everything else that was going on. Naomi came downstairs and shook her head at the three of them shouting on at each other and laughing. Mum was soon ready too and came downstairs.

"Have you got the money, Sean?" said Naomi, looking through her hand bag on the other couch.

"Yer, babe, my bank card is in your purse. Just spend what you need to, babe," said Sean.

The Police and a Fancy Dress

"Oh okay," said Naomi, looking in her purse for the bankcard and soon found it.

"Are you ready, Mum?" said Naomi, getting up.

"Yes, come on then, have a nice time, boys, we will see you later don't expect us back in soon, mind," said Mum, smiling at Naomi, and Naomi smiled back at her.

"Aye, okay, Mum, have a nice day," said Sean, not taking his eyes of the television.

Mum and Naomi looked at Sean, shook their heads, and soon left and shut the front door. Sean saved the game and turned off the computer console.

"Right, come on, we need to put this back in the kitchen for now. Help me get the place put right for when the police come."

The boys jumped up and put the couch and computer console back where they normally were kept.

"Right, you two play on the computer in the kitchen then I can talk to the police in the sitting room when they come, okay?"

The boys nodded and put the console back on ready for their game.

"Hopefully they won't want to talk to you two at all," said Sean.

"I hope not," said Michael.

"Right are you ready?" asked Sean, looking at the house phone.

"Yep, just do it and get it over with," said Damion.

Sean took a deep breath.

"Right, here goes," said Sean, sitting down and picking up the phone.

Sean rang 999 and waited for an answer which was practically straight away.

"Hello, which service do you require police or fire service or ambulance?" said a man's voice on the other end of the phone.

"Police, please," said Sean, looking at the boys.

The boys just stood still and stared at Sean, hanging on his every word.

"Hello, police, can I help you?" asked a woman's voice.

"Eh, yes, could I speak to someone regarding the robbery that has been on the news please," said Sean, looking at the boys.

"Yes and what is your address?"

Sean gave all the details they needed.

"Right, Sean, they won't be long," said the woman officer on the other end of the phone.

"Okay, thank you," said Sean then put the phone down.

"Right, they won't be long," said Sean to the boys.

"Go and play on the games and remember they are not looking for us they are looking for the robbers."

The boys nodded, and went and sat together in the kitchen at the computer table.

Sean took out a cigarette and went into the back garden to try and calm his nerves a bit and tried to show the boys everything would be fine.

It only took the time it took Sean to smoke his cigarette and the police were knocking at the front door.

"That will be them, remember, play it cool," said Sean.

The boys nodded and continued on their game in the kitchen while Sean went and answered the door. When he opened the door, there were two men standing there.

"Can I help you?" said Sean.

"Yes, you rang the police station," said the plain-clothed policeman and showed Sean his badge and then so did the other one.

"Yes, yes, come in," said Sean.

The policemen came into the passage while Sean shut the door.

"This way," the men followed Sean into the sitting room.

"Take a seat," said Sean.

The policemen soon sat down.

"Right, son, just tell us from the beginning what happened," the policemen took out their note pads from their pockets to write down everything Sean said.

"Well, I went out to check on my brothers last night down the woods as they normally camp down there when I saw a white transit van. I didn't think anything of it at first and then I noticed the number plate on the van. It was the same one as the one on the news. Obviously, I was worried about the boys and I went to the normal spot where they camp but they were not there. I panicked, wondering where they were and hoped the robbers had not seen them or something. I went back to where the van was and it was still there. I hid in between the trees and lay on the floor so nobody could see me. I then heard voices and put on my video cam on the mobile phone. Do you want to see it?"

The officers looked at each other and then back at Sean.

"Yes, we want to see it, are your brothers okay?" said one of the officers.

"Oh, yer, they were fine, they had camped up the park instead and didn't bother to tell us," said Sean.

The policemen shook his head as if to say 'kids, eh'. Sean passed the mobile phone over to the closest policeman.

"Just press the screen on it and it should play."

The officer pressed the screen and the video came on. He watched it and passed the mobile back to Sean.

"Could you put that on for my partner to see please?" Sean reset the screen as it had gone back to the cover page and he brought it back up for the other officer to have a look at.

"What's that noise coming from the kitchen, son?" said the officer.

"Oh, it's my brothers playing on the computer," said Sean.

"Do they know anything about the van?" asked the officer.

"No, they don't know anything about it, they never watch the television really, they are either outside playing or they are on their games console."

The video was soon over and the other officer passed it to his partner.

"Right, son, we are going to have to take your phone for evidence and you may not get it back for a long time. Do you need any numbers out of it?"

Sean thought.

"Yes, I will just get a pen and paper," he opened the door of the kitchen and the boys took no notice of him as they were now into the game and were oblivious to what was going on around them.

The officer stood up, looked in the kitchen and looked at the boys. He then stood for a while, came back into the sitting room, sat back down and looked at his partner. Sean soon came back with the pen and paper and wrote all the numbers he needed out of his phone.

"I would suggest getting all your numbers re-directed to another phone for now. Do you work, son?"

Sean looked up at the policeman. "Yes."

The policeman nodded.

"What do you do, son?"

Sean looked up again.

"I am a plasterer."

The policemen nodded.

"Handy trade to be in. Do you know that there is a reward for catching the criminals, son?"

Sean handed over his phone. "No, I didn't know that."

The policeman smiled.

“Well, let’s hope this evidence gets them then you could get a nice reward coming your way, son, thank you for getting in touch. Oh and by the way, we may need you to testify in court against them would you do that, son?”

Sean looked worried.

“They won’t know who you are. We have a special screen now so the accused cannot see who it is in special circumstances to protect your identity.”

Sean didn’t look as worried anymore.

“Yes, that will be fine then,” said Sean.

“Right, well, I think that’s all then, son, we will be in touch with you soon hopefully,” said the officer.

They both raised up out of their seats and walked towards the front door.

“Okay, son,” the officers soon left and Sean watched them jump back into the car.

The woman over the road was watching out of the window at the men getting into the car and driving off. Sean looked at her then shut the door and walked into the kitchen.

“They have gone.”

The boys looked around at Sean and stopped the game.

“So what’s happening, Sean?” said Damion.

Sean told the boys everything that the police had said.

“So do you have to go to court?” said Damion.

Sean shrugged his shoulders.

“I am not sure yet, they have to catch them first.”

Sean sighed a sigh of relief, went into the sitting room and sat down, pleased it was over with.

“Do you want a cup of coffee, Sean?” said Michael.

Sean nodded and Michael walked off into the kitchen.

“Damion, bring the console back in here, will yer, bro?”

Damion was soon back with the computer console. He plugged it back into the big television and pulled the couch back up as close to the television as he could.

“Right, you just need to talk to your mates now and then we should be home and dry, bro,” said Sean, getting up and moving onto the other couch.

“Can you help me though?” Sean nodded yes at Damion and Michael was soon back with three cups of coffee.

"Thanks," the brothers said as Michael handed them each a cup.

"Right, I am going for a quick tab and then I am going to whoop some arse on the fight and flight," said Sean.

The brothers all started to laugh.

They played the rest of the morning until there was a knock on the door.

"Answer that, will yer, Damion."

Damion jumped out of his seat and answered the door. It was all the lads.

"Come on in, last one in shut the door," said Damion.

Everyone came into the sitting room and sat down on the corner couch and made themselves comfortable. Sean switched off the television and pushed the couch back to where it normally was.

"Right, lads, I have something to tell you all, I wanted to wait to get you all together in here where no one can hear us. We took all the money back and filled the bags back up as I didn't think it was worth us all going to prison over."

Everyone looked at each other.

"We did, however, keep a small amount and we are going to share it between us all now then it is up to you to keep it safe and out of the way from anyone getting their hands on it. You can spend it on what you like as long as it is in reason like going on the trips with the youth club but don't take great amounts out with you remember, as otherwise, it will look suspicious. If you need help, ask Damion or Michael and they will help you or if they have to get in touch with me. I know you lot are not stupid to get caught out. I am just saying be careful, that's all, think before you do. Can I trust you all?" said Sean, looking around the room. Everyone was nodding.

"And don't spend too much at the shop here in the village either."

Everyone nodded.

"Damion, go and get the bag out of the shed, will yer?" Damion jumped up off the couch, went into the kitchen, got the keys out of the draw and went to the shed. He was soon back with the bag and passed it to Sean. Sean emptied the bag in the middle of the room.

"Shut the curtains, son, will yer."

Byron got up off the couch and shut the curtains then sat back down.

Sean chucked a bundle of twenty pound notes at everyone so they all had their first bundle each and then he chucked the next bundle at everyone. The lads were flicking through the bundles. There was one bundle left and he split the bundle between everyone to make it fair.

"Right, are you all happy with that?"

Everyone was happy as they all had over four thousand pounds each.

"Right, put it away and open up the curtains. Damion, go and put the bag in the cupboard."

Byron jumped up and opened the curtains and Damion went and put the bag in the cupboard in the kitchen and came back in the sitting room.

"Does anyone want to discuss anything now while we are all here?" said Sean.

Everyone looked at each other and nobody said anything.

"Right, that's it then, lads, have fun and keep it safe," said Sean, getting up off the floor and putting the television back on.

"Come on then, you lot," said Damion. "We will go upstairs in my room and look on the internet to see what we are going to get for the disco."

Everyone got up and trailed upstairs. Sean watched them all and Damion was the last to leave the room. He looked at Sean then smiled a very large smile and Sean smiled back as they both knew that the lads had believed what Sean had said. They were all soon on the laptop and some were on their phones looking for their outfits.

"So are we all going as what we said we were last night then? I am going to have to get some cardboard boxes and some paint for my outfit. I might have a walk around the shop to see if they have any," said Michael.

"Oh, yer, you are going as a creeper, aren't you? Ring Mum and she will pick you up some boxes and the paint you need while she is out shopping," said Damion.

"Aye good thinking," said Michael, running down the stairs to use the house phone.

“Mum, can you pick me up some large boxes while you are out and two lots of green paint one dark green and a black paint as well,” said Michael.

“Oh okay, son, what for?” asked Mum, looking at Naomi, confused.

“For my costume for tomorrow night as it’s fancy dress at the youth club,” said Michael.

“What are you going as?” asked Mum, raising her eyebrows.

“A creeper,” said Michael.

“Oh okay, son, what is Damion going as?”

Michael smiled.

“Oh he is going as Jack Union. We are looking on the internet now at some stuff so he may need some money as well, Mum.” Michael looked at Sean.

“Well, what does he wear?” Michael shook his head.

“Mum, ask Naomi, will yer, she knows who he is, just I want to get back to the lads, Mum, bye,” Michael put the phone down.

“What was all that about?” asked Naomi, looking a bit puzzled.

“Oh they are going to a fancy dress at the youth club on Friday night and they are looking at costumes. Who is Jack Union?” asked Mum.

“Oh he wears a dark blue suit white shirt and a union Jack tie,” said Naomi.

“Do you think we will be able to get it in the fancy dress shop up park street?” said Mum.

“You might be able to or something similar. They should know who it is and they should have a suit,” said Naomi.

“Come on, we will go and get the paint and boxes first and then we will take the car up to park street,” said Mum.

Naomi nodded and they were soon off shopping again.

Michael had gone back upstairs and was looking on the laptop with Jake on the fancy dress website.

“There it is. What do you think?”

Michael took a good look.

“Aye, looks good, you will look funny.”

Everyone crowded around to see the Beatle outfit and they started to laugh. Sean could hear them laughing from downstairs over the television. The costume was thirty-nine pounds and ninety nine pence.

"Oh look at these costumes," said Byron as he pointed at The Shan, Big Ben, Knocker, and The Blue Monkey.

"Four of us should go as them," said Joe.

"I have changed my mind. I want to go as Big Ben," said Byron, looking around at the others.

Michael thought the suits looked great and changed his mind about going as a creeper.

"I am going to go as Despicable. Ha, ha, that's mint," said Michael, getting up and leaving the room to go and use the house phone to ring his mum again.

"Mum, can you scrap the paint and boxes and can you pick me up a Despicable costume please."

Mum shook her head.

"Where from and how much is that?" asked Mum.

"From the fancy dress shop, Mum, it is forty pounds," said Michael, all excited.

"Okay, son, do you want me to keep the boxes and paint?" asked Mum, shaking her head at Naomi.

"Just take them back, Mum, and get your money back thanks, bye, Mum," Michael went off back upstairs.

"I don't believe this. Michael wants now to be Despicable the superhero, so we need to go to the fancy dress shop," said Mum.

Naomi started to laugh.

"Come on then."

They soon set off on their travels to the shop to buy the Despicable costume for Michael.

They had managed to get the Jack Union outfit for Damion and Mum was hoping Damion wasn't going to change his mind as well.

"I am looking forward to seeing the boys dressed up. We will have to get some photographs of this," said Mum.

Michael had run back upstairs to see the others. Sean just laughed at him as he left the sitting room. Luke had changed his mind too, when Michael got back upstairs and now wanted to be Baddy long legs instead of a policeman.

Joe had decided he was going to be the Wey eye man and Jake had changed and now wanted to be The Shan.

"I am going to be the Blue Monkey," said Conner, pointing to the outfit on the computer.

"Damion, you should be The Knocker or Nicky Nacky Nine Arms," said Conner.

"No, I want to stick to what I said," Conner nodded.

"Right, are we all sorted then? Should we go to the town now to go and get the outfits?" said Damion.

Everyone was in agreement and they all made their way downstairs. Damion opened the sitting room door.

"Sean, we are all going to the town to get the outfits for tomorrow night so we will see you later," said Damion, starting to shut the door.

"Damion, do you and Michael want to stay over at ours on Saturday night? We can have a few games and get a take away if you want?"

Damion looked at Michael and Michael nodded to say yes.

"Yes, okay, bro, right we are going to catch this next bus."

Damion shut the door and Sean started watching his film again. The boys decided to just use one twenty pounds to pay for all their bus fares into the town and it wasn't long before the bus came and they were off to get their costumes.

The journey to town only took twenty minutes and they all kept themselves busy by play fighting and looking at girls out of the windows by waving at them then laughing when the girls waved back. The bus pulled up in the bus station and Jake wanted to go to get some cigarettes as Jake and Conner were going halves again on a twenty pack.

"I won't be long, you lot, just stay here as I want to see if I can buy them myself," said Jake, walking towards the shop inside the bus station.

"We will wait for you here, okay?" said Conner, keeping his fingers crossed that Jake could get served.

"So what are we going to do once we have the costumes?" said Michael.

"We will need to get straight back to the village. Remember, we are going go karting at five o'clock. It was supposed to be two o'clock but Alan told Byron to let us all know the time had changed now to five o'clock instead."

"You never said anything, Byron," said Luke, looking at Byron funny.

"I forgot. At least I told Damion, anyway, I wouldn't want to miss it either, yer know," said Byron, sticking up for himself.

"I should have told you all. Well, you all know now. We should have time for a coffee and something to eat if you like before we get back," said Damion as his stomach had started to rumble.

"Was that your belly?" said Luke, listening carefully.

"How could you hear that over the noise in here?" said Damion, laughing.

"I couldn't, mate, only joking," said Luke.

Damion jumped on Luke to give him a dead arm.

"Ow, man," Luke started laughing too.

"Jake is back," said Conner, waiting patiently for his return.

"Did you manage then?" said Byron, looking at Jake disapprovingly.

"Well, aye man," Jake waved the cigarettes in front of Byron's nose just to annoy him. Byron shook his head.

"Great, giza one, have you got a light as well? And no, I don't want you to smoke it," said Conner as Jake always came back with a sarcastic comment if he didn't have a lighter.

"Here, squirt, come on because we can't smoke it in here we will get threw out," said Jake, passing him a cigarette and lighter.

They all made their way outside and Jake and Conner lit up their cigarettes.

"You two really need to pack in smoking. I am thinking of getting our Sean to help as he could get the stuff from the chemist for you and now you have the money it will help you to save it in the long run, yer know," said Damion as he hated that his friends smoked.

"Do you think he will help us, Damo?" said Conner, quite interested.

"I will talk to him later, I know he will. Why should you spend all your money on them?" said Damion, wafting the smoke away from his face.

They all started walking in the direction of the fancy dress shop.

"So are we going to get something to eat or what?" said Damion as his belly was quite loud now.

"Yes, fancy going to Sub like or McGee Dee's?" asked Michael as he was now feeling hungry too.

"Look, there is your mum!" shouted Byron at Damion and started waving at her.

"Oh yer, I wonder if she got my costume. Come on, we will go and see her," said Damion as they all started walking towards Mum and Naomi who were looking in a shop window and pointing.

"Mum, did you manage to get my costume? Did you get mine too?" said Damion and Michael together.

"Yes, I got them, they look really good," said Mum, looking in the bags she was carrying and pulling the costumes out to show them.

Mum handed the costumes to the boys for them to have a look.

"Oh they look great, Mum," said Michael, looking at his and then at Damion's.

"Where are you lot going, and where is Sean?" said Naomi, looking at Michael and then Damion.

"Sean's at ours, watching a movie and we are going to the fancy dress shop, so this lot can get their costumes," said Damion.

Naomi nodded.

"Do you want me to take them home for you? And what time will you be home for tea?" asked Mum.

The boys looked at each other.

"We won't be long but we were going to McGee Dee's with these in a bit," said Michael, giving Mum back his costume.

"Do you need any money?" asked Mum, putting the costume back in the bag then taking Damion's costume off him as well.

"No, Mum, we had some pocket money left, we will be fine thanks," said Michael.

"Okay, you lot, see you a bit later. Oh, I forgot to tell you we seen Kim not long ago heading to the fancy dress shop with some friends for their costumes and they were asking where you lot were," said Mum, pointing in the direction of the shop.

"Mum, we are going go karting at five o'clock, so we will be back soon," Mum nodded and Naomi and her walked towards the car park to go home.

The boys hurried to see if they could catch up with Kim and her friends and they got to the shop just in time as they were just coming out.

"We were just talking about you lot. We saw your mum not long ago too," said Kim, looking at Damion.

"Yer, we have just seen Mum and Naomi they are off home now. We are just coming to get sorted for the disco tomorrow and then we are going to McGee Dee's. Are you three going to come?" said Damion, looking at the girls.

Kate looked at Conner and Conner started to blush as red as a beetroot.

"Are you okay, Conner?" said Kate.

Conner nodded and went all shy.

"Yer, we will come, we will just wait out here for you," said Kim.

The boys all went into the shop Joe smiled at Beth.

"Won't be long, Beth," said Joe, smiling at her.

Beth smiled back at him.

They went to the counter, wrote down the numbers of their costumes and rushed to get in the queue that had started to accumulate around the made path of stretched out bollards and thick rope.

They all got what they wanted and one by one went outside to wait for the others. Jake, Michael and Damion were the first back out of the shop.

"So what are you three going as?" said Damion, trying to look into Kim's bag.

"Get out, it is a secret, you will have to wait and see," said Kim, smiling at Damion.

Damion tried to look in the bag again and Kim hit him with it.

"Pack it in, Damo, I mean it," she said as she hit him again with the bag, carrying on.

"Well, what are you two going as?" said Damion to Beth and Kate.

"None of your business," they said together, laughing at Damion.

The others were soon back and they all managed to get what they wanted in the shop and they were all happy with their choices of costumes.

"Come on then I am starving," said Michael nudging Joe.

They all walked along together through the crowds of people all rushing around and shopping. They spotted one or two of their school friends and gave them a wave as they were on the other side of the road.

They were soon at McGee Dee's and it was heaving full to the brim of people. They waited patiently though in the queue and eventually made it to the counter. Everyone got their order and there was a party of people getting up from a large table at the back of the room.

"Come on over here. We all can sit there," said Beth, pointing to where the table was.

They squeezed through the people queuing and they managed to get to the table as the last few were just leaving it. A lady came over and wiped the table down so it was nice and clean for them.

"Thank you," said Kim to the lady.

The lady nodded and smiled back at her. They all sat down and made themselves comfortable. They just sat where they could to make sure no one got the seat's that where available.

"We have been lucky getting to this table first, I can't believe how full it is in here," said Kate, looking around.

"So, Kate, are you going go karting this afternoon with us lot?" Kate looked across the table at Conner.

"Yes, the time's changed. It's now five o'clock, they rang this morning," said Kate, dipping a fry into some barbeque sauce and putting it into her mouth.

Go-Karting

"Mm this is lovely. It's been ages since I've had a McGee Dee's," said Kate.

Kim flashed her eyes at Kate as she couldn't talk as she had a mouth full of chocolate milkshake.

It is more ice cream than milkshake, she thought, *it is nice but too cold.*

"We should come down the city more often, you know, my mum gets a paper and it tells you what's on over the summer. I will have to have a look and see if there is anything good on," said Kim.

Everyone nodded as they were all eating and tucking into their burgers and fries.

"So are we all just meeting down the youth club at five then?" asked Conner.

"Aye, that might be better, are we all going after this?" said Michael, looking around at everyone.

"Yes, because we don't want to be late or they will go without us. They did that to us last year. Can you remember, Conner?" said Damion, looking at Conner.

"Yer, we stood ages as well and Damo's watch was wrong," Conner started laughing and then started to choke.

Joe jumped up and smacked him on the back really hard and it freed whatever Conner had stuck in his throat.

"Wow, I thought I was a goner there," said Conner then took a drink of his milkshake.

"Well, stop wolfing it down, Conner, you think you had never been fed before," said Joe shaking his head.

"Thanks, Joe mate, what would I do without you?" said Conner.

"Choke, Conner."

Everyone started laughing and so did Conner.

"Right, are you lot ready or what?" said Jake as he had finished his meal.

"I want to go and try on my stuff when I get home to make sure it fits. Because if it doesn't, I will have to come back in the morning to change it."

Jake started to put on his jacket.

"Aye man, you're so impatient, Jake," said Beth.

Jake just looked and raised his eyebrows he knew better than to argue with a girl.

"Come on then. Just bring your drinks with you," said Kim, looking around as everyone was finished their food.

They all grabbed their trays, took them over to the bins and put their trays down. They walked through the town and stood waiting for the next bus to the village. Jake and Conner went for a quick cigarette and stood outside the bus station. They were chatting away and they heard a voice behind them.

"I thought it was you two, caught you again."

The boys swung around quickly and Mr Hunter was stood, looking at them shaking his head.

"Have you got a light, Jake?"

Jake pulled out his lighter and gave it to Mr Hunter and he lit up his cigarette.

"Thank you. Are you two enjoying your holidays then?"

They both nodded.

"Yes, sir."

Mr Hunter smiled.

"Good. Have you been anywhere nice?"

The boys looked at each other.

"Yes, we have been to the shows, camping, and this afternoon we are going go karting," said Conner.

"That's good," said Mr Hunter.

"Well, we are going to have to go, Mr Hunter, as our bus has just pulled in, see you when we get back to school, sir," said Jake.

"Yes, have a good time," said Mr Hunter, waving at them as they walked away.

"Bloody hell, he scared me there. I got the feeling I was at school for a sec," said Conner.

Jake started to laugh.

"That's because he always catches us out at school, that's why," said Jake.

They all got on the bus and sat up the back as they normally did. As they entered the village and came past the wood, they saw a white van. Everyone looked to see if it was the van of the robbers.

"No, it's not them. I don't think," said Damion.

"Who are you on about?" asked Kate.

"Oh nothing, just thought I saw a friend go into the woods then," said Damion, trying to think quickly and it worked.

Everyone made their way home and they were to all meet up at four thirty outside the youth club. It was now four o'clock so they didn't have long. They went into the house and everyone was in the kitchen eating a meal.

"Yours are on the bench if you want them now," said Mum, getting up.

"You're okay, Mum, we have had something to eat in town, we are going out in a minute coz we are going go karting with the youth club. We forgot all about it."

"Do you need some money?" asked Mum, starting to look for her bag and purse.

"Yes, Mum, if you don't mind," said Damion.

Sean smiled at him and winked. Damion smiled back.

"Here there is twenty quid ten pound each," said Mum, handing it to Damion.

"Okay, Mum, thanks," Michael had gone to the toilet and Damion went and got a drink of water.

"Are you ready, bro?" said Michael as he came back into the kitchen.

"Aye, come on then," said Damion.

"Have a good time, boys, and I will see you when you get in," said Mum.

The boys soon left and made their way to the youth club. Conner spotted them and ran to catch up with them. They knocked for Byron on the way past but there was no answer.

"He is probably there already man with his dad," said Conner.

The lads walked along and could see Joe and Byron stood against the wall.

"Is Jake here yet and the girls?" Byron shook his head.

"No, na, not yet," they all watched along the street for their friends coming.

"They want to hurry up," said Byron's dad, locking up the club now.

Everyone looked around to watch Alan lock the door when they turned back. Jake and Luke and the girls were walking along.

"Great, they are here," said Damion.

"Come on, you lot!" shouted Alan, opening up the doors on the minivan.

A few others started to turn up too.

"I hope we can all fit in," said Alan, looking at everyone climbing into the bus.

"Thank god for that," said Alan, then told them all to get their seatbelts on and put his own on and they were soon off to the go karting arena. The girls sang songs on the way and soon the lads joined in too.

Before they knew it, they were pulling into the car park at the go karting centre and everyone jumped off the bus.

There was a sign above the door with black-and-white checked fags and everyone was getting excited. Alan went in first and everyone followed behind him in through the door. Everyone was allocated a helmet each at the reception and then they entered the glass doors. The track looked great with bright colours on the track of yellow and white. There was tyres everywhere around the circuit against the walls in case of any impacts and the go karts where lined up all different colour's even pink which made Beth happy as this was here favourite colour.

"I want the pink one, mind," said Beth, showing Kate and Kim.

"There is a purple one too, that one is mine," said Kim.

"Ladies first, boys, to pick," said Alan from behind everyone and starting to make his way to the front.

"Right, no bumping into each other. The man over there will help you get strapped into your karts."

They all walked over to the man.

Beth was first to get strapped in then Kate then Kim. The lads went next. Once everyone was in and had their helmets on, there was a loud hoot from behind them and they started their engines and they were off around the track.

There was a hill to climb and it swooped around with a squiggly turn and then back down the hill and along a straight and then a sharp bend and then another sharp bend, up another straight and up the hill again. The girls were in front for a short time until the lads came racing past them laughing and waving. Beth tried hard to catch up but was a bit unsure about the bends and slowed down as she reached them. They were all in their elements, whizzing past each other. You could hear the engines of the go karts and the large building echoed with the noise of engines and laughter.

They went round and round and round. Alan stood on the side-lines waving at them all and taking photographs for the youth club as they drove passed him but they were all too busy trying to catch up to their friends and enjoying their experience. The time flew over and the two hours went really quickly. Not one of them wanted to come out of their go kart but they did eventually.

"Alan, that was great, I really enjoyed it," said Kim, smiling at him.

"Oh well, I am pleased you enjoyed it, all of you."

Everyone started talking at once but they all enjoyed it and wanted to go again in the future.

"Will we be able to go next year, Alan?" asked Conner.

"Well, I don't see why not," Alan said, smiling at Conner.

"Great, we can come next year, you lot!" shouted Conner to the others who had made their way over to the vending machines.

"Thank you for having us," said Alan to the man behind the counter.

"Anytime, so we will see you next year by the sounds of things then?" said the man.

"I guess so, see you then," said Alan, walking over to where everyone was stood getting drinks and sweets out of the machines.

"Are you lot ready to go home then?" said Alan, looking at the drinks and got himself some pop.

"Yes, we are ready," they all said together.

"When we get back, do you want to help put up the decorations for tomorrow night's disco or what?" said Alan then taking a drink of his can of pop. Everyone looked at each other and all agreed they would help.

Alan unlocked the minivan and everyone climbed in and put their seat belts on.

"ARE WE ALL STRAPPED IN, EVERYONE!" shouted Alan over all the shouting and talking.

"YES!" everyone shouted together.

Alan placed his seat belt on and they were off again on their travels back to the village and the youth club.

"So have you all decided what you are going as then?" shouted Alan up the mini bus.

"YES!" shouted everyone back at him.

"That's good, I can't wait to see you all tomorrow it will be good." Alan then concentrated on the road and everyone sang as the bus drove on.

It took about half an hour to get back to the village and everyone jumped off the bus. Byron took the keys off his dad to open up the youth club doors.

"There are boxes on the table inside and there is Cellotape and drawing pins to put up the decorations," said Byron, pointing inside then following everyone in. Alan locked up the mini bus and went inside.

Everyone had got to work straight away, so Alan went and put the kettle on and rang Damion's Mum.

"Fancy coming down to give us a hand with the decorations at the youth club?" he said, laughing.

"Okay, Sean and Naomi have just gone over home so I will pop down now," Mum said, grabbing her coat off the peg in the hallway.

"See you in a bit," said Alan, putting the phone down.

He went into the kitchen, put on the kettle and made everyone a cup of coffee and left the sugar on the top so everyone could all put their own in. He even made Mum a coffee. Mum took about five minutes to walk down and everyone shouted at her when she walked in.

"MUM, MUM, WE HAD A GREAT TIME GO KARTING!" Damion and Michael shouted across the hall at her.

"THAT'S GOOD. IT'S LOOKING GOOD IN HERE!" she shouted back at them.

Alan came out of the kitchen and handed Mum a cup of coffee.

"Have they all been good then?" asked Mum then took a drink of her coffee.

"Yes, they have all been really good. I was wondering if you fancied doing some balloons with me? Seams you're the expert in balloons," said Alan, smiling at her.

Mum smiled back at Alan and looked around the room.

"What were you thinking?" said Mum.

"It's up to you, whatever you think," said Alan.

Mum nodded.

"I hope you have plenty of them mind," said Mum.

Alan walked over to a cupboard and pulled out three carrier bags full of different coloured balloons and an electric pump.

"I am pleased you have that otherwise it could have took us all night to decorate this room," said Mum, looking through the bags.

Mum started straight away and started making a large balloon arch for around the door. It looked fantastic when it was finished and the colours swooped around it. She then sorted out the balloons for the table decorations, three balloons in different colours to each table for where the children were to sit. She blew up loads to go on the floor, all in different colours. She then made four tall arrangements to go in the corners of the dance floor that swirled around the same as the arch on the door and they looked great.

"Have you got any helium?" said Mum to Alan.

“Yes, I got it just for you,” he said, dragging it out of the cupboard.

“I will come down tomorrow afternoon and do some arches to go over the dance floor that will finish it off lovely,” said Mum.

“Would you like another cup of coffee, everyone, as I think we all deserve another?” said Alan, collecting the cups off the tables.

“Yes, that would be lovely,” said Mum and everyone else agreed.

They all stood back to admire their handy work and the place had been transformed and now looked like a disco everyone was happy and looking forward to the disco now.

“So do you fancy coming down tomorrow night to give me a hand?” said Alan to Mum.

“Yes, I will come down and help,” said Mum smiling at Alan.

Damion and Michael watched them closely.

“Do you think Alan and Mum like each other?” Damion asked Michael.

“Yes, just as friends,” Damion wasn’t sure and thought he would have to keep an eye on them just to make sure that’s all it was: friends.

Everyone started to talk about the costumes but no one wanted to tell anyone who they were going to be.

“We will all just have to wait till tomorrow,” said Beth.

Alan and Mum went into the kitchen to do the washing up before they left for home. Damion kept a close eye on them all the time through the serving hatch.

“Right, you lot, come on we will get home and have a good night rest for tomorrow,” said Alan.

Everyone made their way outside.

“We are all walking up together,” said Damion speaking for the others.

“Okay, Byron, it’s nine o’clock now, mind, so straight up home and I will see you in a bit,” said Alan then he turned to lock the doors.

The kids all walked up together and Mum stayed with Alan till he had finished locking up then walked up with him.

"Thanks for giving me a hand with the decorations. The kids love them and they look really good," said Alan.

"You're welcome any time, you know that. I am just pleased I am off work and able to help you," said Mum.

"You know you should try and set your own business up doing your flowers and balloons," said Alan.

"Well, you never know maybe one day when I can get some money together then I would, but until then I will just have to wait. You never know I may win the lottery then I would open up a little shop, I think," said Mum.

"You will get there one day, I know you will," said Alan, smiling at Mum.

"Well, we can all dream, can't we. Well, this is you," said Mum as they had reached Alan's house and the lights where all on.

"Byron must be in. Do you want me to walk you up to yours?" asked Alan.

"No, I will be fine, you get yourself in and I will ring you tomorrow afternoon when I am ready to finish the balloons," Mum smiled.

"Okay, see you tomorrow," said Alan then turned and walked up his garden path.

Mum walked on to the house and the lights were all on there too. Damion and Michael where upstairs when Mum went in and shut the door as she could hear them upstairs, banging about.

The Fancy Dress Disco

Mum went into the kitchen and put the light on and then the kettle then went and put the television on and sat down.

Damion came running downstairs in his costume.

"So what do you think, Mum?" Mum looked at Damion and started to smile.

"You look great, son. I wish I got a fancy dress outfit myself now," said Mum.

"Well, why don't you go and get one tomorrow. Alan always gets dressed up. It will be fun."

Michael then came into the sitting room with his Despicable out fit on and everyone laughed as it looked really good.

"What do you think?" said Michael, trying to look at himself.

"Well, I like it, son," said Mum.

“I am not sure now, I am thinking about changing it to Nicky Nacky Nine Arms,” said Michael not convinced.

“Well, let me know in the morning and if you want it changed I will pop into the city and change it for you. I may pick something out for myself. Go and get the catalogue and we will have a look.”

Damion ran upstairs, picked up the laptop and the catalogue, ran back downstairs with them and gave Mum the catalogue while Michael and Damion looked on the laptop.

“What do you think about *Atargatis*? What do you think? Then again, the superhero Ironic dress is a lot longer, I think Ironic will be better for me,” said Mum, looking at the boys.

“I am not sure, Mum, now coz this costume looks better than Nicky Nacky Nine Arms, I can’t decide now,” said Michael.

“Well, you have until the morning to think about it. I will get you up when I get up and then you will have plenty of time,” said Mum.

“What do you think, Damion?”

Damion took another look.

“I like the one you have. It’s great but it is up to you,” said Damion, getting up.

“Right, I am off to get ready for bed,” said Damion, pulling off his mask on his costume.

“Okay, son,” said Mum then looked at Michael who was still looking at the costumes on the laptop.

“Oh I don’t know, right, I am getting ready for bed too,” Michael made his way upstairs to get ready for bed.

Mum picked up the remote and flicked through the television channels and the news came on.

“Tonight on the news police have got some good leads on the robbery that took place in London which had led them to the North East of England then back to London again. Scotland Yard who is leading the investigation have now confirmed they have detailed descriptions of the robbers and are working around the clock to find their whereabouts.”

“Oh they still haven’t found them yet then,” said Mum as Damion and Michael looked at each other again as they came down the stairs.

"Mum, fancy watching a film?" asked Damion, coming through the door and sitting back down on the couch. Michael followed closely after.

"Yes, in a minute, I just want to hear this. It's about that robbery again," said Mum, staring at the television.

Damion and Michael looked at each other and went quiet while they listened to the news with their mum.

"Oh they mustn't have much more information then. Right what do you want to watch then, you two," said Mum, looking at them both.

"A good comedy, Mum, before bed," said Damion.

Mum smiled and went to the movie channels.

"How about watching *The World Is Going to End*?" said Mum.

"Yes, okay."

So they all watched the film before going to bed.

The next morning they all laid in till ten o'clock. Mum woke Michael to see if he was going to change his costume and he decided to change it to Nicky Nacky Nine Arms. Mum got ready and went off into the city while the boys stayed in bed a bit longer. Mum returned and they were still in bed. She went upstairs and Michael was fast asleep so she decided to wake him up as it was twelve o'clock.

"Come on, Michael, time to get up. I got the costume you wanted and I need you to try it on and make sure that is what you want," Michael sat up in bed and rubbed his eyes.

"Okay, won't be long," he climbed out of bed and tried on the suit. He liked it.

Mum woke Damion up too then went downstairs and Damion followed her down. He sat on the couch and looked at Mum as she had her costume in her hands.

"Are we going to Sean's on Sunday for dinner? Sean was on about it yesterday."

Mum nodded as she was looking at her costume and took it out of the plastic.

"Yes, he asked me yesterday, so I said we would go for dinner," Mum stood up and put the dress up against her.

"I am going to go and try this on," said Mum.

Michael had made his way into the sitting room.

"Is it okay then, son?" said Mum as she passed him.

"Yes, I like that one better than the other one."

Mum smiled.

"I am quite looking forward to this now. It should be fun," she went upstairs to try on the costume and the boys were left in the sitting room.

"Do you think the lads believe what we told them, Michael?" Michael looked at Damion then sat down on the other couch.

"I don't see why not and they were happy to get the money, weren't they?" Damion nodded.

"I just feel a little guilty, that's all, lying to them," Michael sat up.

"Why? At the end of the day, you found the money so it should be yours. You didn't have to tell anyone and they all should be thankful for what they got. If it had been me that found the money I would have only told you and our Sean. So don't beat yourself up everyone is happy with their cut," said Michael, picking up the remote and changing the television channel.

"Should we go and give Mum a hand today at the youth club to finish the decorations?" said Damion.

"Yer, okay, let me watch this first and then I will get ready," they both sat and watched a movie.

Mum came downstairs to show them her outfit for that evening.

"What do you two think?" said Mum, doing a little twirl in front of the television.

"Aye, Mum, it looks good. What time are you going down the youth club?" said Damion.

"I was thinking about half past three, four o'clock. I will have to ring Alan to let him know and I wanted to make some cakes and sandwiches to take down you two can give me a hand if you like." The boys nodded.

"Mum, move out of the way of the television, will yer, please just I want to watch this," said Michael, getting impatient.

Mum went back upstairs and got changed. The boys were getting into the film and didn't even notice Mum passing them as she went into the kitchen to make the sandwiches and the cakes for the disco that evening. The boys soon smelt the cake baking in the oven. Michael got up to go and have a look.

"Can we have some cakes now, Mum?"

Mum handed Michael two plates with sandwiches and cakes on and smiled.

"After them we will have to get ready."

The boys tucked into their sandwiches while Mum plated everything up onto a large tray and covered them with Clingfilm. It didn't take long and they were all finished. They both ran upstairs to get ready. Mum took the trays of sandwiches and cakes to the car and put them in the boot. The boys were soon ready and jumped into the car. Mum drove down to the youth club. Alan was there, thankfully, as Mum forgot to ring him. The boys helped her get the trays from the boot and took them into the kitchen.

"Hello there," said Mum to Alan he was in the kitchen sorting out the tuck shop for when the kids come, so they could buy sweets and drinks from the counter.

"Oh they look nice," said Alan as he turned around and looked at the trays.

"Well, I thought I would make some stuff for the kids to eat," said Mum, starting to place the trays into the large fridge at the other end of the kitchen.

"Would you like a cake?"

Alan couldn't refuse cake and took two from the tray.

"Thanks, they look lovely."

Mum smiled and Alan tucked into one of his cakes.

"Is the helium out and I will get on with the decorations?" said Mum.

Alan showed her where he had put it and Mum took some wire out of her bag. She measured the distance she needed and then cut the fishing wire and blew up the balloons with the helium and attached the balloons to the wire. Once all the balloons were attached, Mum tied the balloon arches to the four balloon arrangements she had made the previous night. The balloon arches then came over the dance floor above their heads and looked amazing. She then made table arrangements made of three balloons of different colours with silver ribbons and silver star weights. Alan and the boys placed white table cloths over all the tables and Mum placed the balloon centre pieces in the middles of the tables.

When they had all finished, the place looked amazing and was now all ready for the disco that evening. Mum decided to keep Alan company while he waited for the disco man to come and set up his equipment. Within a dedicated space left within the corner of the room. The boys decided to go home and start preparing for the disco and the first port of call was to ring their friends to see what time everyone was going to be meeting. It didn't take Michael and Damion long to get back up home. As soon as they got in Damion was straight on the house phone.

"Yer all right, Conner? What's happening then?" said Damion.

"Well, aye man, everyone's coming to yours and we will all walk down to the youth club together."

"What time then, mate?"

"I dunno."

"Aye tell you what, meet me at mine at about quarter past six then we will go down for about quarter to seven," said Damion.

"Okay, mate, do you want me to ring Jake and Joe? And then you ring Byron and Luke."

"Aye go on then, it will save my mum's phone bill."

"Right, see you in a bit."

Damion put the phone down and looked at Michael.

"They are all coming here between quarter past six and quarter to seven," said Damion, getting up off the sofa.

"What time is it now?" asked Michael.

"I don't know, put the telly on and have a look."

Michael got up and looked for the remote which was hidden between the cushions.

"It's half past five now."

"Are you going in the shower again?"

"Yes, are you?"

"Aye, do you want to go in first?"

"Well, I was thinking about having a couple of games on the computer like and to see if Olli was on."

"What were you thinking of playing on?"

"Maybe ATA, fancy a game?"

"Aye, it's been ages since I've been on there."

"Come on then, get your console on."

Damion walked up into his bedroom, while Michael's console was in the kitchen. They both got on to their live edition and both put their game of ATA into the console and put their headphones on. Michael invited Damion to his party and then they could talk to each other.

"Can you hear me all right?" said Michael, checking his mike.

"Yer, bro, loud and clear. Is Olli on then?" Michael checked on his friends list and Olli was online.

Michael sent Olli an invite to the party, and it wasn't long before Michael and Damion could hear him.

"You all right, Olli? Fancy a game on ATA with me and Damo?" said Michael, loading up his game to online.

"Yer, why not," said Olli.

"Mate, have you been watching Jack lately? Oh man, he is SO funny," said Michael.

"Yer, man he is great."

"Did you see him on the Virtual Reality, the one where he's on the Cyberspace? OMG, (Oh my god) it is funny, a lot of swearing in it, mind, but seriously my stomach was flipping just watching it and Jack is afraid of heights, man. So funny you will have to watch it later and let me know what you think, mate."

Olli started to laugh as he knew how funny Jack could be.

"Will do, mate, looking forward to it now. So what you up to tonight then?" said Olli.

"Me and Damo are going to a fancy dress disco. Conner, Jake, Byron, and Luke are going too. I will get some photos of us lot and post them online either tonight or tomorrow," Olli started laughing.

"So what are you going as?"

"I am going as Nicky Nacky Nine Arms."

Olli started laughing again.

"Oh Damo mate, what you going as?" said Olli, smiling and tried to think what a Nicky Nacky Nine Arms suit would look like.

"I am going as Jack Union."

"Oh my god, seriously? Where have you got the costumes from?"

"Mum picked mine up at that fancy dress shop on the bank near broom lane."

"Oh yer I know which one you mean."

"Mum got mine from the other fancy dress shop, I think. You should have a look, they are pretty good," said Michael.

"Sounds good."

"So what's the others going as?"

"Byron is going as the superhero Big Ben, Joe is going as The Wey Eye Man superhero," said Michael

"What are Conner and Luke going as again, Damo?"

"Conner is going as the superhero The Blue Monkey and Luke is going as Baddy Long Legs," said Damion.

"I can't wait to see the photos now, make sure you get plenty, Michael."

"Oh don't worry I am going too."

"Are you still going with Kim, Damo?"

"Yes…Oh, I forgot to phone Kim, Michael."

"She did say she would meet you there. I am sure that's what she said last night."

"Oh, yes, I remember now, we are meeting the girls there."

"So when are you coming up next, Olli?"

"I am not sure yet. Mum was on about sometime during the six weeks but I will let you know when and I will come and stay over yours for a night or two."

"Sounds good, we will have a laugh," said Damion.

The time flew by for the boys and before they knew it, it was six o'clock.

"Michael, I am off to get ready, I will give you a shout when I am out of the shower. Olli, mate, speak to you later."

"Okay, mate, speak to you soon. Are you staying on a little longer?"

"Yer, I am just waiting for Damion to get out of the shower, mate, then I will have to go, so I can play a little longer."

"Great."

Michael and Olli played on the computer while Damion got himself ready for the fancy dress. He looked in the mirror. He looked really good and smiled to himself. He came downstairs and into the kitchen where Michael was still playing on the console.

"Right, I have left the shower on for you."

Mum came in through the back door.

"Are you two okay?"

"Yes, Mum, where have you been?" asked Damion.

"The disco has just turned up so I let Alan go and get ready and I stayed with them until he came back," explained Mum.

"So what is Alan dressed as?"

"The Knocker, apparently, Byron gave him the idea, he looks good. Have you been in the shower, Michael?"

"No, not yet, I was going to go in now."

"Well, can I go in first, just I take a little longer to get ready that's all, son."

Michael looked at Mum.

"Yer, Mum, you go in first then no problem," said Michael.

"Thanks, son, I won't be too long, I will shout for you when I am out," said Mum.

Michael smiled at his mum and she went straight upstairs to get ready.

The doorbell went shortly after and Damion went to answer it. The Blue Monkey was at the door. Damion and Conner started to laugh at each other.

"Come on in, Blue Monkey. Where are the others?" asked Damion, looking out of the door and down the street.

"They shouldn't be too long," Damion shut the door and followed Conner into the kitchen, both of them still laughing.

Conner looked really good as The Blue Monkey. Michael started to laugh at him.

"That costume looks good, Conner."

Michael turned around and told Olli Conner was here and he was going to have to go and get ready.

"Okay, mate, speak to you tomorrow sometime if you're online. Don't forget to put the pictures online tomorrow," said Olli.

"I won't forget, catch you later, mate," said Michael then turned off the computer.

Mum shouted down the stairs for Michael.

"Right, I won't be long," Damion and Conner started laughing again.

There was soon another knock on the door and Conner and Damion went to see who it was. When they opened the door, it was The Shan and The Wey Eye Man. Everyone started to laugh at each other.

"Come on in."

They came inside, sat and waited for the others in the sitting room.

Mum came down stairs dressed as Ironic. They all started laughing at her. And when she saw the lads she started to laugh too.

"I am going to have to get a photograph of you all together, you all look great," said Mum.

The doorbell went again and Mum went to the door this time.

It was Baddy Long Legs and Big Ben. Mum shook her head.

"Come on in, we are just waiting for Michael or should I say Nicky Nacky Nine Arms."

Everyone started laughing and Michael could hear the laughter from upstairs. He hurried to get ready. He came downstairs and again everyone started laughing at each other.

"Right has everyone got everything? I am just going to lock the back door and then we can all walk down together," said Mum, going into the kitchen.

She locked up and picked up her small red bag she had bought to go with her Ironic outfit.

Everyone got up off the couches and walked outside. Mum locked the front door and they all walked down the road together.

"Have you got your phone, Michael?" said Damion.

"Yes, Mum, can you put it in your bag? Until I want it later," said Michael.

Mum opened her bag, placed the phone inside it and shut the clasp. People were looking out of their windows and showing their young children as they all walked passed as it was still light.

"Wave at the kids, lads, as you are their super heroes."

Everyone started to wave at three little boys looking out of their window and their faces were a picture and they were so happy to see them.

"Look at their little faces, bless them, it's not every day you see so many super heroes walking down your street, is it?" said mum.

The lads kept waving and the little boys waved back all excited to see them. Even their mum waved at the lads. The boys felt on top of the world and now even more excited about seeing the girls.

They were all soon at the disco and it was starting to get packed already. Mum went straight into the kitchen to help Alan. Alan turned around and took a good look at Mum and started laughing at her.

"Well, hello, Ironic, how are you this fine evening?" Mum giggled.

"Very well, thank you, by, it's getting quite full already, isn't it, and it's not even seven o'clock yet," Alan smiled at Mum.

"Fancy a coffee?" Mum nodded and smiled.

"Yes, thank you."

The music started to play in the other room and it started to get louder and louder.

"Here we go!" shouted Alan to Mum so she could hear him.

He passed Mum her coffee and then they went and stood at the double doors and watched everyone around the room. The lads had decided to get up and dance. All of them had masks on so they weren't so shy to get up and they danced and danced. The youth club by half past seven was full and the boys where all sat around a large round table together laughing and joking around.

"I wonder where the girls are," said Joe, starting to worry.

"They won't be long, you know that they have to be fashionably late," said Damion, looking over towards the main entrance to see if he could see them.

"There they are," said Damion standing up and waved at them to come over.

Kim spotted Damion and the girls made their way over to the table. Joe looked around and could see Beth she was dressed as the superheroine Nessa and she looked amazing. Kate was dressed as Cushdee the superheroine and Kim was dressed as Paradoxical the superheroine and they all looked fantastic. Joe stood up and moved a chair so Beth could sit down.

Damion watched him and then did the same for Kim. Kate went and sat next to Conner who had been talking to Michael and Luke and was too busy laughing on with them.

When Conner turned and looked at Kate he couldn't believe his eyes; he was quite speechless.

"Oh you look lovely, Kate, I can't believe you have come as Cushdee and I am the blue monkey. Did you know what we were all going to be dressed as?" asked Conner.

"No, I didn't," Kate started to laugh and as the girls looked at their partners they all started to laugh at each other's costumes.

"Right, no one is allowed to call each other by their names and must call each other by their characters. Is everyone agreed?" said Michael, looking around at everyone.

Everyone did agree and they started to have fun.

"Cushdee, would you like a drink?"

"Yes, Blue Monkey, that would be lovely, thank you." Both of them started to laugh.

"Right, Nessa, would you like a drink?" Beth looked at Joe and smiled.

"I would love a drink, Wey Eye Man."

Joe and Beth started to laugh.

"Would you like a drink, Paradoxical?" Kim looked at Damion.

"Yes, thank you, Jack Union. I would love a drink from you."

Damion started to laugh at Kim.

"Just call me 'Jack' if you like, my little popsicle."

Kim smiled and started to blush. Thankfully, it was quite dark inside and Damion didn't notice.

Jack Union nodded then stood up with Wey Eye Man and The Blue Monkey, and they all walked over to the kitchens to get their superheroines a drink.

"They look good, don't they?" said Joe, looking at Conner and Damion.

"They look beautiful," said Damion

"I know if I was older I would ask Kate to marry me. She looks fantastic. I love Cushdee, she is one of my crushes," said Connor, beaming from ear to ear as Kate looked amazing.

Mum was at the counter helping Alan serve drinks and food.

"Hello, boys, are you lot enjoying yourselves?"

They all started talking at once over each other but they were all enjoying themselves.

"Mum, can I get two cans of pop please? Any pop will do Mum, thanks."

Mum went to the fridge and pulled out two cans of pop and passed them to Damion.

"Go on, son, I will pay for these, is one of them for Michael?" Damion shook his head to say no.

"No, one is for me and other is for Kim," Mum went back over to the fridge and got another can of pop out.

"Take this one for Michael, will yer?" Damion nodded and waited for Joe and Conner while they got served.

Conner pulled out his money from his socks.

Mum was reluctant to take the money knowing where he had just pulled the money out of, but she did take it and then went to wash her hands straightaway after. She shook her head at Conner and Conner gave her a cheesy smile.

Joe had his money tied in a small pouch tied to his Wey Eye Man Shield. Conner was intrigued.

"Good thinking, Wey Eye Man," Joe looked at Conner and started laughing.

"Well, thank you, Blue Monkey," said Joe.

Joe and Damion burst into tears of laughter and then so did Conner.

They all started walking back over to the table through the crowds of kids dressed up, laughing at everyone else's costumes as there were some really funny characters.

They all handed their girlfriends a drink each and Damion passed Michael his can of pop.

"Cheers, bro," said Michael, smiling then carried on his conversation with Jake and Luke.

Mum was enjoying herself in the kitchen serving everyone and talking to Alan. She didn't realise how fun Alan could be and he was really good with all the kids. The queue for pop, sweets, and burgers had gone down.

"Alan, I just want to say that I am having a really good night, seeing all the kids so happy and enjoying themselves, it is really lovely. I know my boys have been really looking forward to tonight and I just want to say you have really pulled it off," Alan smiled at Mum.

"Yes, with help from you as well, thanks for coming to help me. I couldn't have made the place look this good without your help," Mum smiled.

"Thanks, I am going to go and take some pictures of all the kids to put them online on the website for the youth club, is that okay?"

Alan nodded and Mum went and got her mobile phone out of her bag.

"I won't be too long. If you need me just send one of the kids to look for me," said Mum.

Alan nodded.

"Go on, the kids will love getting their photos taken," said Alan then turned to serve a child that was stood waiting at the counter.

Mum went over to where Michael and Damion where sitting.

"I am going to get some photos of everyone. All huddle together for me, will you, please."

Everyone on the table put their arms around each other and cuddled each other in. Mum started taking photos. She went around everyone's table and took everyone's picture with their friends. Everybody wanted to be on the website for the youth club.

Mum took pictures of the disco and the DJ waving his hands in the air and of everybody on the dance floor. She then went back to the kitchen and took some of Alan serving the children drinks and food. She also took some of the balloons and decorations around the youth club as it did look really good and everybody was having a fantastic night.

"Fancy coming for a drink over mine after this for a bit? It would be nice to have a bit of company and we can put the pictures up on the website? Byron can come and sleep at ours if you like then you don't have to worry about him," said Mum.

Alan looked surprised.

"Yes, I would really like that, thank you."

Alan cuddled Mum and when they turned around Byron, Michael, Jake and Luke were stood watching them, all of them smiling.

"Oh I what's going on here, Mum?" said Michael in a funny voice.

"Nothing and none of your business."

Byron and Michael started to laugh.

Mum shook her head and Alan went a little red.

"Dad, are you okay? Just, you have gone red."

Alan looked at Mum.

"Yes, I am fine, thank you, Byron, right what do you lot want?" Mum gave Michael the look as if to say 'don't you dare embarrass me anymore'.

"Byron, would you like to stay at our house tonight? Just your dad and I are going to have a drink at mine and put the photos that I have got on the internet tonight, so everyone will be able to see them tomorrow."

Everybody looked at Byron.

"Eh, yer, okay then," said Byron, looking at Michael.

Michael smiled and then the kids wondered off back into the disco.

When Michael and Byron went back into the disco, everybody was up dancing on the dance floor. Damion was dancing with Kim and Joe was dancing with Beth. Conner was dancing with Kate. So they all joined in. The dance floor was packed and they danced and danced for quite a few songs. They were all shattered by the end.

"Do you lot fancy going outside for a bit of fresh air?" said Beth.

Everyone agreed and they all walked through the crowds of kids to the entrance of the youth club.

They walked outside and it was quite dark now and cooler than in the club and a little quieter.

"Oh fresh air, it's lovely out here," said Kim.

Jake and Conner lit up a cigarette and went round the corner to smoke it and everyone followed them.

"We have just caught Mum and Alan cuddling each other in the kitchen," said Michael.

Damion looked at Michael.

"Seriously?" Damion was a little taken back.

"Yes, didn't we, Byron?"

Byron nodded.

"Yer, and your mum said that I can stay at yours tonight coz me dad and your mum are having a drink together and are going to put the photos on the website for the youth club," said Byron.

Kim then butted in.

"Well, maybe it's just being friends, they are allowed to be friends, you know."

Damion agreed, but wasn't sure what to think.

"Oh my god, just think if them two got together, that would mean we would be step brothers and we may have to live with each other."

Byron looked shocked and he stood and thought about it.

"Oh my God, me live with you two that means I would have to share a bedroom with one of you." Byron wasn't keen on that idea at all.

“We would have to move to a bigger house like a four or five bedroom that wouldn’t be too bad it’s just putting up with you two all the time.”

Damion and Michael started to laugh.

“And what about us? We would have to put up with you two, you know,” said Michael, putting his hands on his hips and getting a little defensive.

“Anyway, it hasn’t happened yet and we are going to make sure that it doesn’t happen, all agreed?” said Michael, looking at Byron.

Byron nodded.

“I don’t mind them just being friends, but that’s it.”

Michael and Damion looked at each other and agreed with Byron.

“Well, I think you three need to butt out and leave them alone, they are adults and if that’s what they want then that should be up to them. What if someone tried to interfere with our relationship? How would you feel, Damion?” said Kim, looking a little upset.

“It has nothing to do with our relationship but when it comes to our mum then that’s another thing.”

Kim shook her head.

“Right, I don’t want to talk about it anymore as it isn’t going to happen,” said Michael, walking off back into the youth club to see what his mum and Alan were up too.

“Well, I think your mum and Alan would make a nice couple,” said Conner.

Damion looked at Conner and so did Byron.

“No, they won’t, Conner,” said Byron and Damion together.

Conner put his hands up in the air and waved them about.

“Okay, I was just saying.”

The boys shook their heads in disapproval.

“Come on, I want to go back in. I feel a bit cold now,” said Beth, rubbing her arms to try and warm herself up a bit.

They all made their way back into the youth club and back to their table Michael was back sitting in his chair.

“I have just checked on them and they are busy, so we are all right for now,” Kate then pipped up again.

“You can’t watch them all the time. It is probably just innocent and they are just friends,” said Kate.

Michael nodded, but he just needed to make sure as he didn't want anyone living with them at all. He was happy with just him, Damion, Mum and Sean. If Sean wanted to come back home, but that was it.

The girls wanted to get up and dance again and all the lads got up too. Even Michael eventually was persuaded by Beth to come and dance, which helped him to forget about his mum for now.

As what really could happen at a youth club? he thought.

Michael started to enjoy himself again and they were soon all laughing and swinging each other round and trying to outdo each other with their dance moves.

The time flew by and before they knew it, it was eleven o'clock and the last song was on. The boys who had girlfriends went and danced a slow dance while the ones that didn't took a seat and watched the others. Michael and Byron went into the kitchen where Mum and Alan where starting to clear everything away. They decided to help them and eventually the music stopped and it was time for everyone to leave and go home. The DJ started to pack up his CDs and speakers, and Alan and Mum went to say goodbye to everyone who was leaving.

"We have had a great time, Alan. When is there going to be another disco?" said a few of the teenagers as they left.

"Well, I am not too sure yet, but I will let everyone know as soon as I do," said Alan, who got one or two cuddles and so did Mum as they left the building.

Alan, Mum and the boys then helped the DJ to put everything into the back of his van and Alan paid him his money.

"I am sure we will be in touch with you soon for another disco as the kids have really enjoyed this one," said Alan, handing over the money.

"Okay, mate, you have my number, just give me a little notice and it shouldn't be a problem."

Everyone waved at him as he drove off up the driveway and out onto the road then everyone who was left returned inside the club.

"Are we going to get the cleaning done now then? So it is all done and over with?" Mum asked Alan as they looked around the hall.

"Yer…I think that's a good idea."

Mum smiled and headed for the cupboard to get the brush, mop and bucket out.

"Right, you lot, what are you doing? As your mum and I are going to get tidied up before going home."

The boys and girls were now all sat around the table together.

"What do you want us to do? Should we give them a hand?" said Damion to the others.

They all looked at each other.

"Well, I told my mum I was going to be in just after eleven and Kate and Beth are sleeping at mine."

Everyone looked at Kim.

"Well, it's up to you, if you have to go now we will walk you up home and then come back down, to help these out," said Damion.

"Are you sure? You don't mind?"

Damion cuddled Kim.

"Of course I don't mind. Right, Conner, Joe and I are going to walk the girls up to Kim's house then we will come back to help you lot," said Damion, standing up.

Conner, Joe, Kim, Kate and Beth all stood up and started making their way out of the building, which just left Luke, Jake, Byron and Michael.

"Right, Dad, what do you want us to do?" Alan was starting to clear away the stuff from the tables.

"You lot can pop the balloons if you like?"

The lads all jumped up.

"Get in," said Byron.

They started gathering up all the balloons in the centre of the dance floor and then started jumping on them like small children and tried to make as much banging sounds as possible. They dived on them, jumped on them and stamped on them. They even squashed them between their hands until in the end there was a pile of deflated balloons in the centre of the room.

Mum and Alan laughed at the boys having so much fun with just popping balloons. Mum took some photos of them then came over and started to sweep them up into a pile while Alan finished washing the tables. Damion, Conner and Joe were soon back from Kim's and everything was nearly done.

"By, you lot have been busy, it hasn't took you long," said Joe, looking around the room.

"We have had a whale of a time popping the balloons," said Michael.

"Is there anything else to do, Mum?" asked Damion, looking around the room.

"Go and fill the mop bucket with some hot water, son, and we will give this floor a quick mop over before we lock up."

Mum was just picking up the last of the balloons off the floor.

Damion picked up the bucket and was soon back with it full of hot soapy water and the mop.

"You lot can go home now, if you like, there is only this left to do."

The boys agreed they would all walk up together as Mum wasn't going to be long.

"Okay, Mum, see you in a bit."

They all walked up the road together and made their way to their separate homes except for Byron. They all said their goodbyes and went their separate ways.

"Text you tomorrow, Damo!" shouted Conner.

Jake and Joe as they carried on up the road together.

"Okay, see you later."

The boys went in the house and shut the door.

"Right, where is Byron sleeping then?" asked Michael as he walked into the kitchen and put the kettle on.

"He can sleep in my room on the floor with the sleeping bag or on the two-seater sofa, it's up to him," Damion looked at Byron.

"Anywhere. I don't mind where I sleep," said Byron.

"Fancy a game, you two?" Michael picked up his console, took it into the sitting room and switched the television on. Michael set everything up while Damion went upstairs and brought back down two controllers, one for him and one for Byron.

"What do you fancy playing?" asked Damion, handing a controller to Byron.

"Aye, fancy playing COD?" Damion and Michael nodded and Michael went back into the kitchen to get it.

"Do you two want a coffee?" shouted Michael.

"Yer, go on then!" they both shouted back to Michael.

"Give me a hand with the couch and we will pull it up to the telly," said Damion who was already stood next to it waiting for Byron's help.

They pushed it over so they could all sit right in front of the television.

"Give me a hand, bro, will yer please?"

Damion and Byron went to help Michael and brought back their coffees, and Michael placed the game into the gaming console. There were three screens on the telly and the game was about shooting and hiding and they were that into the game that they didn't even hear Mum and Alan come into the sitting room and walk straight past them and into the kitchen.

"Would you like a glass of wine, Alan?" asked Mum, going to the cupboard to get the glasses out.

"Yes, thank you, I would love one, I reckon we deserve it after tonight, as it went really well," said Alan.

Mum smiled, and went and got the bottle of wine out of the fridge. She opened the wine, poured it out into the two glasses and handed a glass to Alan.

"Right, let's get these pictures onto the website for everyone to see," said Mum, walking over to the computer desk.

Alan came over and sat down on the chair next to Mum.

"I can't wait to see these, I bet they are great," she hooked up the USB cable to her mobile phone and started to upload the content on to the computer.

They were soon available to see. Mum put it on full screen and the first picture that came up, Mum and Alan started to laugh. It was a picture of their boys sat around the table. Damion then noticed Mum was back in the house.

"Mum's back, did any of you hear her come in?"

Michael and Byron shook their heads as if to say no, not one of them took their eyes off the game.

"These are fantastic, wait till the boys see them. They are going to think they are so funny."

She had pictures of them dancing, pictures of them eating then dancing with the girls and pictures of all sorts of characters.

They all looked amazing. Mum had even got a picture of the boys at the end of the night popping all the balloons. Mum started to upload them onto the internet.

"This should give the youth club a bit of a boost," said Mum, sitting with her glass in her hand and looking at the computer screen.

"Yes, I think it will. BOYS, COME AND HAVE A LOOK AT THESE PICTURES, THEY ARE GREAT!" shouted Alan from the kitchen.

The boys put the game on pause, went into the kitchen, looked through the photos and they laughed at how funny they all looked.

"I have to put that one on my Facebook profile, the one with us all together posing, it looks fantastic," said Damion.

They all laughed Michael and Byron were going to do the same thing. The boys then went back to their game and Alan and Mum polished off two bottles of wine between them.

It was really late by the time Alan went home and Mum went to bed soon after he had gone. The boys were starting to get tired too. They saved their game and put the couch back, so Mum wouldn't complain in the morning at them. They went upstairs to bed Byron decided to bed down on the floor in the sleeping bag and Damion jumped into bed.

Michael decided to get his sleeping bag too and go into Damion's room with Byron and Damion and sleep on the couch.

"Damo," Byron whispered.

"What?" Damion whispered back.

"Do you think the police have caught the robbers yet?"

"I don't know, maybe. We should watch the news in the morning,"

"I wonder if the robbers will know if any of the money is missing,"

"Probably not," whispered Michael.

"I am knackered now, I am going to sleep," said Byron, snuggling into his pillow.

"Night."

"Night," Michael and Damion said together.

Michael and Damion laid in bed, knowing that the robbers would know about the money being missing by now and didn't say a word. They both found it hard to get to sleep thinking about how the robbers might have reacted to the money not being there.

Byron started to snore and then Michael and Damion started to giggle. They both wanted to talk about the robbers to each other but didn't dare in case Byron overheard their conversation. So instead, they stayed quiet both of them. An hour later, they had both dropped off to sleep. The next morning, Mum was banging about in the kitchen making pancakes for the boys. They all woke up together.

The Swimming Baths

"What are you two doing today?" asked Byron, looking at Michael and then Damion.

The brothers looked at each other.

"Fancy going swimming?" Byron said as he started to sit up and get out of the sleeping bag.

"Yer, it's ages since we have been swimming. I am going to have to have a look for my swimming trunks," said Damion, sitting up on the edge of the bed.

"Me too," said Michael, looking through his Facebook page on his mobile phone.

"BOYS, BREAKFAST IS READY!" shouted Mum from downstairs. All of the boys got up, went downstairs and sat at the kitchen table.

"There you go, Byron, I hope you like pancakes."

Mum then passed Michael the other plate she was carrying.

"There is chocolate syrup and strawberry syrup on the table, just help yourself."

Mum went back, picked up another two plates and put one in front of Damion.

"There you go, son," Mum then sat down on the other chair and squeezed some syrup on her pancakes. It made a funny noise and the boys all started to laugh, even Mum laughed.

"So what are you boys doing today then?" asked Mum.

The boys looked at each other.

"We are thinking about going to the swimming baths, Mum, could you give us a lift in?" asked Damion.

Mum finished her mouthful of pancake first.

"Yes, I don't see why not, will you be going too, Byron?"

Byron nodded.

"Yes, but I am going to ask my dad to take me in then more of us can go," Mum looked at the boys.

"Well, who is going?" Mum looked at Damion.

"We are going to have to text everybody first because we have just thought about it."

Damion then tucked back into his pancakes. Michael started texting everyone to see who was going to go swimming. Soon the texts started coming through, one after another. BLEEP, BLEEP. Michael picked his phone back up off the table and looked through his texts.

"Looks like everyone is coming."

Damion looked up.

"Are the girls coming too?"

Michael shrugged his shoulders.

"All the lads, I meant," said Michael.

Damion got up and went to look for his mobile phone.

He had left it upstairs in the bedroom. He texted Kim to see if the girls wanted to go swimming. Sure enough, the text came back with 'yes, we will all go swimming and what time?' Damion went back down stairs into the kitchen.

"What time are we going? Kim's asking as they are coming too," said Damion, looking at Michael and then Byron.

"About an hour to give us time to get ready," said Michael, starting to text again.

"So how many of you are going?" asked Mum, standing up and collecting in the plates from everyone.

Michael started to count everyone on his fingers.

"Me, Damion, Byron, Conner, Jake, Luke, Joe, Kim, Beth and Kate, so that's ten of us."

Mum had started to wash up.

"Well, I can get another two in my car and your dad could get three in his car so that's eight of you." Mum continued the washing up. *BLEEP, BLEEP.*

Damion's phone went off. He picked it up and it was Kim again on the text, saying:

"My mum is going to take me, Kate and Beth up."

Damion read the text out.

"Oh well, that's good that means everybody has a lift then," said Mum, starting to dry the dishes and putting them away.

"Are we going to hurry up and get sorted then?" asked Michael, getting up from the kitchen table.

"Yer."

The boys followed him upstairs. Mum finished clearing away while the boys got ready. Byron put on his Big Ben costume in the bathroom and went back into Damion's bedroom and put the pyjamas he had borrowed off Damion in Damion's washing basket.

"Damo, I am going, we will take Luke and Jake if you take Joe and Conner with you."

Damion was trying to get his top on and he popped his head through his t-shirt.

"Okay, mate, see you in a bit. Just wait for us near the entrance and then we can all go in together."

"Okay, mate, see you in a bit."

Byron went downstairs, put his shoes on and ran down home, hoping no one would see him in his Big Ben costume.

Damion texted Kim again. 'Wait at the entrance and we will meet you there.'

Kim soon texted back 'Okay, babe', which put a big smile on Damion's face.

He looked through his top draw and soon found his swimming shorts and swimming goggles.

"Yes," said Damion to himself then went to the cupboard on the landing to get a large towel.

"Are you ready, Michael?" asked Damion, knocking on Michael's bedroom door.

"Aye, won't be long," Michael took twenty pounds from his stash of money he had hid in a tin in the back of his wardrobe.

He put it back, hid the tin back under some clothing and shut the door. He then looked for his swimming shorts and they were in the top of his draws with his goggles. He opened the cupboard door, went and got a large towel out and shut the cupboard door again. He followed Damion downstairs into the kitchen.

"Do you two want to go now?" asked Mum, picking up her car keys.

"Yes, Mum."

Mum picked up her purse and they left the house. Mum drove to Conner's house and honked the car horn. Conner came running out and jumped into the car. They then went to Joe's house and Mum honked the horn and Joe came running out of his house. It didn't take long and they were at the swimming baths and they were the first ones there. Mum got her purse out of the glove compartment. She gave Damion and Michael ten pounds each and as she pulled out the money a lottery ticket dropped onto her lap.

"Right, have a good time, do you want me to come and pick you back up?"

"No, Mum, we will just walk home, it's more fun. The weather is okay so it should be fine. Thanks, Mum," said Damion.

Everyone started getting out of the car. Mum soon drove away down the street and the boys stood and waved at her. She didn't notice the ticket on her lap.

"We will just wait here for the others. They shouldn't be long," Damion looked up the street, seeing if he could see any of their cars but he couldn't.

"I need a drink, are you lot coming in or what?" asked Michael, looking through the window of the reception area.

"You go and get a drink and we will stay here," said Damion. Looking up the street again, he spotted Byron's dad's car.

"I am sure they have a drink machine in there. I know they did the last time we came," said Michael, going through the doors.

"There is Byron's dad's car coming."

Everybody started to wave at them and they started to wave back then the car pulled up. Byron, Luke and Jake jumped out.

"Yer, see you later, Dad," said Byron as he shut the car door.

They walked towards the others.

"Where's Michael at?"

Damion pointed to the doors.

"He's gone to the machine for a drink."

"Oh right, I guess the girls are not here yet then?" said Jake, looking back up the street.

"They shouldn't be long," said Joe, quite excited as he was looking forward to see Beth.

"Here they are, I am sure that's Kim's Mum's car," said Joe and it was.

The girls jumped out and they all went into the reception area. Michael was at the desk complaining as his drink was stuck in the machine.

The guy who was on the reception came around with his keys and unlocked the machine and passed a bottle of pop over to Michael.

"Thanks, mate," said Michael, taking the bottle off him.

The man then locked the machine back up and came back to the reception. Everyone got their tickets and went into their changing rooms to get changed.

There were girls and boys changing rooms and they all arranged to meet up to get their armbands together so they went in together and came out together. Conner was the first ready. He found some lockers so all the lads' lockers were together.

"Over here, Michael, Luke, over here," Conner opened the lockers up.

"Cheers, mate," said Luke.

Damion was the next to come out of his cubical and spotted where they were. He put his belongings into a locker and locked the door.

"Where are Joe and Jake?" said Damion, looking back at the cubicles.

Jake and Joe then came out.

"Come on, you two, hurry up."

They were all ready and they went to the waiting area to get their armbands the girls where already there waiting for them.

They all got their bands then went into the baths together. They all walked slowly into the water as it felt quit cold there wasn't many people in at all. One or two others dotting about but that was it. It felt like the two hours were going to be just for them.

"They still do the waves here, don't they?" asked Conner.

"I hope so, are we going to go on the slide in a bit?" asked Jake.

"Yes, I just want to get wet first," said Luke, looking up at the slide that twisted and turned and looked really fun.

It was yellow in colour and had go faster stripes on the side of it. They were all in the water and it wasn't long before they were all splashing each other and chasing each other around the pool. Jake was the first out to go on the slide which led straight into the middle of the pool, when you came out. It wasn't long after that everyone followed him. They all climbed the stairs and stood in line at the top waiting for the pool attendant to let them go down the slide.

"Right, son, you can go," said the pool attendant and Jake was first in line.

"JERONIMO!" he shouted as he sat and pushed himself off down the shoot.

He lay back and he was going really fast, swaying from side to side and around the loop then SPLASH straight into the pool below.

"YAHOO!" Jake shouted as he emerged from the water and took a deep breath.

They all followed in line and then back up the stairs for another go. They were all having a brilliant time. The sirens started to go off and the slide was then closed for a short time as the waves were starting.

They all splashed each other in the water and then the waves got stronger as if they were out at sea. The waves pushed them here and there.

"Fancy a race from one side to the other, you lot?" shouted Conner over the noise of the wave machine.

"YES!" they all shouted back at Conner.

Everybody swam to the side of the pool and held the side.

"Who is going to call it!" shouted Conner.

"I will!" shouted Beth, ready to set off.

"Right, are you ready? Steady, GO!" shouted Beth.

Everyone set off as fast as they could they were all laughing as they swam. The waves were strong and it took some time to get to the other end. Michael was the first to get to the other side followed by Conner then Luke, Damion, Joe, Beth, Kim and last but not least Kate. They all laughed and their laugher echoed around the pool area.

"Right, who wants to go again? Beth, are you going to call it, babe?" said Joe.

Beth nodded, trying to catch her breath.

"Ready, steady GO!"

Everyone swam as fast as they could again to the other side. Joe was the first back this time.

"YES, I'M THE WINNER!"

He shouted at the top of his lungs, which sounded even louder because of the echo. Again, everyone started to laugh as they reached the other side. It was Kim that came in last this time.

"Never mind, princess!" shouted Damion a few mates up.

She did feel a little embarrassed but it soon passed, as she knew that her mates were real mates and wouldn't take the mick out of her. The waves were starting to stop again and the slide was now open, they walked as fast as they could towards the slide trying not to slip over on the way. They all had another few goes. The time went really quickly and before they knew it their colour was flashing up on the board.

"Oh I don't WANT to go," said Beth, walking out of the pool.

They all left and went into the showers in their changing rooms and then got ready. The girls had brought bobbles to tie up their hair after drying it off under the dryers provided in the changing rooms. The lads were out first.

"The girls must still be in the changing rooms, come on we will wait on these tables for them," said Damion.

The tables where in the reception area and they all started to plan what they were going to do next. It was either go back home or have a look round the town window shopping and then maybe go to Starlight café for a hot chocolate, which was Luke's idea.

The Lottery Ticket

"Or we could go to the cafe which is over the river. We can sit outside on the balcony and watch the boats and stuff?" said Michael.

All the boys were in agreement.

"There you are, we have been waiting for ages," said Conner to Kate.

"Right, girls, fancy a look into town and have a look around the shops and then maybe go to the cafe that has the balcony over the river, what do you think?" asked Damion.

"Yer, why not," said Kim, linking her arm through Damion's arm.

He bent over and kissed her on the forehead. Then they all set off.

****

Back at home, Mum had gone into the house and done some housework. She didn't notice the lottery ticket on her knee when she got out of the car and it slipped down onto the mat below the steering wheel. She decided that she needed to go to the shop for milk and was going to pop over to see Naomi for a cup of coffee.

When she got back into the car, she noticed the lottery ticket on the floor of the car and picked it up. Normally, she threw them away if she had checked them. She looked at the date and it was for a few months ago. She put the lottery ticket in the glove compartment, drove to the shop and decided to check it just in case she had forgotten to do so.

"Hello, how are you? By, your lads are getting so big now, aren't they?" said the shopkeeper as Mum was picking up a basket from just beside the doorway.

Mum turned around.

"Eh, I didn't see you there, I am in a world of my own. Yes, the boys are getting big, aren't they?" said Mum.

"I know, and they are all good looking lads," said the shopkeeper.

Mum smiled.

"You couldn't check this for me, could you? Just while I go around the shop," asked Mum.

"Yes, of course," Mum handed the shopkeeper her lottery ticket then wandered off to the fridges at the back of the shop for milk. TING, TING, TING, TING.

"OH MY GOODNESS!" shouted the shopkeeper as she looked at the screen in front of her.

She rushed out from behind the counter and up the isle towards Mum. Mum was bend over picking up some bread buns from a lower shelf.

"You are not going to believe this," said the shopkeeper all in a fluster.

Mum stood up and turned around and looked at her.

"What's wrong? And what was that tinging noise?" The shopkeeper started to jump up and down on the spot.

"Are you all right?" Mum opened her eyes wide and looked at her as if the shopkeeper was a mad woman.

"YOU HAVE WON!"

Mum smiled at her.

"Oh right that's good, how much?" said Mum.

“Eight MILLION POUNDS,” Mum was shocked and just stood there looking at the woman.

“I can’t believe it,” the shopkeeper cuddled Mum and Mum was still in shock.

The shopkeeper guided Mum over to behind the counter and sat her down on the stool.

“I am just going to lock the doors, I won’t be a minute,” said the shopkeeper.

Mum just sat there on the stool, with a blank expression on her face. The shopkeeper came back and all of a sudden, Mum jumped up.

“Oh my god, I can’t believe it, are you sure?” said Mum.

“I am sure, mind, because it also made that noise on the computer, you will have to go to the lottery place to get the money. Obviously, I don’t have that kind of money in my little till.”

Mum started to smile but her heart was beating really fast.

“I don’t want anyone to know mind about it, you won’t tell anyone, will you?” said Mum.

“No, I wouldn’t do that, no way,” said the shopkeeper, smiling like a Cheshire Cat and all excited.

“Thanks,” said Mum, then cuddled the shopkeeper.

“Would you like a coffee before you go home?”

Mum then remembered Naomi.

“Oh. Err, no thanks. I am going to our Sean’s to see Naomi. I will get one there if you don’t mind,” said Mum.

“Are you going to be okay to drive? Just it’s a bit of a shock.”

Mum nodded and was trying to get her head round what had just happened.

“Right, I need to go, I will still take the milk and bread buns thanks,” said Mum, making her way back around the other side of the counter.

“Yes, of course, they are on the house. CONGRATULATIONS!” The shopkeeper put the items in a bag for Mum.

“Don’t worry, I won’t say anything, I promise you that.”

“Thanks, I just can’t believe it.” Tears started to come to Mum’s eye’s.

“Are you sure you are okay?” asked the shopkeeper again.

Mum nodded and the shopkeeper handed Mum the bag and unlocked the shop door.

"Put this in your purse and as soon as you get home ring the number on the back and they will tell you what to do okay?"

"Thanks, I will," said Mum, placing the ticket back into her purse, she walked to the car, opened the door, sat in the driver's side seat and shut the door.

Mum looked back at the woman waving at her then started the car up and slowly drove away heading towards Naomi and Sean's house. Mum was soon there and she jumped out of the car and ran up the path and stood and composed herself at the door then walked in. Naomi was in the kitchen sitting on the bench as she normally did on her mobile phone.

"Hello, is Sean home?" asked Mum.

"He shouldn't be too long. Actually, he has just texted saying he has finished the job and he is on his way home now. Would you like a cup of coffee?" asked Naomi.

"Yes that would be nice thanks pet," said Mum, sitting at the kitchen table.

Naomi jumped down, put the kettle on and made them both a coffee.

"Are you all right, Mum? Just you seem a bit quiet has something happened?" asked Naomi.

"Yes," said Mum, looking like she was in some sort of trance.

"I knew there was something. Are you all right?" said Naomi.

"Yes, yes, I am fine," said Mum.

"What is it?" Naomi came and sat at the table.

"I have won the lottery," said Mum.

"WHAT, OH MY GOD!" Naomi started to smile and she jumped up and cuddled Mum.

"That's GREAT NEWS! So how much have you won? If you don't mind me asking, that is?" Naomi was happy for Mum thinking it was about fifty pounds or something like that amount.

"Eight million pounds," said Mum.

"EIGHT MILLION, ARE YOU SURE?" shouted Naomi.

Mum nodded. Then Mum smiled a big smile, jumped up from the table, grabbed Naomi and started jumping around the kitchen.

"YES, WE'VE WON. WE'VE WON!" Naomi and Mum cuddled and danced again.

They didn't hear Sean coming in.

"What are you two doing?" said Sean, starting to laugh at his mum and Naomi dancing around the kitchen.

Mum smiled a big smile at Sean.

"WE WON, SON, WE WON," shouted Mum.

"Right what have you won?" said Sean.

"THE LOTTERY, I WON THE LOTTERY, SON!"

Sean's face dropped.

"How much have you won, Mum?" asked Sean, quite shocked.

"EIGHT MILLION!"

Sean stood and just looked at his mum and then Naomi.

"Are you sure?" said Sean.

"Yes, son, I am sure."

Mum grabbed Sean's cheeks then they all started dancing around the kitchen, holding each other's arms and going round in circles.

****

Back in the city, Damion, Michael and their friends were looking through the shop windows on their way down towards the cafe. Everybody decided that when they got there they all wanted a hot chocolate and a sandwich each. They took their trays through and onto the veranda outside. There were three small tables with twelve chairs so they could all sit out there quite comfortably.

"This is the life, we could be in France sitting here, it is so lovely," said Kim.

"I have never been abroad before, I hope to go one day," said Damion, trying to imagine what it would be like in France.

Kim smiled then took a drink of her hot chocolate.

"Can we smoke out here?" Conner asked Jake.

Jake shrugged his shoulders.

"I don't know," said Joe.

"Don't spoil it, you two, no one is allowed to smoke out here, there is a sign up there, look," said Beth, pointing to a sign above the door.

Conner sighed.

“You two need to pack in smoking, it’s not good for you, you know this,” said Damion, shaking his head at the pair of them.

“Well, you can get Sean to get me some patches from the chemist or something,” said Conner, putting his cigarettes back in his bag.

“Let’s just enjoy the views and finish our sandwiches and hot chocolate then you two can have your cigarettes.”

Damion pulled out his mobile phone and texted Sean.

‘Sean, could you do me a favour and buy some Nicorette patches for Conner and Jake. They want to pack in smoking, thanks, bro. Will pick them up tonight when we come over yours,’ Damion pressed send on the message.

“There, I have sent a message to Sean to pick you two up some patches from the chemist so you can pack in smoking.”

Conner and Jake where shocked at Damion and didn’t think he would have done it yet.

“You two will have to pack in now because Sean is getting your patches and he will be pretty upset if you don’t so you better get your heads round it now. I will get the patches off Sean tonight then pack in on Monday.”

Conner and Jake looked at each other and everyone started to laugh.

“Okay, mate, I will pack in,” said Conner.

“Me too, to be honest I hate smoking, it was other kids egging me on to start in the first place and sometimes I get a bad chest,” said Jake, looking at Damion.

“Well, this is your chance to get rid of it for good, I know our Sean smokes but I know he sometimes hates himself for ever starting and wishes he had listened to Mum. Funny that Mum is always right in the end.”

Michael started to laugh as he knew Damion was right. Everyone then sat for a while and reflected, while watching the people walking passed over the cobble stone bridge.

They just sat and watched the river and the birds. The sun was out and felt warm, the hot chocolate was sweet and comforting as they sat and watched the world go by.

****

Back at Sean's home, Naomi had made a fresh cup of coffee and they were sitting in the sitting room discussing what Mum was going to have to do next. Mum had a hold of the lottery ticket and was reading the back of it to find out what she had to do.

"It says here: *Guidance on how to claim a prize. If you believe you have won over £50.000 telephone the (Lottery Line.) For all claims over £500 and up to £50,000, please claim your prize at the lottery post office, take a photo ID and proof of address. The post office can pay up to £500 cash, above this amount the remainder in a cheque or the whole amount by cheque if you prefer. Telephone the Lottery Line on this number. Claims over £50,000 must be made in person. Telephone the help line*. It looks like we are going to have to phone them, son," said Mum, looking up at Sean.

Sean jumped up out of his chair.

"There is the phone, Mum, ring them now."

Mum took the phone and dialled the number on the back of the ticket and it started to ring.

"Hello, you're through to the National Lottery to get you to the right place listen to all your options:

Dial 1 if you have won £500 pounds and under.

Dial 2 if you have won £500 and over.

Dial 3 if you have won £50,000 and over.

To hear this option again press star."

Mum pressed three on the phone and it started to ring. It didn't take long and there was a voice of a woman at the other end of the line.

"Good afternoon, you're though to the lottery help line and can I firstly say congratulations on you win."

"Oh eh, thank you, I was just phoning as I have won over £50,000 pounds and I don't know what to do next,"

"Oh that's great, right, do you have any transport?"

"Yes, I have a car."

"That's fantastic. What you need to do now is keep your ticket in a safe place and come to Watford. I will give you the post code WD18 9TT."

"Sorry, I will just get a pen and write this down," said Mum.

"It is okay the post code is on the back of your lottery ticket."
Mum took a look.

"Oh yes, I see it."

"Right you need to bring your driving licence and proof of address and bank details with you so the money can be transferred into your account as quickly as possible."

Mum started to write everything down on a scrap piece of paper Naomi had handed her.

"Could I now take your name and address for our records, thank you?"

Mum gave the lady her name and address.

"That's great, now can I take the numbers on your winning ticket and the date of purchase please?" Mum gave the lady the details.

"That's fantastic, right the last part now, we need to arrange a date for you to come to the offices, as soon as you possibly can."

Mum tried to think. It was Saturday now.

"I think the best time will be Monday, if that's okay with you?"

"That's fine and what time would you like?"

"Oh it will have to be on the late afternoon, as I live in the north east of England,"

"Well, our opening hours are from nine am to five pm Monday to Friday,"

"Okay and what is your latest appointment?"

"That will be four thirty on Monday."

"Oh, yes that should be fine, thank you," said Mum.

"You are very welcome and can I just congratulate you again on your win? We will see you on Monday at four thirty, Mrs Howard."

"Thanks, that's great, see you then," Mum put the phone down and looked at Sean and Naomi who were sitting quietly listening to the conversation.

"Well, we have to be there for four thirty on Monday with ID and the ticket,"

"Well, I will come with you Mum and Naomi will watch the boys. I wouldn't tell them just yet, Mum, wait until after Monday."

Mum nodded.

"Well, I could do with another coffee how about you two?"

Naomi got up and followed Mum into the kitchen. Sean sat for a little while trying to take it all in with a very large smile on his face. He wanted to tell Mum there and then about the money in the wall, but didn't know how to. He though the best time to tell her would be on the way back from the trip to Watford on Monday.

Back in the city, everyone was walking over the bridge.

"Come on, you lot, fancy a look in the game shop?"

Everyone piled in to the shop. Michael and Luke headed towards the new games for their consoles and picked them up off the shelf to have a look.

"I fancy this game, do you, Luke? It looks really good," said Michael.

"Yes, I have seen it advertised on the telly a few times. The UK Protectors, it looks fantastic," said Luke.

"Should I get it and we can have a game later. If Mum asks I can just say it's your game and vice versa," said Michael.

"Yer, okay then," Michael took the game to the counter and gave it to the man. Damion and the others looked around the shop at the other games.

Damion picked up Far 4, Joe and Conner picked up the same game to have a look.

"That's not bad, thirty nine ninety nine, I am sure it was forty five when I last went shopping with Mum the other day at the supermarket," said Joe, examining the box thoroughly.

"Joe, shh, do you think I could pass as sixteen?" Joe looked at Damion, examined his face and nodded.

"Yes, I don't see why not."

Damion took the game over and placed it on the counter. The man picked it up and looked at Damion.

"How old are you son?"

"Sixteen."

"When is your birthday?" Damion had to think quickly.

"Eleventh of December two thousand."

The man looked at Damion and you could see him trying to work it out.

"Okay, son," he picked up the box and put it through the scanner at the till.

"That will be thirty-nine ninety-nine please," Damion pulled out the money from his tracksuit pocket and handed it over. The man then placed the game and receipt in a bag for Damion and handed him the bag with a penny change. Damion spotted a Pudsey Bear canister on the counter and placed a penny in it.

"Thank you," said the man.

Damion nodded and everyone left the shop.

"What have you bought?" said Michael, trying to see through the plastic bag Damion was carrying.

"Far 4," Damion started to laugh.

"How have you got that? You're not old enough," Michael wasn't happy at all.

"He asked me how old I was and when my birthday was," Damion showed Michael inside his carrier bag.

"You jammy sod, if I knew that, I would have got you to get me an older game, something like Warfare 2050 the next gen, I am fed up now," Michael started to sulk.

"Well, get it next time we come into town," said Luke, patting Michael on the shoulder.

Michael nodded and placed his new game into his backpack and flung it back over his shoulder. They walked up the steep bank and down the other side and along the road towards the milk market as they walked passed Conner noticed a water hosepipe dripping all over the road and ran towards it.

"Conner, what are you doing?" Conner turned around, squirted water all over Kate and then pointed it at the others.

"I AM GOING TO GET YOU FOR THAT, CONNER!"

Everyone started laughing they all put their bags over the other side of the road and then ran towards Conner.

"AHHHHH!" shouted Conner, as the cold water hit his face.

They all scrambled to get the hosepipe off him and Jake managed to get it first and soaked Conner till he was dripping wet. Everyone laughed at Conner as he stood there his jumper hung on him and his sleeves covered his hands and he flapped them around at everyone as if he was a seal. Jake decided to then turn his attention onto Michael, Michael jumped back then ran at Jake.

"CHARGE!" shouted Michael and everyone charged at Jake, including Conner.

By the time they were all finished, they were soaked to the bone with their hair stuck to their heads and freezing cold but they laughed and laughed at each other.

Eventually, it was time to set back off on their travels again. The girls dragged their towels from their back backs to dry their hair.

"Well, I should have just kept my bathing costume on," said Kim, rubbing her hair with her towel.

"If I knew we were coming here, I would have," said Beth, trying to tie up her long dark hair into a bobble to get it out of the way of her face.

"I'm freezing, come on, I need to get back home to get dry," said Kate, rubbing her arms.

Conner placed his arm around her and she started screaming.

"Get off me, you are wetter than I am!" shouted Kate.

"Oh don't be like that," said Conner, trying to put his arm around her shoulder again and flapped his wet jumper onto her chest.

"Conner get off me NOW, you are making me COLDER."

Conner looked a little sad.

"Sorry, babe, you know I love you," said Conner.

"Conner, you suck up," said Michael, jumping on his back.

"Ahhh, man," Michael started to mess Conner's hair up.

"Behave," Conner grabbed Michael's legs and ran off down the street with Michael on his back.

"Giddy up, Conner," Conner started to laugh and had to stop to catch his breath.

"Get off me, you're heavy, yer know," said Conner.

"Cheeky," said Michael, jumping down off Conner laughing.

They all walked along the winding road towards the village. The teenagers decided to take another way home through the lines which are public walkways which go through the woods.

The girls cuddled each other and linked their arms. Everyone was soon at the small bridge. They all stood in a row on the bridge and watched the stream going under them.

"We should come and camp down here one night. What do you think?" said Conner, looking at his mates.

"Conner, it's a little far away from home don't you think? What if something happens? It would take ages to walk in the dark back home and you don't like the dark, do you, Conner?" said Luke, smiling.

"Yes, I do!" Conner gave Luke a look, as if to say 'you're embarrassing me now in front of Kate, man'.

"Oh right, Conner," Luke rolled his eyes at him and Conner stuck his fingers up as he felt a little silly about being afraid of the dark.

They decided to get off home again and soon said their goodbyes till later. Michael and Damion got in, shut the door and put the heating straight on.

"I am freezing," said Michael.

"Me too," said Damion

"MUM, MUM!" shouted Damion through the house.

"Mum, isn't in yet, fancy a game on Far 4?"

Michael couldn't refuse that.

"Do I, let's get out of these clothes and then I will whoop your arse on it."

Damion started laughing at him.

"Yer right," Michael ran up the stairs to get in the shower first.

"Oh this is lovely and warm in here!" shouted Michael through the door.

"Leave the shower on for me, will yer?" said Damion

"Aye!" shouted Michael back through the door.

Damion stripped off his wet clothing, piled them up in the middle of his bedroom floor and wrapped himself up in his fluffy dressing gown Mum had bought him last Christmas. Damion soon started to warm up. He picked up his haversack and dragged out his wet towel and shorts and plonked them on the pile then carried them downstairs.

"I'm out!" Michael shouted down the stairs at him.

"Okay," Michael ran into Mum's bedroom to grab the hairdryer from her dressing table and then ran into his room with it and shut the door.

Damion could hear the dryer as he came back upstairs and went into the shower. Michael was soon ready. He went downstairs and set up the game in the sitting room as they always did when Mum was out. Damion was soon ready and they settled down to play the game.

It wasn't long and everyone was online and the messages started to come through on the console for Michael and Damion to play ATA. They sent a message back to their friends saying in an hour as they were playing their new game first.

The new game was good but they both decided to play with their friends and put on their headsets. Everyone was online, even the girls. Everyone played for hours, laughing and calling each other names but in a joking friendly way as they always did. Mum came back eventually and brought in pizza for everyone.

"Where have you been, Mum?" said Damion, not taking his eye off the game.

"Oh just over Sean's, son, talking. I lost track of time a bit, so I thought I would get us all pizza."

Damion told his friends they were going offline to get something to eat.

"Are you two coming back on after?" said Jake and Joe.

"Well, aye man, of course, see you in a bit," said Damion and Michael together then they started laughing at each other.

"Jinx, you're not allowed to talk now. The first one that does has to give the other one ten pounds," said Michael.

"Yes, well, you two can play for another hour then I want the telly, as there is a good film coming on that I want to see," said Mum as she plated up the pizza, chips and garlic bread.

The boys tucked into their pizzas and were soon back online playing with their friends.

Their game time was soon at an end. Mum put her film on and they all sat and watched it together. After the film, Mum explained that she was going away on Monday with work and Naomi would be watching the boys while she was away.

They all retired for bed, after chatting with their mum about their day and what fun they had while at the baths with their mates.

Sunday soon came and the boys enjoyed their dinner over Sean's that Naomi had made for everyone. Mum helped with the dishes and the boys played on the game with Sean the day seemed to fly over and it was time to go back home.

Monday soon came and Sean picked Mum up for their journey down south and to collect her winnings from the lottery.

Sean followed his satnav all the way to Watford. There was a massive car park, thankfully, when they got to Watford. Sean parked the car and they both got out and looked up at the building.

"Are you okay, Mum?" asked Sean as Mum looked terrified.

The Robbers Back Again

"Yes, I think my nerves are just getting the better of me, Sean, that's all. I still can't believe I have won some money."

Sean smiled and they walked into the reception area together.

"Good afternoon, can I help you?" said the lady at the reception desk.

"Yes, thank you, we have an appointment," said Mum, looking quite worried.

"Is your name Mrs Howard?" asked the receptionist, looking back at Mum and Sean.

"Yes, that's right, Mrs Howard," said Mum.

"That's great, Mr Smith won't be long, just take a seat, thank you."

Mum nodded.

"Thank you," said Mum, then walked over to the seating area to sit down and Sean followed her.

They both sat and waited patiently for Mr Smith to come and get them.

The receptionist decided to put the telly on for them while they waited. "This is the afternoon's news at four thirty. Last night, there was another robbery in London's Mint. The same robbers are believed to be involved, as in the last robbery a few weeks ago. Scotland Yard are leading the investigation into the robbery with the help of MI5 and MI6 intelligent agencies. There is going to be a reconstruction of the events in a couple of days on crime stoppers to try and jog the public's memories of anything suspicious that could help to find the perpetrators of these events. The number for crime stoppers will appear on your screens and police are urging anyone with any information to come forward. The mint has decided to give a CASH REWARD of anything leading to the persons involved in the robbery of quite a considerable sum of money!"

Sean and Mum listened carefully to what was being said.

They both said nothing about the news but both looked at each other each in deep thought about what was going to happen next.

****

Back at the village, Gaz had now driven up from London and decided to check the crime scene again, making sure there was no police or anyone else knocking around before he got out of his car.

He eventually left his car and went into the woods to check the place again for anything that may lead him to who may have the money off the first robbery he had done.

Gaz's friends were back celebrating at the hideout as this time, they had managed to get away with the money and they had it all.

They decided to keep the money in the flat and divide it equally as soon as Gaz got back, hopefully with the rest of the money.

They all went home to their families and friends and kept their secret to themselves.

Gaz couldn't let the other money go. He knew someone had it who was local. It was just trying to find out who. They must have left a clue and if he couldn't find anything then he would go and visit his sister to see if she knew of anything as it was a small village. He knew that it wouldn't be long before the whispers started and someone would open their mouths about finding some money.

Maria, his sister, was his one and only chance of finding the money again.

Gaz had drove to the woods to check around to see if there was any clues to where the money might be.

Someone must know something about it, he thought.

He looked around in the woods and went back to where the money had been stashed but he couldn't find anything at all.

Gaz grew up in the village where they had stashed the money. His mother and father were Italian and had gone back to Italy after he went to prison the first time and took his five brothers with them. His sister, however, decided to stay in England in Durham City as she had fell pregnant and wanted to make a go at it with her boyfriend, whom she later married and had another two children.

Gaz didn't know his sister had been divorced as he never stayed in touch with her. He didn't know she was left alone with the three boys to bring up on her own.

He hadn't kept in touch with her as he was moved from prison to prison and he knew how upset she was with him.

Gaz hoped that maybe his sister would forgive his past and what he needed from her now was only going to upset her even more but he had to try. He needed to get the money back not just for him but for his friends.

Gaz searched and searched in the woods, hoping he could find anything to help him but there was nothing. He had searched for hours. He eventually gave up and made his way back through the woods and towards the car. Then all of a sudden, he saw a card on the floor. He picked it up and saw that it was a business card. It had a mobile number on it. (Plasterer, no job too big or small, phone Sean on 07752398109).

Gaz smiled to himself and looked around. There was no one there. He quickly jumped back into his car and rang the number.

"Hello, I can't answer the phone right now but if you can leave a message I will get back to you as soon as possible. Please leave your number after the beep."

Gaz put the phone down and put the card in his glove compartment. He had a hunch that Sean the plasterer might know something about where his money just might be.

****

Sean's phone had just rang, but he didn't want to answer it as he knew it wouldn't be long before they had to see Mr Smith in his office.

"You should have answered your phone, son, it might have been Naomi," said Mum.

"No, Mum, it won't have been. She knows I can't do anything until I get back home anyway. I will check my messages when we get out of here."

"Hello, there," said a gentleman. "I am Mr Smith."

Mum and Sean stood up and shook Mr Smith's hand.

"Hello, pleased to meet you," said Mum, shaking his hand.

"Hello, Mr Smith," said Sean.

"Could you follow me into my office, please, it is this way?"

Mum and Sean followed him into the office and he shut the door.

****

Back at home, there was a knock at the door.

"Oh who's that knocking at the door?" shouted Michael but he got no answer as Damion had fell back asleep on his bed watching Netflix.

Naomi had decided to go to the shop for more cigarettes, as she had ran out.

Knock, Knock, Knock.

"Oh, I better answer it then," said Michael to himself.

Michael paused his game, got up and answered the door. When Michael opened the door, there was a man stood looking at him.

"Hello, son, is your mum there?" said the man.

"No, she not here at the moment. Can I help you?" said Michael.

"Is your mum's last name Cooper?" Michael had to think.

"Yes, that's her maiden name. Why, who are you?" said Michael, wondering how this man knew his mother.

"I am her brother, Gaz," said Gaz with a big smile on his face.

"Okay, well, she has never mentioned you before," said Michael, looking at him strangely.

"Oh I wonder why?" said Gaz.

"I don't know WHY, she hasn't mentioned you before," said Michael.

"Look…why don't you come back tomorrow in the morning. She is on holiday from work at the moment and she should be back by then," said Michael.

"Oh okay, kid, I will come back to see her tomorrow then."

Michael nodded and gave Gaz a smile then Gaz walked away up the street. Michael shut the door and went back to play on his game.

The Burglar

Damion had started to wake up as he had overheard voices at the front door. He heard Michael shut the door and wondered who it was so he got off his bed, went downstairs and went into the kitchen.

"Who was that at the door? Also where is Naomi?" said Damion.

"Naomi has nipped out to the shops."

Damion went and put the kettle on.

"So who was at the door?" said Damion again and looked at Michael.

Michael swung around in his chair.

"Oh yer that was strange."

Damion turned to look at Michael.

"What do you mean it was strange?" said Damion.

"Well, this man was at the door and he said that he was Mum's brother. I didn't know Mum had a brother, did you?"

Damion thought it was weird.

"No, I didn't know Mum had a brother. That's fucking weird. Where has Naomi gone?" said Damion, starting to get a bit freaked out about it.

"I told you, she has gone round the shop," said Michael.

"Why would Mum never mention her family?" Michael shrugged his shoulders.

"I don't know why. It is weird. Should we ring Mum and find out?"

Damion stirred the coffee and sighed.

"No, we can ask her when she gets back from wherever she is," said Damion, puzzled to what was actually going on.

"Okay, maybe it's for the best. I wonder where Mum and Sean have gone. Did you ask Naomi?"

Damion looked at Michael who was now blowing up something on his screen.

"Boom, you fucker, no I didn't ask her anything. To be honest how interesting can it be? It's Mum remember?" Michael took a quick glance at Damion.

Damion looked in deep thought.

"Yer, your right, it's Mum, it can't be that interesting. It's probably something to do with her job, as per usual," said Damion, walking past Michael and sitting down in the sitting room.

Naomi came back in and Damion switched the telly on and put it on the cartoons.

"Oh you're awake now," said Naomi.

"Hey, Naomi, does my mum have a brother?"

Naomi went into the kitchen and took the wrapping off her cigarettes.

"No, not that I know of. She has never said to me about any family before and I never thought to ask her, to be honest," said Naomi.

Naomi took out a cigarette from the box and lit it up then went into the back garden.

"See, it is weird," said Michael.

Naomi popped her head back inside the back door and blew the smoke out into the garden.

"Why, what's weird?" said Naomi.

"There has been a man at the door saying he is my mum's brother," said Michael, still playing his game and not taking his eyes off the screen.

"What, while I have been at the shop?"

Naomi was freaked out a bit.

"Yes, while you were at the shop," said Michael.

"That's weird, I have never heard your mum mention a brother or any other family at all. I think we should keep the doors locked."

Naomi stumped her cigarette out, went and locked the front door and walked back through into the sitting room.

"No friends in today, mind, as I think this is a bit strange to say the least. Thankfully, your mum will be back later and we can ask her then," said Naomi.

Naomi didn't like the sound of him and was a little worried. She knew that Sean and Mum wouldn't be back until late that night and she wasn't taking any chances in case this man came back while they were still away.

****

Back in Watford, Sean and Mum were just signing some documentation and Mum had all her identification on the table. Mr Smith photocopied all Mum identification and said that the money would be in her account within seven working days and, if there were any problems, to contact him straight away.

"Wow, I can't believe it was that simple," said Mum.

“Yes, we like to keep it all very simple. We will have a financial adviser be in touch with you soon to help you invest your money wisely and can I congratulate you on your win,” said Mr Smith, giving Mum a large box of chocolates and some flowers.

A photographer came into the room and took a photo of Mum, Mr Smith and Sean.

Mum didn’t want people to know about her win and she wanted it kept out of the papers. Mr Smith said that he would do his very best for the papers not to find out about it. Mum shook Mr Smith’s hand again before leaving the premises and so did Sean.

Mum and Sean went outside and Mum started laughing then cuddled Sean and sighed.

“I don’t know what to do with the money, son, what would you do?” Sean unlocked the car door and then looked at Mum.

“Mum, you do anything you want with the money, it’s your money. Why don’t you get your passports and go on holiday? You have never been on holiday for as long as I can remember.”

Mum smiled at Sean.

“How about we go to Italy, all of us?” said Mum.

“Okay, that sounds great, Mum.”

Mum smiled to herself, climbed in the car and put her seatbelt on.

“I have been abroad years ago when I was a little girl. I lived in Italy.”

Sean looked at Mum and was shocked he never knew that.

“Wow, you never said,” Mum smiled.

“Yes, I was born there then we came to England to live.”

Sean was quite shocked Mum had never spoken about this before.

Mum told Sean about her mother and father and about her brothers and she was the only girl. She also told Sean about her brother who was a criminal but she didn’t say what he had done. All she said was he disgraced the family and that her mother and father had gone back to Italy because they were ashamed of what he had done. Mum had kept in touch with her mother and father over the years and she had promised that one day she would go back to Italy and bring her children with her to meet their grandparents but had never mentioned them to the boys in case she could never get the money for them to meet them.

"I honestly never thought I would be able to take any of you to meet them. I miss them so much. It has been over twenty three years now since they left and I had just fell pregnant with you, Sean. I couldn't leave your dad." Sean looked across at Mum and smiled as she had started to cry that she was now able to take her children to meet their grandparents after all this time.

"First thing's first, Mum, passports for all of us then. I will look for flights after that and a hotel for us to stay near to them," said Sean.

Mum smiled a happy smile and she wanted to keep everything secret from the boys. Mum wanted them to be surprised they were going on holiday for the very first time and she wanted to keep their grandparents a surprise for them too.

Sean drove back to Durham City and he couldn't believe the last two weeks of his life. He had never had so many secrets to keep ever. He was happy for Mum and that he was eventually going to meet his grandparents for the very first time. That meant more to him than all the money in the world.

****

Gaz decided to book into a cheap hotel for the night. Not too far away and he looked up all the plasterers in the area. He did find the number again but no address for this plasterer. He had a hunch that this might be the person who had the money. At least it was some sort of lead to where it might be.

Gaz left his things in his room and decided to mingle downstairs in the hotel and have a drink. He sat at the bar and ordered himself a pint. He thought and thought about how he could find this persons address then it hit him. The company's house. He might be registered with them. He sat and smiled to himself as he finished his pint.

****

Sean and Mum were finally home and Mum couldn't wait for a coffee.

"Put the kettle on, will you, Michael, please," said Mum, going upstairs and taking off her good Jacket and dress. She put her pyjamas on and dressing gown. "Oh that's better."

Sean and Naomi went outside for a cigarette and Naomi told Sean about the man who came to the door saying he was his mother's brother.

"It's funny you should mention that, my mum has just been telling me all about her family for the first time ever and she wants to visit them in Italy she doesn't want the boys to know though because she wants it to be a surprise for them. I am older so I am just happy to find out I have got grandparents after all. So did you see him?" Naomi shook her head.

"No, I had gone to the shop for some cigarettes and when I came back he had been and gone apparently he is coming back tomorrow to see your mum."

Sean looked and gave a slight smile to Naomi. He wasn't sure if this brother of his mother's was a good thing or a bad thing especially about what his mother had said about him being in prison.

Why was he coming back now after all these years? thought Sean.

"Right, well, we will have a quick cup of coffee and then I need to get home as I have work in the morning. Once I have done that then I will be over to meet my mother's brother hopefully," said Sean, finishing off his cigarette.

"I am tired to babe," said Naomi.

Michael had made everyone a coffee and Mum had come back downstairs.

"Thank you, darling, I have been looking forward to this for the last three hours," said Mum.

"You're welcome, Mum," said Michael with a smile.

Mum picked up her coffee and sat down at the kitchen table. Naomi and Sean did the same.

"Mum, I have something to tell you," said Sean, then looking at Naomi. Mum took a drink of her coffee.

"What do you have to tell me, son?" said Mum, looking at Sean and then Naomi.

****

Back at the hotel, Gaz had his laptop on, looking for companies with the same number as on the business card he had found in the woods. He was logged into company's house and he typed in the company number which was on the card.

"Got you now," he said to himself as he matched it up and all the details came upon the screen of the laptop.

****

Back at the house, Sean told Mum what Naomi had told him.

"Naomi said the boys had a guy at the door today saying he is your brother," said Sean, looking at his mum's reaction.

Mum took a deep breath.

"Well, I wondered when he would show up," said Mum, taking another drink of her coffee.

"So did you know he would come here?"

Mum looked at Sean.

"I wasn't sure to be honest with you."

Sean looked at Naomi.

"Mum, what has he been to jail for?" asked Sean.

"Sweetheart, it's a long story and I don't really want to talk about it tonight."

Sean nodded.

"Okay, Mum, I know it's been a long day for all of us we can talk about it tomorrow when I come over."

Sean finished his coffee and so did Naomi.

"Mum, try not to worry too much hopefully he has changed his ways now and a changed man, leaving that other life behind him."

"I hope so, son, I hope so."

Sean went and kissed Mum on her forehead.

"See you tomorrow, Mum, try and get some sleep."

Mum smiled at Sean and then Naomi.

"I will, son, go on now you two get away home and we will see you tomorrow," said Mum.

Sean and Naomi left and drove home and locked the doors. They were soon both in bed, snuggled up.

Mum went to bed as well as soon as Sean and Naomi left the house.

Michael went into the sitting room and woke up Damion as he had started to snore and didn't hear most of the conversation.

"Damion, Damion, wake up it's time for bed."

Damion started to wake up.

"Did you hear the full conversation between Mum and Sean?" said Michael, starting to wonder exactly who his uncle really was and what he had done to be locked up.

"Damion, I think he is a bank robber or something, what if he is one of the bank robbers?"

Damion started to laugh.

"I am sure he won't be, Michael, I think your imagination is running away with you now."

Damion stood up.

"Come on, get to bed, go and lock the back door and I will lock up the front door. I am sure we will find out everything we need to know tomorrow when we meet him, or in your case meet him again," said Damion.

"Yes, you're probably right, I am just a bit on edge, that's all."

Damion patted Michael on the back.

"Come on, what is he going to do? We are all family," said Damion, smiling at Michael.

Michael nodded and took a big sigh.

"Okay I guess you are right." Michael started making his way to bed and Damion followed behind him turning off the lights on his way up the stairs.

The boys were soon asleep but Mum was having problems sleeping, as she knew her brother and what he was capable of.

****

Gaz had decided to go out in the car to see if he could find the address of the plasterer. He put the postcode of the address in his satnav and it wasn't that far away from where he was staying. He reached over into the glove compartment, pulled out a black balaclava and placed it on the seat. He then reached back in for a torch and then a gun but he put the gun back in the glove compartment. Gaz started the car and followed the satnav to the location.

He drove past the house, parked the car a few streets down and then walked back to the house. There was no one around and it was very dark. Gaz was quiet and he looked at the windows and doors. He wanted to get inside the house to take a look around to see if he could find any money stashed in there. He picked the lock and he was as quiet as a mouse. The door clicked and he was able to open it and he went inside. He put on the torch, opened the cupboard doors and looked inside each cupboard but he couldn't find anything. He then went into the sitting room and went through draws and cabinet's but he found nothing.

Sean had woken up and was rubbing his eyes. He then heard something downstairs. He looked across at Naomi and she was fast asleep. Sean then heard another noise. He decided to leave Naomi asleep to go and investigate what was going on. He had a feeling someone had broken into his house. He picked up the house phone and rang the police.

"Hello, emergency, which department police, fire or ambulance please," Sean whispered to the woman.

"Both please, because someone is in my house and I will beat his arse, believe me," said Sean, looking for something he could use as a weapon.

"Okay, sir, what is your name and your address?" said the woman on the other end of the phone.

"My name is Sean and I live at 23, Oxford Street, County Durham. Dh1 1CB."

Sean put the phone on the bedside cabinet and kept it on. The woman could hear everything but at that time there was nothing but silence. Sean reached down and from under the bed he picked up a rounder's bat he had since he was younger. He went and opened the bedroom door and closed it behind him. Sean knew that whoever it was was still downstairs as he heard the cupboard under the stairs open.

It had a very distinctive squeak to it. Sean knew he had him now. Sean was like stealth. He knew where every squeak was on the staircase and he knew how to move without them making a sound. He had mastered this when Naomi had been working night shift and was asleep during the day. Sean was then standing right behind him. He grabbed at the man's mask and pulled it off then jumped back and switched the light on.

"Who the fuck are you?" said Sean, holding the bat ready to swing at his head. Gaz turned around and looked at Sean.

"Where is my money?" said Gaz to Sean.

"I don't know what the fuck you are taking about, you fucking arsehole. I don't have any money and if I did I wouldn't leave it here."

"You know what money I am on about. You found it in the woods, didn't you?" said Gaz.

Sean then knew exactly who he was and he knew how dangerous and desperate he was as well.

"I don't know what the fuck you are talking about," Sean didn't take his eyes off him.

Gaz moved towards Sean and Sean raised his bat.

"Go on, you fucker, and it will be the last thing you do because I won't stop believe me." Gaz knew he wasn't lying and put his hands up above his head slowly.

"Right, you bastard, get in the sitting room now. You know where it is."

Gaz moved slowly and started walking slowly towards the sitting room.

They both heard the sirens going in the distance and Gaz then took off running in the direction of the backdoor the way he managed to get in.

Sean ran after him and threw the bat at him which hit him on the head. Gaz didn't stop running though and legged it as fast as he could down the street towards his car. Sean was right on his heels behind him. Gaz jumped in his car and started it, leaving the lights off, and he drove away down the street.

Sean stopped running and tried to see what type of car it was and the colour. He couldn't, however, see the number plate because it was too dark.

Sean stopped running and bent over and held his knees to try and catch his breath.

****

Gaz then put his lights on when he was well away from Sean and drove off in the distance back to the hotel. He got out of the car and locked it up. He then went straight to his room and locked the door. He looked in the fridge and there were small bottles of vodka and whiskey he went to the sink and poured one on his head. It stung like hell.

He gritted his teeth and then took his wet t-shirt off. He drank the other bottle down and lay back on the bed. His head was pounding with the blow he had took off the bat Sean had threw at him.

****

Back at Sean's house, there was police and an ambulance with its lights flashing outside his home. A policeman stood at his front door.

"Can I help you, sir?" said the policeman.

"Yes, I want to get into my house," said Sean, pissed off at the fact he didn't catch the bastard who broke into his home.

"Okay, sir, could I have your name please?" said the policeman.

"Yes, I am Sean, I rang you lot to come out, as we were being burgled," Sean said, his patients wearing very thin.

"Yes, okay, Sean, you may go inside," said the policeman and let Sean passed the entrance of his front door.

The police had gone in and woke Naomi up. The police were out looking for Sean and the burglar. Sean walked into the sitting room and Naomi jumped up, ran to Sean, cuddled him and started crying.

"I guess you're Sean then, son," said an older looking policeman stood near the fireplace. "I am PC Thompson. I will need to take a statement off you, Sean."

Sean nodded.

"Babe, could you make everyone a coffee please?" Naomi nodded and a policewoman followed her into the kitchen to help her. They knew Naomi was a bit shaken up as the police officer had to wake her up and Naomi got quite a shock.

"So, Sean, can you tell me what happened but first where has the robber gone?"

Sean sat down on the couch.

"I ran after him onto Linden Park but he jumped into a car and drove off. I couldn't see what car it was because it was too dark and he didn't turn his lights on so I couldn't get the number plate either."

Sean sighed.

"What did he look like, Sean?" said the police officer.

"He looked normal, brown hair, average height of about five eleven, normal weight, dressed all in black. He did have a balaclava on but I ripped it off his head so I could see who he was."

"That's good, Sean, do you know where the balaclava is now?"

Sean stood up and walked into the passage to the cupboard. The policeman followed him.

"There, that's it, on the floor," said Sean, pointing to the black object in front of him at his feet.

The police officer put on some latex gloves, took a bag out of his pocket, picked up the item and placed it into the bag.

"Well, hopefully we will be able to get some hair fibres from this down at the labs and find the culprit who did this," said PC Thompson.

"Sean, do you have any idea why this person may want to break into your home?" said the police officer.

Sean knew exactly why but he wasn't about to tell the police now, was he?

"I haven't got a clue, I never keep money in the house. Other than money, I don't know. I am a self-employed plasterer, maybe my tools," said Sean.

"Have you upset any of your customers, Sean?"

Sean shook his head to say no.

"No, he wasn't one of my customers. I would have remembered him," said Sean.

"So if you saw this man again, Sean, would you definitely recognise him?" said PC Thompson.

"Yes, I would definitely recognise him," said Sean, frowning as it brought back the memory of the guy's face when he pulled off his mask.

"Right then, Sean, what we will do is, send over forensics in the morning to dust everywhere. We will need you and Naomi to come down to the station in the morning at nine o'clock so we can get your fingerprints on file, so at least then we can eliminate yourselves from the crime scene."

"Thanks, okay, we will be there, I will just phone my clients in the morning and explain to them what has happened. I am sure they will understand," said Sean, starting to worry a little about his work.

"I am sure they will understand, I just need to ask what time did this happen, Sean, can you remember?"

Sean didn't know what time it was when it happened as he didn't think of looking at the time. He just thought of phoning the police.

"I am not sure what time it was, but I rang the police straight away. So it should be on your records of when I rang I would have thought," said Sean.

"Yes, it will be, Sean. I will take a look and see what time you called it in when I get back to the office. Also if we get a match back from forensics you might have to come in to take a look through some photographs," said PC Thompson.

"Okay, no problem," said Sean who was now starting to feel tired from his ordeal.

"Okay, Sean, can I just get you to sign your statements and we will leave you in peace and let you two get back to bed. Don't forget nine o'clock in the morning at the police station to get your prints done," said PC Thompson.

"I won't forget. We will be there," said Sean.

Naomi came in with a coffee for Sean and handed it to him.

"Thanks, babe," said Sean and took the drink off Naomi then put it on the table.

"Okay, thanks for coming so quickly," said Sean.

"You're welcome, the ambulance crew checked over Naomi as she got a bit of a shock when we woke her up to try and find out where you were. Naomi is okay as well, Sean, do you need any medical assistance while they are here?" Sean looked at the officer.

"No, I am fine," said Sean, who then thought about the burglar as he had hit him with the bat on his head and he wondered if he was okay.

Sean didn't tell the police that he had hit the guy over the head because then Sean might have ended up in trouble with the police as well if he told them that. So instead, he said nothing and kept that bit to himself.

Sean had a feeling that this guy wasn't about to give up so easily. As he had found his card in the woods and he obviously had his suspicions that Sean had took the money and it was also a lot of money that was missing. Even Sean would have done the same thing if the shoe was on the other foot. Sean, however, had the upper hand now as he knew exactly what the guy looked like and he was defiantly one of the robbers. Thankfully, he didn't find anything to lead him back to his mother's house otherwise the situation might have turned out quite different.

Sean locked all the doors and kept the key in the lock so no one could pick the lock again. Sean and Naomi went straight back to bed and it didn't take them long and they were both asleep.

****

Back at the hotel, Gaz was now in bed trying to think of what he needed to do next in his plan to get the money back.

He wasn't about to give up that easily on leaving millions of pounds to some jumped up kid, he thought. Gaz had decided he was going to have go back and break in to the house when everyone was out. Next time, he had less chance of being attacked by the fucker who hit him over the head with a fucking bat. He rubbed his head as it was still hurting like a bitch.

Gaz sat up in bed and drank all the complementary bottles of alcohol that was left to try and take away the pain, so he could get some needed sleep to help him recover from his ordeal.

****

The next morning soon came around. Damion was the first one up out of the bed, showered and ready for the day. He decided to wash the dishes for Mum and tidy the cushions in the sitting room.

He put the kettle on and Mum must have smelt the coffee through the house as it wasn't long after she was showered and ready with just her hair to dry.

Meeting Mum's Brother

Mum picked up the newspaper off the floor near the front door which had been delivered by the paperboy and then she went into the kitchen and put the kettle back on. Damion was at the kitchen table and Mum didn't notice him until she sat down with her cup of coffee.

"Morning, son, by you are quite this morning, I didn't even realise you were there. I knew that one of you were up, because you had been in the shower before me. So the big day today, the first time you will have met my brother. How are you feeling about meeting him, Damion?" asked Mum.

"I don't know to be honest with you, Mum. What did he actually go to prison for?" said Damion, quite interested in what his uncle had actually done to warrant prison.

"I don't know if I should be the one to tell you, he might eventually tell you himself," said Mum and then sighed at the thought of her brother being a criminal.

"How long was he in prison for, Mum?"

Mum looked at Damion.

"He has been inside for ten years."

Damion's eyes grew wider. He was now even more curious than ever about what his uncle had done.

Was he a murderer or a robber or what else could he actually be, thought Damion. *Ten years was a long time to go to prison by all accounts. he must have done something really bad.*

Michael came into the kitchen and poured himself a coffee and then a bowel of breakfast cereal.

"Okay, what are you two talking about?" said Michael walking towards the kitchen table to sit down with his breakfast.

"Uncle Gaz. I asked Mum how long he had been in prison for and he was in for ten years," said Damion, looking at Michael concerned.

"Ten years, that's a long time to go to jail. He must have done something really bad to get that sort of time," said Michael then put a spoonful of breakfast cereal into his mouth.

"I think you should tell us, Mum, I really do, then we never have to ask him."

Mum looked at her boys and she could see concern on their faces.

"Okay, okay, he did a bank robbery, he got caught and went to jail, that's it, really, he was in and out of jail before then as well, for other stuff," said Mum.

"You don't think he has anything to do with the bank robbery in London, do you, Mum?" asked Damion, starting to wonder.

"I don't think so. Why on earth would he want to go back to jail for another ten to fifteen years? He would be crazy insane for even thinking about it," said Mum but she also had her suspicions that he could have done it.

"Anyway, just don't say anything for now and let's just see him and spend a bit of time with him. He's okay and he is easy to get on with but I don't know any more as prison might have changed his way of thinking, hopefully, for the better. Right, Damion, you can come with me, and we can go and pick up some shopping so we can make a nice tea for him coming. It will be nice us all having tea together with Sean and Naomi coming over to meet him as well."

Michael smiled at Damion as if to say 'ha, ha, I don't have to go'.

"Michael, when you have finished that you can go and make your bed and hoover through the house and clean the sinks and toilets," said Mum.

Michael's face soon changed.

"That's not fair. He helps you and I have to do all the housework?"

Mum looked at Michael.

"Damion washed the dishes for me this morning and tidied up the sitting room. He also made his bed. I will polish through the house when I get home. It's not that hard. I bet you have it all done by the time we get back," said Mum, walking past Michael to go and dry her hair before going shopping.

Damion smiled at Michael.

"It's not fair," Michael was in a huff.

"Okay, then you go with Mum and I will do the housework. I don't mind," said Damion.

Damion knew he would have it done in no time and still have plenty of time to play on the console with his friends while they were out.

"Okay then, I will go with Mum," said Michael, smiling, thinking he was getting the best part of the deal.

Mum came back downstairs and put on her cardigan and shoes.

"Are you ready, Damion?"

Damion smiled at Michael

"No, Mum, I am not going. Michael is going with you and I will clean the house for when you get back."

Mum was surprised at Damion.

"Okay, son, thank you. Is there anything you want while we are out?" asked Mum, looking through her bag to make sure she had everything she needed before setting off.

"Yes, Mum, could I have a can of pop?" asked Damion.

"Of course you can, I will get you a big bottle if you like and then you can have some for later too," said Mum, smiling.

Damion smiled at Michael.

"Thanks, Mum," Michael still thought he was getting the better deal.

As soon as Michael and Mum had gone, Damion rang Joe and Conner to come over to help him.

It wasn't long and they were at the door.

"Conner, you can hoover and Joe can you polish though the house while I do the bathrooms and make Michael's bed then we can have a few games while they are out," said Damion.

Its wasn't long and they all were at the ready. Joe loved polishing and making everything smell nice and Conner loved to use the hoover win for Damion.

"Mum is going to bring back some pop for us to share as well," said Damion.

"Sweet," said Conner.

Damion put some music on and away they went. They had the whole house cleaned and polished in thirty minutes.

Damion put the game on and he pulled the couch up to the television.

The lads all sat down and played on COD. Luke, Byron, Jake were also online so they all played together while Michael was still shopping with Mum.

"We won't be coming out today, lads, because my uncle is coming to meet us for the first time so we will be out tomorrow hopefully," said Damion.

"I didn't realise your mum had a brother," said Connor.

"Yer, we didn't either, Connor, we have just found out, it's complicated," said Damion, not really wanting his friends to know he had an uncle who had just got out of jail for robbery, especially with them knowing about the money and who actually had spent some of it. They might panic and put two and two together and come up with five as they did. Damion tried not to think about it anymore and carried on with the game.

****

Over at Sean's house, Sean and Naomi had been to get their fingerprints done and were now back home dealing with forensics covering the place with dust and taking samples. Naomi and Sean sat in the kitchen waiting for them to be finished.

"Should we tell your mum what's happened, babe?" said Naomi, lighting up a cigarette. Sean wasn't sure if he should or not.

"Maybe after meeting her brother as I don't want to spoil the reunion for my mum. This would just make her upset and not enjoy seeing him again. We can tell her the day after, babe," said Sean, getting a cigarette out of the box and lighting it up.

Sean decided to text Mum to see what time was best to come over for tea.

****

Mum's phone went off and Michael looked at it as Mum was driving back home after two hours shopping as she decided to go to the metro centre in Newcastle and to look in every book shop in there. Then to the wholesalers to pick up some lovely cakes, buns and meats for sandwiches.

Michael was happy about getting the cakes but not happy about the time it took.

"Mum, it's Sean asking what time was best for him and Naomi to come over?"

Mum thought about it.

"Message back 'four o'clock', son, will yer, thanks," said Mum, trying to concentrate on the road.

Michael messaged Sean back.

'Bro, Ma said 4pm k', then a message came back through.

'K, off, Sean.'

Mum was really looking forward to seeing her brother. She thought about the times when they were younger playing at the park with their mum and dad and how she really missed them all it had been so long. She wondered how he had changed and if he looked older like she did as they were now in their forties. Mum actually felt sorry for Gaz as he had to start everything from scratch even a family.

That's maybe what he needed to have a family and be settled once and for all, thought Mum.

Michael and Mum were back home and Damion came to help with the shopping bags out of the car. Michael looked at Damion.

"So did you get the housework all done then?" Damion smiled at Michael.

"Yes, of course I did. They don't call me Michael," Said Damion.

"So how long did it take you?" said Michael curiously.

"I have just finished it," said Damion, lying through his teeth as he knew if he didn't say that and what he did do then he might get stuck shopping with Mum instead next time.

"Oh okay," said Michael, feeling a little happier that it was actually worthwhile going with Mum instead of housework.

They all helped to empty the bags of shopping and Mum took her new books upstairs to read later on in bed.

Mum came back down and started to make up sandwiches and put them onto trays then covered them in Clingfilm to keep them nice and fresh and placed them into the fridge.

"There, all ready for everyone to come," said Mum, pleased with herself.

There was then a knock on the door and Mum went to answer it and when she opened the door it was a policeman stood there.

"Oh, can I help you, officer?" said Mum, quite shocked to see him stood at her door.

"Yes, I wonder could I come inside?"

Mum didn't want to offer him inside but she thought she had better to stop the neighbours looking at her from across the street.

"Yes, yes, please come in," Mum showed the officer into the sitting room.

"I am here to see your son, Sean, we have had his phone and I am just returning it to him."

Mum was shocked.

"Oh, why have you had my son's mobile phone?" said Mum, looking at the officer puzzled.

“Oh, he has been helping in our investigations about the robbery in London and he may be receiving a cash reward if the evidence he has convicts the men involved. Would you be able to pass on the message for me please, thank you?”

Mum nodded, still not quite sure if she had heard the policeman right.

“Yes, yes, okay, I will make sure he gets the message and his phone, thank you,” said Mum, trying to rush the officer out with her brother coming soon.

“Oh, thank you,” said the police officer.

Mum opened the door for him and he smiled and left.

Mum shut the door quickly, leant up against it and let out a sigh. She looked at the phone and tried to open it but it had a lock on. She wondered what was on the mobile phone and what evidence could Sean possibly have on his phone about the robbery in London. None of it made any scene. She went and took the phone into the kitchen and the boys were on the game, oblivious to what had just gone on or so Mum thought.

She put the mobile phone on the windowsill and just left it there. The time was now four o’clock and there was a knock at the door again.

Hopefully, this will be him this time, thought Mum as she went to answer the door again.

Mum opened the door and Gaz was stood there, as large as life. Mum smiled and flung her arms around him, she was so pleased to see him, after all the time which had passed.

“Come on in, Gaz,” said Mum with tears in her eyes.

“Come on, come and sit down. DAMION, MICHAEL COME AND MEET YOUR UNCLE GAZ!” shouted Mum from the sitting room.

Michael and Damion looked at each other then got up and went through to meet their uncle Gaz.

Damion went and shook hands with him first.

“Hi, I am Damion,” said Damion, still shaking his hand.

“Pleased to meet you finally, Damion,” said Gaz then nodded and smiled.

“Hi, I am Michael, pleased to meet you,” Michael shook his uncle’s hand and smiled at him.

"Oh yes, we met yesterday, didn't we? I bet you got a bit of a shock when I told you I was your mother's brother," laughed Gaz.

"Yes, just a bit as she has never mentioned you before," said Michael then everyone sat down on the couch.

"Well, so how long have you been out for?" said Mum, straight to the point.

"A few weeks, that's all," said Gaz, smiling.

"Okay, you're not involved with any of the robberies, are you, in London?" asked Mum straight out.

Michael and Damion looked at Mum shocked as they couldn't believe she had just come out with that. The boys then looked back at Gaz to see what he was now about to say.

"No, of course not, I have done enough time inside, don't you think? I certainly don't want to go back there," said Gaz reassuringly.

"You're lying, Gaz, aren't you? I could always tell when you were lying and I know you are lying now."

Gaz looked at the boys and he looked a bit embarrassed.

"I knew it, you have done the robbery and that's why you have come back this way. It's not about seeing your family, is it? No, it's all about the money. Have you hid the money up here?"

Gaz again looked at the boys. Then so did Mum.

"Boys, go into the kitchen and get the sandwiches out of the fridge and get the table ready for tea while I talk to my brother please." Mum got up as well and shut the door.

"I know you, Gaz, just tell me the fucking truth, for goodness sake," said Mum.

Gaz looked at Mum and nodded his head.

"I fucking knew it. Why have you done it again?" Mum was so disappointed in him.

"I just know I can get away with it this time, Maria."

Mum shook her head and put her head in her hands.

"So where is the money?" said Mum, looking at Gaz disapprovingly.

"I put it down the woods and left it there hidden under the leaves and sticks, we came back up for it a few days after we did it and we took the bags back to London. When we opened up the bags most of the money was gone. I have come to ask you if you know of anyone that might have the money?"

Mum didn't understand.

"How would I know who has the money? It could be anyone in the villages or surrounding areas who has it, Gaz, what the fuck." Mum couldn't believe it.

There was then a noise from the passage. The sitting room door opened and Sean and Naomi walked in.

"I think maybe you should go home, Gaz, as I don't think I want you here after what you have just told me," said Mum.

Gaz looked around at Sean and Sean looked at Gaz.

"Mum, he is not GOING ANYWHERE, ARE YOU, GAZ?" said Sean.

Gaz stood up quickly.

"Who's this, Maria?" said Gaz to Mum.

"This is my eldest son Sean, Gaz."

Gaz looked at Sean and he shook his head.

"What's wrong, babe, what's wrong?" said Naomi.

Sean didn't take his eyes off Gaz.

"Mum, Naomi go into the kitchen, please, thanks. I need to talk to Gaz a minute."

Mum looked at Sean; his face was like thunder.

"Sean, what's wrong with you? Please, son, what's going on? Just tell me?" said Mum.

"Why don't you tell my mum what you did last night, Gaz?" said Sean.

Naomi had just opened the door to the kitchen then she turned back around.

"Is this the guy who broke into our home last night, Sean?"

Sean looked at Naomi.

"Yes, babe, now go into the kitchen and make a coffee please."

Naomi nodded and went into the kitchen.

"What the fuck is going on in there? We have been trying to hear but Mum made us come in the kitchen out of the way," said Damion then sighed.

"That man in there broke into our house last night and we had to get the police out and everything," said Naomi, putting the kettle on.

Michael and Damion looked at each other in shock.

"What the fuck, seriously?" said Michael.

"Yes, seriously, son," said Naomi as she was so mad with Gaz for doing that to them.

Naomi went into the garden and lit up a cigarette she was shaking with anger.

"So, Gaz, you broke into my son's home last night, why? What the actual fuck is wrong with you?" said Mum.

"I told you I hid the money in the woods and most of it is missing, yer? Well, I found Sean's business card in the woods and on a hunch, I thought he might have the money. I didn't realise he was your son, Maria, and my nephew, honestly, I didn't." Gaz put his head in his hands.

"I am so sorry. I truly am, Maria. I don't know what to say."

Sean looked at Mum and he could see she was upset with Gaz and what he had done.

"I am just so disappointed with you, Gaz, I really am, I know you and I am not sure I can forgive you for what you have done to my son." Mum shook her head.

"Sean, do you know anything about the money at all?"

Sean looked at Mum and he knew that she would be able to see straight through his lies.

Naomi then came into the sitting room with a coffee for Sean giving time for Sean to think.

"Naomi, I am so sorry about what happened in your home last night," said Mum, ashamed of her brother.

"You know what? I don't care if Sean knows anything or not about what has gone on or where the money is. You don't deserve it anyway. Just go now before I call the police and have them come and arrest you for the robbery in London. You will never change and I never want to see you again. Just get the fuck out of my house now. If you go anywhere near my son or his home again God help me, I will do time for you believe me. I just want you to leave and never come back."

Sean looked at Gaz and Gaz knew he was beat. He loved his sister and he was gutted for what he had done to his nephew.

"I am sorry, Sean, I honestly didn't know it was you. Sorry, Naomi," said Gaz, looking at her for any sort of sympathy but Naomi just turned away from him and walked into the kitchen and put her back to him.

"Look, mate, if you know anything about the money just let me know now and then I will go away for good."

Mum just looked at him.

"Get the fuck out of my house now, GET OUT!" screamed Mum at the top of her lungs.

"Right, okay, I am going, Fuck it, keep the money and split it between the three of you. I suppose I can always do another bank job," said Gaz on his way out of the door.

Sean followed him out. Gaz turned around and Sean punched him in the face and knocked him to the ground

"Don't ever come back because next time I won't be as nice believe me, Gaz, also you want to hope that the police don't recognise you up here as I gave them a video tape of you and your cronies who did the bank job. That's how you found the card. I had gone past on the bus and noticed the white van at the woods, with the same number plate as the robbers had on the news C.C.T.V. So I got off the bus and videotaped you all. The van had the same number plate as the robbers. I then videoed you all getting into the van, that's how you must have found my card it must have fell out of my pocket when I was on the ground," said Sean, watching Gaz getting up off the floor.

"I didn't know it was you, I didn't even know you existed until yesterday. I just wanted the money the banks were offering for any information about the robbers, to help my mother out, as she has worked hard all her life and she deserves some sort of happiness. So I would say I am sorry about grassing you all up but to be honest after what you did to me last night and my girlfriend, I hope you rot in hell. Especially for upsetting my mother as well. She was so looking forward to you coming to see her after all these years but don't worry, I will look after your sister. As I have always done because I love her. She is my mother."

Gaz understood where Sean was coming from and respected him for what he was trying to do.

"I am just sorry it was like this as I would have loved to get to know you all properly. Look, kid, I know you are doing your best and trying to stay on the right side of the law. You do what you need to do to take care of your family. Maybe one day you might see it in your heart to forgive me." Gaz then turned and walked away down the street.

Sean watched him as he got into his car and drove away. Sean sigh a very big sigh, went back into the house and shut the door and walked into the kitchen where everyone was now sat at the table.

"Sean, did you know anything about the money?" Sean looked at Damion and Michael.

"Mum, I don't want to talk about it at the moment," said Sean, picking up his cup of coffee that Naomi had made him and taking a drink.

Mum went and put the kettle back on to make herself a coffee.

Sean looked at Damion and Michael and pointed for them to go outside. They both got up from the table and went outside. Sean picked up a cigarette and lit it. Naomi picked a cigarette up too.

"Naomi, wait a minute, will you talk to my mother a bit. I just want to talk to my brothers about what is going on," said Sean, getting up from the table picking up his coffee and going outside. He shut the door so his mother or Naomi couldn't hear him. Sean walked down the bottom of the garden and sat down at the table and the boys followed him and also took a seat.

"I want to tell Mum about the money you found in the woods. Obviously, you now know your uncle is one of the robbers, who stole the money. I don't believe he will be back and he obviously hasn't changed his ways. I just don't want Mum thinking bad of us three as well for keeping the money that you found, Damion, knowing that it is from the robbery that he did. What I am trying to say is maybe we should tell Mum everything." Damion and Michael didn't know what would be best to do.

"Look, maybe we should get it out now and then it's over and done with. No more secrets from Mum and Naomi and then they know everything that's been going on. This is a good time as I don't really want Mum to be disappointed any more than she already is," said Sean, looking at Damion.

"Okay then let's tell Mum what's been going on," said Damion and Michael nodded to agree.

"Sean, the police brought your phone back. It's on the windowsill," said Mum as the boys came back into the kitchen.

"Why have the police had your phone, Sean?" said Naomi, puzzled.

“Damion, make a coffee please as it looks like we might be here for a while.”

Naomi and Mum looked at each other and then back at Sean. Sean and Michael sat down at the kitchen table while Damion made the coffee. Damion passed everyone a cup of coffee then Damion sat down with his cup of coffee as well at the kitchen table.

“Damion, start from the beginning please,” said Sean.

Damion took a deep breath in.

“Mum, I found the money from the bank robbery.”

They all told their stories to Mum and Naomi and by the end of the night everyone was in agreement of saying nothing about the money and to leave it exactly where it was behind the wall in Sean’s bedroom. Mum had her own secret to tell about the eight million pounds she had just won on the lottery that nobody but the shopkeeper knew about and them.

A few weeks later, all the robbers were caught and the evidence against them was overwhelming, especially the video evidence that Sean had given to the police but Sean wanted to stay anonymous. Everyone was caught, including his uncle Gaz. The money from Mum’s lottery win had been transferred into her bank account and she was looking to invest it in to real estate and decided to buy Sean’s council house for him as a present.

****

One Sunday afternoon, during Sunday’s dinner at Mum’s house, there was a knock on the door. Sean got up to answer it and there was a man dressed in a black suit at the door.

“Hello, can I help you?” said Sean.

“Yes, are you Sean Howard, sir? And do you have any identification on you to prove who you are?” The man took out his mobile phone, took a photograph of Sean and saved it to his phone.

“Yes, can I ask why you have just took a photograph of me please?” said Sean, going to his jacket in the hallway and pulling out his wallet to find some identification.

“Once I can see your identification everything will be revealed,” said the man.

Sean was starting to get worried in case Gaz had changed his mind and decided to send a hitman to kill him. Sean pulled out his driving licence with his photo ID on it.

"Is this okay?" asked Sean.

The man took a photograph of Sean's licence and then he reached inside his jacket slowly and pulled out a white envelope.

"From the bank of England, we thank you, Sean Howard, for your evidence in convicting the bank robbers and in this envelope is your reward for doing so."

The man held out his hand and shook Sean's hand, nodded, then jumped back into his black car and drove away up the street.

Sean shut the door and opened the envelope and there was a cheque inside he looked at it and nearly fell over. The cheque was for two million pounds. Sean took the cheque into the kitchen where everyone was quiet and looking at Sean.

Sean held the cheque out to show his family and everyone was shocked.

"They say things come in threes," said Sean, smiling.

The End